2478

BK. ST.
DAVIS, DOROTHY S. &
ROSS, JEROME   4.95
GOD SPEED THE NIGHT

BOOK STORAGE

God Speed the Night

OTHER BOOKS BY DOROTHY SALISBURY DAVIS

NOVELS

Enemy and Brother
The Evening of the Good Samaritan
Men of No Property

CRIME FICTION

The Pale Betrayer
Black Sheep, White Lamb
Old Sinners Never Die
A Gentleman Called
Death of an Old Sinner
A Town of Masks
A Gentle Murderer
The Clay Hand
The Judas Cat

GOD SPEED THE NIGHT

Dorothy Salisbury Davis and Jerome Ross

CHARLES SCRIBNER'S SONS · New York

A–7.68[VB]

PRINTED IN THE UNITED STATES OF AMERICA
Library of Congress Catalog Card Number 68-17330

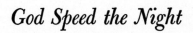

God Speed the Night

1

THE HARVEST TIME OF 1943 WAS AS BITTER A SEASON AS THE people of France had known since the Prussian victory of 1871. The *Boche* was in total and greedy occupation and too often he was aided, even abetted, by the Frenchmen of Vichy. In the vicinity of St. Hilaire, a small town in the southwest, the orchards were heavy with fruit, the fields turning gold with grain. Many a woman toiling alone with no man left to help her wished the land, and sometimes herself in those times, barren.

That day the peasant women of St. Hilaire worked steadily with scythe and sickle, indifferent to the approach of the noon train from Bordeaux. Once they would have rested while it passed, stretched their backs and folded their arms. They would have nodded to the travelers whose faces swarmed in the windows, and it would have been in their minds to say, Yes! Isn't it beautiful? This land belongs to us and we to it, for their nationality was in the very scrapings of the soil from beneath their fingernails. But the train then squealing through the valley would bring only strangers, fat Nazis, Vichyite officials, and haunted refugees with empty pockets. The women did not look up when it rattled to a stop on high and open ground where a platoon of German soldiers probed the undercarriages for unenumerated passengers; they merely steeled themselves for the racketry of automatic rifle fire and went on working. There was no rifle fire that day.

Some near the road, however, paused and shaded their eyes at the appearance of a conveyance unusual for even those times of transport oddities. From out the hilltop gates of the Convent of Ste. Geneviève came an ancient barouche of faded elegance. A grey-clad novice was perched on the driver's seat, her veil streaming in the wind as she urged the

ploughhorse into an elephantine trot. As the barouche passed
the women bowed low, for the passenger was Reverend
Mother St. Charles, superior of the house. There had been a
time when both farmers and townspeople gave to the nuns,
whereas today the religious community was known to deprive
itself on behalf of the plundered citizens of St. Hilaire.

For her part, Reverend Mother was beset by misgivings
for having herself ventured beyond the convent grounds,
much less at having brought with her one of the novices who,
by strict construction of the rule, should have been shielded
from the outside world. But the times were stricter than a
rule, she reasoned, and Gabrielle was a sturdy vessel of the
Lord. The harnessing of a ploughhorse to a barouche instead
of a hayrack would not make her vain. And if it did, the
carting of a hundredweight of luggage at the railway station
would humble her again. There was this also in Reverend
Mother's mind: Gabrielle would study and some day teach
history, even as she herself had done, and to Reverend
Mother history was to be understood not only in the study
of parliaments and tyrants, but in the people of the times, in
these very women in their fields to whom she waved, for it
was they who would sow tomorrow's seed from the bitter
harvest of today.

"Look, Reverend Mother!" Sister Gabrielle turned in the
seat, her eyes wide with discovery. She pointed to the roadside shrine, a white cross with a braided wreath of flowers
hung on it.

"A memorial to someone in the Resistance," Reverend
Mother said, raising her voice above the clatter of the horse's
hooves.

"I know," Gabrielle said, and turned her attention again
to the road.

Did she know? Or was it a manner of speaking? And how
much more would she know before this journey was com-
pleted? In the distance they could see St. Hilaire, the spire of
the cathedral rising like a hand toward God. Along the road
banks before them, the memorials grew numerous. Gabrielle

would mark them in her mind and whisper of them to the other novices, and they would pray for the souls of the Resistance fighters as, during Reverend Mother's own noviceship, she had prayed for the unknown soldiers fallen at Verdun. She put her hand to the beads at her side, and at every memorial repeated thrice: *Requiescat in pace.*

Sister Gabrielle gave herself up for the moment to the delicate maneuvering of the reins along the horse's rump in order to dislodge a fly Poirot could not reach with his slashing tail. To concentrate on such a common thing was comforting. She had always loved the sky, but now there was too much of it, and never before that she could remember had she looked down at crosses. Always up at them. Her first thought when Reverend Mother had told her that she was to hitch Poirot to the barouche and drive her to meet their sisters from the north had been that afterwards she would be homesick again. The homesickness had already come, but not for the house of her father nor the farm of her childhood. No more than a few minutes from its gates she wanted to turn back to the convent. But not for the world would she let Reverend Mother know that. She would be equal to the duty and worthy of the trust—with the help of Ste. Geneviève and Our Lady—for was it not likely that this was a test of her true vocation? As Reverend Mother had said in one of her talks to the novices, extraordinary times impose extraordinary duties. If God tests us, He also gives us courage. Reverend Mother spoke often of the need for courage.

Gabrielle did not hear the automobile approach until almost the moment Reverend Mother called out to her to make way. She pulled hard on the rein in time to turn Poirot's head aside before the car surged past raising a curtain of dust. It screamed to a halt a few meters ahead. The horse balked just as two German officers leaped out and slammed the car doors behind them. Both men started across the ditch and up the bank toward a trio of the memorial crosses, but one of the men, seeing the horse about to bolt, came running back. He caught the bridle in both hands, allowing the beast by the upward thrust of its head to lift him from the ground. When he came down he brought the horse under control with a vicious yank of the bit. He pulled again and again as though he would saw the tongue from its mouth.

Sister Gabrielle cried out, "You don't have to do that!"

He stood for a moment by the quivering animal and grinned up at her. He was a handsome young man with insolent eyes. Gabrielle met them, foregoing modesty in anger. Both were sins: her realization was immediate and she cast down her eyes.

Reverend Mother cried out: "Merciful God!"

Gabrielle and the soldier also looked then to where a peasant woman, her scythe raised, and her voice cracking with rage, lunged toward the German who had torn the crosses from the ground and was in the act of breaking them over his knee. He swung around in time to avoid her, and then with one backward step, he drew his revolver and fired point blank.

Poirot plunged forward again at the sound of the shot. The young officer once more grabbed the bridle. By the time the horse was subdued, the other officer had returned to the car.

The young one called out to Reverend Mother, "Please, madame, continue your journey." Gabrielle turned around.

Reverend Mother stood steadying herself before climbing down. Ignoring the German, she said, "Sister Gabrielle, you will remain where you are." She stepped awkwardly from the barouche.

Gabrielle looked at the soldier.

"God's fools," he said, and saluting her, he ran to the car, slid into the driver's seat and drove off.

Gabrielle reined in the restive horse and watched the converging of other women on Reverend Mother where she knelt beside the fallen one. Gabrielle was ashamed of the trembling in her knees; she feared she could not walk if Reverend Mother called her to come. But Reverend Mother rose and stood a moment praying, and the women stood with her silent through the prayer, then they raised a lamentation like the crying of wolves at night. Four of them bent and lifted the woman in their arms and carried her over the crest of the hill to the house where she had lived. Another of the women, for five of them had come, picked up the scythe and started to follow. She stopped, turned back, and ground the handle of the scythe into the earth where the blood had marked it, and there it stood looking from a distance like a broken cross.

Reverend Mother returned to the carriage, her habit swirling the dust. She climbed in, her face as white as the wimple on her brow. "A walking pace will do from here, Gabrielle. Our sisters will wait in the station until we come."

2

THÉOPHILE MOISSAC, PREFECT OF POLICE, ORDINARILY LOOKED forward to meeting the train from Bordeaux, but that day he would have preferred to absent himself from the station. The Germans had recently taken their own census of the department's able-bodied men, a procedure in which he had necessarily co-operated. The labor conscriptees would go out from St. Hilaire on the noon train. This at the very time the landowners' syndicate was recruiting volunteers for the harvest. He had tried to persuade Colonel von Weber, the Occupation chief, to delay the conscription. To this Von Weber had responded, "My dear Moissac, they are going to Germany to work. The Germans are going to Russia to fight."

Moissac could have found other duties at that hour, but the district prefect of agriculture had informed him that he would arrive by the noon train, and in any case it was Moissac's duty to be on hand. He wondered if it would be appropriate for him to invite the prefect of agriculture to dinner. It was a gesture he particularly wanted to make, so he stopped at home before going to the station to see what Maman could provide.

"It will do you honor," she said, avoiding a direct answer as to what she would serve. She was often mysterious in these matters, and most of the time he preferred it so: she did such wonders on their food coupons. It crossed his mind that the prefect of agriculture might be of the same opinion. He did not want him to be overly impressed. But how to say this to Maman he did not know. He tried to think of the right tack while he got the clothes brush and brought it to her where she was cutting the leaves from a head of cabbage. Maman dried her hands on her apron and took him out into the sunlight where she could brush him properly. She had, now that she was bending with age, to stand on the step in order to inspect his shoulders. She made a little clicking sound with her tongue while she brushed him.

"I am losing my hair. I can feel the sun on the top of my head," he said.

"I can't see where, but I will get more of the tonic."

"Where will you get it?"

"Never mind."

"The last you got made it fall out the faster."

"Dead hair. You are healthier without it."

He turned and looked down at her. "And handsomer, maman?"

"Handsomer than most," she said, and he wondered if there were any more conviction in her words than there would have been in his, paying a like compliment to a shriveled old pouch of lavender like herself. Lavender and cabbage, lavender and garlic, lavender and sweat.

"There will be roast pork for dinner, my son."

Moissac almost wished she had not told him. "Butcher's pork?"

"I shall cook it well."

"Which does not answer my question."

"I have answered it," she said. Then, turning back as she started into the house: "René brought it if you must know."

He had guessed as much. Having removed Maman from the district of St. Hilaire known as the Old Town when he became prefect, he had thought she would make new friends. She had complained since his childhood—his father had been killed in an accident when Théophile was six—of having to live over a drapery shop. But now that she had the cottage she wanted with a view of the river at the front of the house, she rarely left the kitchen at the back, and the only new friend was Monsignor La Roque whom Moissac himself had cultivated. The only old friend who still came, but never when Moissac was home, was René Labrière, a jack of all trades who presently advertised himself as a photographer. Moissac followed his mother into the house. "I'm not sure René wouldn't poison me these days if he had the chance. Did he tell you where the pork came from?"

She shrugged impatiently. "A pig. He took a wedding photograph. It was his payment. He did not lose money, bringing it to me."

"I wouldn't think he had. All the same, call the registry in my name and be sure there was such a wedding in the district." Moissac knew he was making René and not the unrationed pork the issue. But he knew too that if there had indeed been such a wedding, his own conscience would be untroubled explaining their table to the prefect of agriculture.

Maman said, "Théophile, I cannot live with such suspicion. René was my friend when we lived in the Rue de Michelet. When you were away at school he brought me wood every day."

"That was almost forty years ago, maman. We no longer live on Michelet. René does. I am prefect of police and he is a photographer when practically no one wants to get their picture taken. I will wait until you call the registry."

3

WHEN THE TRAIN JOLTED TO A HALT ON THE PLAINS ABOVE ST.
Hilaire, Marc Daridan came violently awake. He recognized
no one at the instant of waking, not even the woman trying to
hold him against her. The eyes upon him were the eyes of
strangers, always the eyes of strangers and always fixed on
his as though challenging his recognition: it was a repetitive
dream that occurred when he was about to waken, the dream
of faces, almost literal in its meaning, and this time it merged
with consciousness, for the other passengers were staring at
him.

"It is all right," Rachel said over and over. Her voice and
then her whole presence became familiar, and he knew at
once why she was on the other side of the dream: they had
married less than a week ago, and the dream had commenced
before. "He has bad dreams," she explained to the others in
the compartment.

"Who does not?" a man said.

Marc turned to the window. Close alongside the train,
their helmeted heads bobbing up and down, the German
soldiers moved forward. The tremor of fear ran through him.
Rachel said, "They are outside, we are inside."

The man opposite overheard although she had spoken
softly. "No, madame. They are inside everywhere."

Marc looked at him: a mournful, sweating face. He was
wearing far too many clothes for the summer day. He too was
on a one-way journey, Marc thought, and his wife was trying
to elbow him into silence.

Another man trod on their feet, trying to climb over the
luggage to the window. "What are they looking for?"

Marc looked out again. The soldiers had squatted down,

their rifles poised. "For the traveler without an *Ausweis*," Marc said.

"Inside everywhere," the man repeated.

"We are almost there," the man at the window said. "I can see the spire of St. Hilaire."

"You should have wakened me," Marc said, leaning close to Rachel.

"You never sleep enough."

"Never is too big a word. You haven't known me that long." He spoke lightly, wanting to forestall more tension if he could. He brushed her forehead with his lips.

The color rose to the pale girl's cheeks. It pleased him to see it. It meant her fears were less than his, he thought, and he had mastered his before.

The woman opposite Rachel said, "You are just married, madame—monsieur?"

"No, madame," Marc said. The papers they traveled on showed them to have been married for a year. The fact was their marriage had been a compact in the presence of a witness: there was no public record of it.

"Do not ask questions," the woman's husband said. "Leave the questions to the *Boches*." He curled the sweat from his forehead with his fingers and whipped it onto the luggage at his feet. The splash of it crawled through the dust like something alive.

The man at the window stumbled back to his seat.

"There is no more conversation anywhere," the woman lamented.

"Soon it will be different," Rachel smiled at her. It was almost impossible for Rachel not to smile, Marc thought, and for just an instant he conjured a picture of what she would be like in the daylight of their lives if that time ever came: a laughing girl who loved the sun.

A whistle sounded, a gutteral command and the soldiers scrambled up the embankment. A moment later the train lurched forward. The soldiers waved. No one in the compartment waved back to them. Those with a view of the aisle began to grope in their pockets for their papers. The team of inspectors soon arrived, the French conductor, a German in the uniform of the French railways, and a national policeman. Marc steeled himself and watched what happened to the couple opposite who he suspected were also in flight. They were passed without question, their papers stamped for arrival at St. Hilaire. Marc gave over his to the conductor.

The German asked at once his military status. Marc was the only man under thirty in the compartment. He described another's history. His identity card showed him to be a medical student. The German watched him closely, and in the midst of his recitation, interrupted. "Why do you travel now, monsieur?"

"It is between terms and we are permitted to go home to assist in the harvest," Marc said.

"Let me see your hands, palms up."

Marc showed them like a beggar seeking alms, but they were steady. "They will harden quickly," he said.

The German moved on to the next compartment, the gendarme following him. The conductor returned the papers to Marc but without the terminal stamp on the travel permit. If the omission was observed by anyone except Marc it was not commented on.

A few minutes later the conductor returned alone, stuck his head in and announced, "St. Hilaire, the end of the journey. Everyone must exit forward."

Over the grumbling of the passengers Marc asked, "Are we on time?"

"Monsieur, it will depend on what you wish to be on time for."

The others laughed, but for Marc the words signaled his next move. While the other passengers gathered their luggage, Marc took the one small valise he and Rachel shared, moved into the aisle and kept the conductor in sight. He saw him try the water closet door, then presumably lock it. Marc moved quickly but not fast enough to pass before two nuns pushed into the aisle ahead of him, shepherding four small children.

Time and eternity were but one to them. Marc followed on
their heels. He slipped into the washroom and locked the door
behind him. The stench was such that he breathed through
his mouth, shallow gulps of the foul air. He used the valise as
a table, and with his penknife, a blade honed to the sharpness
of a razor, he removed his and Rachel's photographs from the
identity cards of a couple named Marie and Jean Belloir. He
pocketed the photos and put the cards along with the travel
permit—unstamped, so that it could yet be used by the
Belloirs themselves—into an old envelope of the French railways.

He opened the valise, pried away the lining, and took
from behind it his and Rachel's own papers. It had been
many months since he had used his, and Rachel's was new, at
least the photograph was, for she had grown from schoolgirl
to woman since the Occupation. Both I.D. cards bore the Star
of David.

The conductor tried the door and rapped three hard
knocks.

"One moment, monsieur." Marc was ready. He closed the
valise and unlocked the door.

The trainman came in loudly abusing him for waiting
until the last minute to use the cabinet. He closed the door
behind him.

Marc gave him the railway envelope. "Thank you, monsieur. You have helped save my life."

The trainman put the envelope in his pouch among the
official records of the journey. "What do they want you for?"

Marc said, "I am a Jew for one thing."

"What else do you need?"

"The *Milice* are also looking for me."

"Nazi bastards," the trainman said. "They are worse than
the Germans."

"Far worse. Do you know where I can find a Monsieur
Lapin in St. Hilaire?"

"I would look first in what they call the Old Town. But

watch yourself. The prefect of police is another bastard." He opened the door. "Out, monsieur. Out!"

Marc had now to push his way among the crowd. He saw Rachel twist and turn, trying to watch for him. Alone and unburdened by luggage she had been shoved far ahead. He edged toward her. Everyone had too much luggage, particularly the nuns. There were several of them now and they were trying to get the children to hold onto one another's hands. Refugees, Marc thought at once; even at that age they did not trust one another.

He reached Rachel's side. She prisoned his hand between her arm and her breast as together they stared out at the shabby environs of the town. Some of the buildings had the look of being carried away, piece by piece. And it might be so, Marc realized, for he could see the torn plaster where iron-railed balconies might once have hung, and the unweathered places where shutters had been removed. Like other northerners before the whole of France had been occupied, he had cursed the south as the garden of Vichy, and he had shared in a cruel satisfaction when the *Boche* knocked down the check-points and moved in.

"Look!" a woman cried and pointed with a desperate repetition, her fingers against the glass. "The trees are gone from the promenade. They're all gone."

The barren stumps, two rows of them, looked raw and somehow obscene.

"Madame, so are the men," an old gentleman said.

The whole town looked to be dying, the houses with their tall chimneys lolled against one another, the limestone yellowing, the roof tiles askew. Only the cathedral stood in high and serene arrogance, a Gothic invader where the Romanesque had ruled in humbler dignity. Once in his student days, before he had taken his certificate in architecture, Marc had wanted to visit St. Hilaire cathedral. Now he doubted he would ever see more of it than this glimpse from a train window, and it no longer mattered a whit to him.

The train, having only gained a little speed, slowed down again. He was better able to observe what he was sure was the Old Town. The cobbled streets were narrow, twisting into one another, and the two-story buildings hunched over the streets vaguely suggesting old men at chess.

The train rattled across a viaduct and abruptly they were in the station yard. The sweat went cold on Marc's back. Nazis were everywhere, green uniforms and black.

"What does it mean?" Rachel whispered.

Everyone was asking the same question.

Marc studied the soldiers. There was something strange about them, something in their stance, in the quality of their alertness; he realized what it was. They were more concerned with a crowd of people outside the fence than with the train and its arrivals.

"It will not concern us," he said to Rachel.

The train ground to a halt, the aftersounds of steam and air pressure like a vast sigh. Everyone pressed toward the platform. The passengers were ordered by the police, military and municipal, to proceed single file into the station building. Marc tested their vigilance by moving up alongside Rachel. He was ordered back into line. A few steps further on he bent down and, on the pretense of retying his shoelace, looked to see beneath the train to what lay beyond the tracks. A cement parapet. He tried to inquire of a French policeman why the people had gathered outside the fence. They were mostly women.

"Move on, monsieur. Move on."

When all the passengers were out of the train, a civilian official came down the line with a megaphone and spoke to a section of the arrivals at a time: "Messieurs—mesdames, will those with harvest work permits kindly step out of line?"

Rachel glanced back at Marc. He shook his head. They no longer had such permits. He watched the straggle of workers, men and women, fall out and follow the official to where two policemen were waiting. They entered the building by the baggage entrance.

The line moved ahead at a snail's pace, an ominous sign. The nuns and the children were taken from the line, the children now helping with luggage that weighed more than themselves. They were taken forward, but when some minutes later Marc and Rachel drew near the building, both nuns and children were still on the platform. They were being questioned in French and in German: the children's papers showed them only to be the adopted wards of the nuns. It did not satisfy the Germans.

Marc shut his mind to them. He was coming close to a window. The waiting room was milling with people because of the delay at the other end. A taller man than most, Marc saw over their heads to the courtyard doors where yet another inspection was to be got through, this time both luggage and papers. He had seen enough of the Gestapo in his time to recognize them among the inspectors. And he had been told that St. Hilaire was a "safe" town. Perhaps it was if they could reach it, but there was no safe passage through the station exit for them. But neither was there escape except through the building. Marc calculated their best chance to lie in the confusion of numbers. He pressed Rachel forward as they approached the door, forcing her to force the woman ahead of her. He had only managed to wedge himself inside the station when guards came up and sealed off the entrance until those inside the building were processed.

Rachel's face was the color of old newspaper. Marc maneuvered her toward a window as far as possible from the inspection. Children were crying, families abusing one another. The flies swarmed overhead. A loudspeaker blared unheeded instructions. There were but three doors in the room, Marc observed, the street and platform exits, and one to the Departures waiting room. He guided Rachel toward the latter drifting slowly as with the surge of the crowd. There was no barricade between the two rooms, but no traffic either. The departures, from what Marc could see, were a stolid lot, patiently waiting the prod of bureaucracy. Then he thought he knew why: two policemen conducted a protesting woman into the far room. She would go back to the town she came from, her papers not in order. Marc watched and waited, riding the perimeter of the crowd, holding Rachel's hand. Her color was no better and he saw her bite her lip.

Suddenly she said, "Marc, I have a bad pain in my side. I wish I could sit down."

"Perhaps it will be useful," he said coldly. Then he put his arm around her and whispered, "We've got to get out of here safely. That's the first thing."

"I know. It's letting up a little. I'm all right now."

They were near the door when the loudspeaker's blare of "Attention, attention!" coincided with the removal of another traveler turned back from St. Hilaire. A pretty girl, she was weeping and she had the sympathy of the policeman who was trying to justify himself for doing so rotten a job. Marc and Rachel followed them into the Departures room.

As soon as he passed through the door Marc saw the soldiers out of the corner of his eye. They were armed and stationed along the wall between the waiting rooms. He pressed forward in the close wake of the policeman as though he and Rachel were also to be deported.

Just before reaching the platform gate, Marc held back. He sent Rachel into the washroom, and waited outside the door. The policeman and the woman went on, disappearing down the platform. Marc measured time, his back to the waiting room: he had to be prepared for the hand on his shoulder, the prod in his back. Neither happened. Slowly, taking first a few steps toward the gate, he turned around. They seemed to have passed safely from one room to the other. But no one would pass unchallenged from this room to the Arrivals. Some thirty or forty men were waiting, sullen and silent, under the military guard. Too many, he thought, to be political prisoners. Labor conscriptees, which accounted for the angry women outside the fence. How ironic if they were ordered out at this minute and he were swept with them, probably all the way to Germany. His fear when Rachel was so long in coming became more of his own panic than anything else. His only control was through action. He dropped the valise on the floor and gave it a little kick toward the washroom. He walked toward the courtyard entrance. There were soldiers out there too, but in the entranceway the ticket-taker sat on his stool, his punch in hand. He yawned while Marc was watching him and took out his watch. He put the punch between his knees and wound the watch. It was the normal in the midst of so much abnormality that sometimes panicked a man, and at other times reassured him. A petty official might not question a show of authority, Marc thought, only the lack of it.

He strode back to the washroom door, his head high, his shoulders back. When Rachel came out he said, "Take the bag and do not speak to me until we are outside."

His hand firm at her elbow, he steered her to the ticket-taker. "Monsieur, this woman is too ill to travel." He clipped the words as a German might.

The man looked from him to Rachel. "But monsieur, I cannot give her back her ticket. It is not allowed."

"Then she may apply to the French railways. For now she should see a doctor." He and Rachel moved out into the courtyard.

The ticket man got off his stool and followed them hesitantly. Marc saw the grey-clad nun even as the railway man called out to her.

Sister Gabrielle was on her way back to the barouche when the man spoke. She and Reverend Mother had been permitted to go through the baggage room to where the northern sisters were detained. Reverend Mother, she was sure, had not expected the children, but Sister St. André spoke as though it had all been arranged and Reverend Mother pretended it was so. The Germans wanted to know who the children's parents were, where they were, everything about them, but mostly they wanted to know if the children were Jewish. There were three little girls and a boy. Everyone

spoke as though the children did not understand what was
being said, almost as though they were not there at all. Which
was why Gabrielle had suggested that she be allowed to take
them out to see Poirot, the horse, and bring them back later.
At that point Reverend Mother had sent her back by herself
to see that the horse was all right.

When the man spoke, saying, "If you please, Sister,"
Gabrielle looked around to make sure that it was she to whom
he spoke. There was no other nun in sight.

"Yes, monsieur?"

The man in the railway uniform said, "This woman is ill,
Sister. Perhaps you could take her to a doctor."

The woman did look ill, but she also looked frightened,
her eyes darting to the face of the tall man. Gabrielle glanced
at him: his eyes seemed to have been waiting for hers. She
looked away quickly. "Madame could rest in the barouche," she
said. "I must wait for Reverend Mother."

"It would be a charity, Sister," the trainman said. His
voice quavered just a little.

Marc realized what had happened: his show of authority
to get them past the man had aroused his concern for Rachel,
he was trying not to leave her in Marc's hands. Marc took the
valise from Rachel's hand, and said to the railway man, "I will
see that madame is taken care of, monsieur. Believe me, I am
not unconcerned."

The man started back to his post, then stopped again.
"Monsieur."

Marc told Rachel to go to the carriage with the nun, and
went back to meet the trainman.

"May I see your identification, if you please, monsieur?"

Rachel, about to climb into the barouche, stopped dead
still when she saw Marc take his I.D. card from his pocket.
Gabrielle put out her hand to help her. Rachel caught it and
held onto it for dear life.

Marc watched the man's face, the shock at seeing the
Star of David. "She is my wife," Marc said. "We are on the
run."

"Get out of here quickly," the man said. "Things are bad in St. Hilaire."

"Can you tell me where to find Monsieur Lapin?"

"Please, monsieur. I have three children. It is against the law to help you."

Marc turned back and saw the women standing, their hands joined. He went back to them having to move now among the people coming from the station. At the gate to the courtyard they were having again to show their permits. He said to the nun, "We are Jews, Sister, and we must find a place to hide."

Gabrielle prayed that Reverend Mother would come, but she knew that she would not. The woman still clung to her hand, the first time any hand had touched hers in almost a year. "But madame is ill," she said.

"I am not that ill," the woman said, and removed her hand from Gabrielle's. "It is more important that we find a place."

"I do not know the town. Wait and I will go to Reverend Mother."

"We cannot wait," the man said. "There are Nazis everywhere. Do you know what it means if we are taken?"

"I think so, monsieur."

Please, dear Lord, let me help, Gabrielle thought. Perhaps to pray instinctively is to concentrate in a way not otherwise possible. Once as a child she had come to St. Hilaire with her father, bringing grain to the mill. While her father drank wine with the miller, she had climbed to the loft with the miller's son and there from the window they had taken turns spitting down into the canal. She and Reverend Mother had passed the mill. It was a ruin now, but she could see the loft in her mind's eye as if it were illuminated by the light of God. "There is an old mill with a loft on Rue Louis Pasteur," she said. "It is not far."

"Take my wife there, and I will find it."

"No, Marc," Rachel said. "I will stay with you."

"You must do as I say. I am safer alone. If you walk out

together the guards won't question you. Take the valise."

"I will carry it," Gabrielle said, and by taking it from the man's hand she committed herself.

"If you are stopped say you are taking her to a doctor."

Gabrielle did not know a doctor, but she nodded. She glanced back toward the station.

"I will tell the sisters if they come and I am here," Marc said.

They walked, the two women, unchallenged through the gate. The policemen stationed there touched their caps to them. The German guards ignored them. Marc watched them disappear from sight at the intersection. He did not like it that they were going away from the Old Town, but he doubted that anywhere was safe now in St. Hilaire. He saw the ticket-taker watching him and he could feel the man urging him to go. The women of the town had come along the fence from the railway yard to the courtyard and the soldiers had moved along with them. The women were jeering now, not only at the soldiers, but at the strangers coming into the town. A band of men and women came from the station on the march, swinging their luggage, mostly sleeping bags. They were the strangers, he realized, the harvesters, some of them younger than himself, students likely, among them a boy with a guitar. The man in the lead carried a white paper in his hand which he waved at soldiers and police alike. When they came abreast of him, Marc fell in with them. They did not care in the least; one of the women winked at him, and Marc took her bag and carried it. He marched through the gate with them, and at the intersection, he gave the woman back her bag and dropped from the ranks. He followed the way Rachel and the nun had gone.

Gabrielle did not speak to the woman until they had turned into Rue Louis Pasteur. "I wish I knew a doctor in St. Hilaire," she said.

"You are very kind, but I would not go until we have new papers."

"I do not understand," Gabrielle said.

"Papers that will enable us to go on from St. Hilaire."

Gabrielle still did not understand, but she did not say so. "If the Germans find you, what will happen?"

"I do not know. A concentration camp in Germany. I have heard that most of my family are there. For Marc it is worse: the French collaborationists want him, and they will kill him if they find him."

The words were strange to Gabrielle. She thought about them, particularly the word "kill." It was like reading or hearing about the martyrs: you believed it because it was written and because their suffering made them holy; you wanted to believe it, but at the same time you did not really understand. She had seen a woman killed and yet what she had felt more deeply was the cruel way the soldier had hurt Poirot.

In brief glimpses she looked more carefully at the woman. She had never before spoken with a Jew to her knowledge. Neither the woman—the girl really—nor her husband looked like Jews. But what did Jews look like? The only ones she could judge by were the pictures of Jesus and Mary, and nobody else looked like them either. She saw the woman put her hand to her side. She looked around to see if there was a place they could rest. They had just passed the church of St. Sébastien.

"We could go into the church for a moment and rest, madame."

"No. I must go and wait where Marc can find me, and please, if you see him again, do not mention my illness. I do not want him to have to think of that now."

Gabrielle said, "If we go to the wall, I think we could see the mill from here."

They were at the parapet when Marc overtook them. Rachel gave a little sound of joy. Only briefly did Gabrielle look at them, catching the flashing smile of the girl, the dark eyes dancing. She looked down the canal toward the mill. "If you look this way you will see the building," she said. "I hope you will be safe there. I must go back."

Marc said, "That black stone building, is that it?" It
resembled an old fortress in the distance.

"Yes, monsieur."

"We shall not forget," he said.

"Godspeed," Gabrielle said, and left without looking at
them again.

There were not many people on the street, only a few
men in work clothes. It was a factory district, brickworks,
blacksmith shops, tile makers, a Citroën garage with several of
the cars outside it. They all bore official license plates. Across
the street was a box factory where, through the open windows, the women could be seen at their work.

Rachel said, "I can wait in the church and then come
when the street is busier."

"Yes," Marc said, "that's what I was thinking, that we
should not go together."

As he held the heavy door for her he wondered if she had
ever been in a Christian church before. He held the door also
for an old woman going out. Her going left the church empty
except for the graven images. A spangled haze hung in the
chancel, the many-hued light coming through the stained
glass. There was the smell of incense. And there was almost a
sound to the stillness. Marc left Rachel on a chair near the
wall. In the vestibule, he removed his coat and rolled up his
shirtsleeves. He ran the sleeves of the coat through the handle
of the valise and then slung both over his shoulder, the coat
covering the valise, and returned to the street.

Gabrielle went back to the train platform by the way she
had come. Only the nuns and the three girls were still there
with the officials. The little boy was gone. Down the platform
men were lined up, boarding the train. Sister St. André's large
round face was flaming red and there were tears in her eyes.
Gabrielle went to the children and the other sisters where
they waited with the luggage a little distance apart. She
heard, nonetheless, the protests of Reverend Mother and
Sister St. André, part of which she would remember and

think of many times again: Sister St. André saying, "But, *Monsieur le Préfet,* our Lord Himself was circumcized. The feast is a holy day of obligation."

"And our Lord was crucified by the Jews, Sister. That also is a holy day." This the policeman, and then the German officer saying that he was right.

Reverend Mother said, "Peace, peace, Sister. The prefect has promised to do what he can."

"You will let them have the child, Reverend Mother?" St. André said.

"They have already taken him, and we may lose the others if we do not go, Sister."

"Exactly," the policeman said.

Sister St. André came then and picked up two of the roped suitcases herself. "God save France," she said. "Herods, all of us."

4

MONSIEUR DORGET, THE PREFECT OF AGRICULTURE, MOISSAC DIS-
covered, had been summoned to St. Hilaire by Colonel von
Weber. He had informed Moissac of his coming in order to
facilitate, on the same journey, the security processing of the
harvesters. It was a matter they discussed first at the station,
then in Moissac's ancient Peugeot on the way to Von Weber's
headquarters in the *Hôtel de ville*. Monsieur Dorget had wit-
nessed the affair with the nuns, but neither man spoke of it.
There was implicit in Dorget's manner, in the very way he sat
in the car, his distaste for the policeman. Moissac did not
suggest the luncheon.

He went round to the police prefecture further disgrun-
tled, for the mayor of St. Hilaire, the local commander of the
gendarmerie, and several department officials were gathered
for the meeting. He had not been asked to attend. Von Weber
often called him in for private consultation, but not when
there was anyone important around.

He was at his desk but a few minutes when a terse com-
munication, handwritten, was brought to him. *"Wo bist du?"*
His own staff had neglected to tell him of the meeting. He
skittered along the polished corridor to Von Weber's office,
once the chambers of the justice of the peace. In the old days
these floors had been safe to walk on. In the old days, too, the
corridor had been lined with busts of the heroes of 1918—
Foch, Clémenceau. . . . Now the only occupant of his marble pedestal was Marshal Pétain.

Von Weber suspended his remarks until Moissac had
found a chair to suit his bulk. He started to sit on the one
nearest the door, decided that it was too fragile, and moved
across the room on tiptoe to a sturdier one.

"A bumble bee should not covet a violet," Von Weber
said in perfectly accented French.

Everyone laughed which rarely happened when a German made a joke in St. Hilaire.

Von Weber proceeded with his usual lecture on the ingratitude of the people in his district, on the benevolence of his command. It was not the day for it what with the labor conscriptees and word having reached the Frenchmen of the peasant woman's death. They sat in an unresponsive silence that even Von Weber could not overlook. He stopped abruptly. Then, "What is it, gentlemen?"

"There was a woman shot in her field this morning, Colonel," the mayor said.

"She attacked the officer. There were witnesses, two members of the religious community, I understand. Nonetheless, the man is under arrest at this moment. He will be tried before court martial."

He waited. No one said a word. "What more do you want?" he demanded.

Still no one spoke.

Moissac felt something should be said. Also, he saw an opportunity to justify himself with the prefect of agriculture. "You will not call on the nuns to testify, Colonel? It would not be fitting."

"If it should become necessary, Monsieur Moissac, I shall ask you to take their testimony. Perhaps that would be fitting. Shall I proceed with the purpose of this meeting?"

"Please," Moissac said miserably.

Von Weber detailed his latest policy directive. There was to be every co-operation with the harvest. Since there were itinerant workers, he would see that their travel was facilitated, provided the prefect of police cleared them in St. Hilaire. He had already arranged the necessary fuel for the transport and operation of the syndicate's machinery. "I find it interesting—why a syndicate and not a co-operative, Monsieur Dorget?"

The prefect of agriculture was slow to answer. "It is an ancient association, Colonel."

"Of very rich men."

"For the most part they have been."

"It is not our purpose to impoverish them. I had hoped you gentlemen would take that message from me today. Let us have peace during the harvest. Allow us that much co-operation with one another. Do you agree to that?"

The mayor stirred uneasily. "The woman's death," he said again, "it was a bad omen."

"I do not suppose she was a member of the syndicate," Von Weber said bitingly. "But I personally offer you, the mayor of St. Hilaire, my deepest regrets."

"What will happen if there is a reprisal?"

"That would be a great pity, but no hostage will be taken. I give you my word on it."

"Then," the mayor said, leaning forward to see the faces of his colleagues, "we must do our best to see that there is no reprisal."

The others murmured assent.

"I would have hoped for more enthusiasm from you gentlemen. I cannot understand why a country under peaceful occupation arranged by solemn treaty condones so much violence. You may go, messieurs."

He did not rise. Nor did he look up again from the desk until he heard the click of the guards' heels as they came to attention before opening the doors to the departing Frenchmen. Then he called out, "Moissac, a moment, please."

Moissac shuffled back and waited. Von Weber continued the study of the papers on his desk. He instructed the sergeant who would prepare the memorandum of the meeting. Finally he looked up at Moissac. "So you do not wish me to embarrass the religious ladies?"

"It is not our custom to call them in civil or criminal matters," Moissac said. Von Weber had asked him once to inform him on local custom.

"Interesting," the German murmured. He took off his glasses and polished them. "I had no intention of calling them and you know it. Whom were you trying to impress?"

Moissac could feel himself coloring. "It seemed like a way of making peace, that was all."

Von Weber smiled. If he could not get the answer he wanted, he was content to embarrass a man. He put on his glasses again. "You don't live in Old Town, do you, Moissac?"

"I did for many years, Colonel. I was born on Rue de Michelet."

"That's where we need to make peace if it's to be made in St. Hilaire. Otherwise the whole district should be cleared out."

"What do you mean, cleared out?"

"The *Maquis* breeds there, wouldn't you say?"

"Not the *Maquis*, Colonel. Not in St. Hilaire. We are a religious people."

"I keep forgetting that, don't I? What was the incident with the convent ladies at the railway station?"

"*Monsieur le Colonel* is quickly informed," Moissac ventured. He wondered how much Von Weber knew.

"I overheard. That is why I wish to be informed now."

"Some sisters arriving from Normandy brought four children with them. Captain Mittag wished to detain the children."

"Why?"

"Refugees. Their papers were questionable."

"Were they Jews?"

"The nuns did not admit it."

"And they called on you to come to their aid."

"Yes, Colonel."

"Poor Moissac," the German said. "You would think that if they had passed this far Captain Mittag would not have been so zealous."

Moissac said nothing.

"Wouldn't you?"

"Yes, Colonel."

"Well. I am sure Monsignor La Roque will put in a soothing word on your behalf with the religious ladies. Or were the children given over to them?"

"Three of them were. The male child was detained."

Von Weber smiled. "On your suggestion?"

"Yes, Colonel."

"You have a genius for compromise, a true Frenchman."

"Thank you, Colonel."

Von Weber just stared at him. "These agricultural workers," he said finally, "you will process them yourself?"

"Yes, Colonel, but they have been screened already by request of the prefect of agriculture."

"The friend of the syndicate. Tell me about the syndicate."

"It is a group of large landowners. Most of the holdings are hereditary. They own certain machinery in common, and on a share basis they harvest also the smaller farms along the way. They dine together formally tomorrow night with the mayor—certain officials. It is a ceremony to begin the harvest season. And they feast the workers."

"Will you dine with them?"

"I have not yet been invited," Moissac said.

Von Weber rubbed his hands together. "Then I was right. You were hoping to impress the prefect of agriculture with your defense of the religious ladies. He was present at the railway station. Isn't it so? Ah, Moissac, Moissac, do not deny me the pleasure of knowing you. There are so few Frenchmen I can truly understand. Now. These harvesters—where do they come from?"

"Mostly students, but this year there are not so many students. Flotsam and jetsam."

"Exactly. And yet one does not want Section Four interfering. It is I who must provide the grain quota, not Captain Mittag. I assume you understood my self-interest in the pacification program. Between ourselves, I will say the officer was right to shoot anyone who attacked him. But I can afford an officer if that is the price of the harvest. And I would rather work with a Frenchman than the Gestapo. After all, you too are an officer of the peace, wouldn't you say?"

"Yes, Colonel."

"Then see if you can use some of that genius for pacification in the Old Town."

5

RACHEL CAME AT LAST, MOVING AMONG A CROWD OF GIRLS ON their way home from work. She walked, Marc thought, as though she too had a home to go to. He glanced around the loft. It was almost in darkness, the glassless windows boarded up. Once it had been a home of sorts, and he was pleased with his salvage. He turned back to the broken board through which he watched. When Rachel dropped from among the girls and seated herself on the parapet, Marc went down thinking how well she had learned the pattern of flight.

The street was a clamor of voices and bicycle bells and the clopping of wooden-soled shoes. The air was tainted with gas fumes, coal smoke, and the stench of the tannery up the canal, but the haze was golden in the late sun and it gave the hoveled town a kind of beauty. Marc waited in what was now a hollow shell of stone from which everything worth removing had been taken away, grinding wheels and machinery, even the door to the office. The whole structure trembled when a heavy truck rolled along the street and chunks of mortar plopped into the murky water.

As a transport of military trucks approached and everybody scattered to make way, Rachel ran down the ramp. Marc called out to her from the shadows. He opened his arms to her, but she came with such slow shyness that he knew they would have to begin all over again, almost from their discovery of one another.

He showed her his acquisitions of the afternoon piece by piece. He had ventured twice into the streets, moving along the wall with a bargeman's pole in his hand, and hiding the pole each time beneath the bridge for his return. To the matches and candles, to the bit of soap, to the bread and the cheese, to the pot on the charcoal burner, Rachel put her

36

fingers tentatively and whispered her wonder at his having managed them.

"You don't have to whisper," he whispered teasingly.

"I feel like I'm still in the church."

"I know."

But when she stroked the flour sacking on the planked bed as she might a silken sheet, he laughed aloud.

"What?" she said.

"You're like a child in a confectionary."

"I am."

He put his arm around her. "No. We cannot be children any more."

"Not even for a little while?"

He shook his head and kissed her.

"We must be gentle, Marc," she said after a moment.

"When was I not?"

"I know. I didn't mean it that way. But I've hurt myself somehow. It's a little pain mostly, but I don't want it to come back again."

"It won't." He moved away from her well aware of the sudden coldness he had not tried to keep from his voice. It was virtually a reflex with him: in three years of trying to get stubborn Jews safely out of Paris, he had learned that the timid of them used your sympathy as they might a crutch: they magnified their infirmities in proportion to the concern you showed. It was not fair, even this momentary abandonment of her, but fairness measured nothing in their lives, if indeed in the life of man. He moved to the boarded window and picked up the voluminous serge skirt he had found in the flea market. "Serge in July, monsieur?" "After July, November is not long in coming." "Such a thought for so young a man!" "Madame, I have an ancient mother." And so he had. Somewhere.

"Rachel, are there scissors in the valise?"

She found them and brought them to him. He opened the pleats and the seams and then hung the heavy cloth over the window and fastened it with a strip of molding he had torn loose in the office below. He used a brick for a hammer. When he was done the room had the darkness of night.

"You may light the candle now," he said.

The flame flickered up and wavered in the draft. She cupped her hands to protect it, the light making briefly luminous her fingers. She glanced at Marc. "I do not even know what day it is."

"Let us say it is whatever day you want it to be."

And so she prayed silently with a little bow and the touching of her forehead with her fingertips.

Marc said, "Amen."

She looked up in surprise, then her whole face broke into a smile.

"Tradition," he said.

"It will do."

They washed in the water he had brought up in a borrowed bucket, sipped a little from the flask of cognac given them for their wedding, and ate the plums and cheese and black bread while he told of the gypsy-dark woman at the corner bistro with whom he had exchanged his ration coupons and a little money for all the food she could give him.

"Did you tell her anything about us?"

"I did not even tell her there was an us, but I asked her if she knew a Monsieur Lapin. 'Monsieur,' she said, 'if I did, I would have him in the pot.' She gave me the matches and the soap—which she makes herself, I must say the place has the smell of it—and the loan of the bucket."

"You have a very sensitive nose," Rachel said.

"Is that bad?"

"You must tell *me*," she said and her own nose crinkled.

He put his hand on hers where it lay on the table and pressed it just a little. They sat silently and looked into each other's eyes. Very slowly her hand turned until the palm was upward beneath his.

6

IN THE MIDST OF THE EVENING MEAL THAT NIGHT AT THE CONVENT
of Ste. Geneviève, the electricity failed. The lecturer suspended
her reading and there was a small clatter of knives and forks
that would not have occurred had there been light by which
to set them down more carefully.

Sister St. André broke the community silence to declare:
"In Normandy this happened every night. Then very soon we
could hear the planes droning like bees in the distance."

Her words, together with the awareness of the children
now having supper with Sister Agathe in the infirmary, gave
the nuns of the house an eerie appreciation of the events
which had brought their sisters from the north among them.

Reverend Mother said gently, "There will be no planes,
so we shall keep our discipline."

Outside, darkness had not completely fallen, but the
walls of the refectory, which was in the oldest wing of the
building, were over a meter thick, and the windows so small
as to give no more than a necklace of light at the height of
noon. Now they seemed but pale stones among those black-
ened with age. Sister Marguerite, the refectorian, arose from
her place and glided toward the vestibule where the lighting
staff was kept. She trod with a ghostly quiet, for the flagstones
were as familiar as the shoes on her feet.

A vigil lamp burned before the statue of Ste. Geneviève,
and on this thirteenth-century sculpture of a seventh-century
saint, its colors faintly luminous, Sister Gabrielle gazed in
attempted meditation. Reverend Mother had suggested on
their return from St. Hilaire that, in order to overcome the
day's distractions, she contemplate the life of the convent's
patroness; perhaps Reverend Mother forgot at the moment
that Ste. Geneviève was also the patron saint of Paris where

she had foretold the invasion of the city by the Huns and, her prophecy fulfilled, had led the people to safety on the Island.

Gabrielle rarely found it difficult to think about Ste. Geneviève, but now she found herself thinking more about the Huns. Her father had always spoken of the Germans that way and that day she had learned herself how terrible they could be. She would not exalt herself to say that God had chosen her as His intermediary, yet she could not get over the fact that she had seen the mill of her childhood on the way to the station. Nor could she forget the Jewish woman's face, her fear when her husband had to show his identification. All the way home, with the children sitting at her feet, their legs dangling at Poirot's rump, she had wondered what their mothers looked like and if they had been as frightened as the woman she had helped.

The refectorian returned and lighted the candles overhead. The lecturer resumed her reading, the other nuns their meal. No sooner had Sister Marguerite returned to her place than the lights went on again. A whisper of mirth escaped the novices. Reverend Mother did not look up.

After the thanksgiving Sisters Gabrielle and Ursula stood up at their places along with Sister Marguerite until the other nuns had filed out. Gabrielle asked the refectorian if she might extinguish the candles. The older nun, rheumatic in her arms, gave permission but in a way that made Gabrielle think she was deliberately giving up an opportunity for greater sanctity. Gabrielle's motive was sensitive if not holy: Sister Ursula was a robust girl from the Dordogne whose perpetual distraction—and the distraction of all those around her, for her stomach complained loudest at the most solemn moments—was hunger. That she fought her appetite for food, Gabrielle knew. She also knew, although she pretended not to be aware of it, that Sister Ursula often lost the struggle. If there was a scrap of food left on the plates they cleared, Ursula would slip it into her mouth. Gabrielle, putting out the candles, rightly supposed that the other novice would first remove to the scullery such plates as contained so much as the husk of a bean.

Again Gabrielle thought of the Jewish couple. If they were hiding, how would they get food? And more important, if the woman was seriously ill, and Gabrielle felt that she was, how could they hide and find a doctor for her at the same time?

Sister Ursula turned off the tap and tested the water in the tub. "Why did Reverend Mother take you with her today?"

They whispered. Sister Marguerite was mending linens while she supervised them.

"Because I am strong and I can drive a horse."

"Anybody could drive Poirot. You are Reverend Mother's favorite."

"That's not so. It would be a sin."

Sister Marguerite looked at them over the top of rimless glasses. She spoke with resounding clarity: "Sisters, do you think we are deaf?"

"*Mea culpa,*" the novices murmured, glancing over their shoulders toward her.

A few minutes later Ursula whispered again, "Then why did she take you?"

It no longer seemed important to Gabrielle, so much had happened. "I don't know."

"Maybe it was because of the children."

Gabrielle did not say anything.

"Will they stay here?"

"I don't know."

"You do know, but you aren't telling."

"Truly I don't," Gabrielle said. "The Germans may come and take them."

"Reverend Mother would not permit it."

Gabrielle thought of the little boy and the words she had heard at the station, and she thought of Reverend Mother in her stall in chapel that afternoon when the novices and lay nuns had filed out after vespers. She had never before seen her bowed down, her face concealed entirely from view. Gabrielle did not mention the boy to Sister Ursula.

They did not speak again until the tub was drained and the places set for morning at the polished refectory tables. By then the nuns were passing from the chapel through the cloisters into the recreation room in the new building. The two novices hurried to be on time for recreation, but in the end they had to wait while Sister Marguerite put away her linens and inspected their work, almost dish by dish.

"I wish it had been me who went," Ursula said, and then added, "*Mea culpa.*"

At recreation Sister St. André did not mention the boy either. She described the bombings in the north and the flight of the refugees as the Germans pressed their security measures in the coastal cities. She told how her convent had hidden as many as twenty children at a time. "And when we had to leave, ourselves, we decided to take along as our wards the ones that were left. Our chaplain, God keep him safe, made out baptismal papers for them. 'If Our Lord wishes them baptized,' he said, 'they are now baptized in His eyes.' And so we brought them. We commend them as well as ourselves to your loving hospitality."

Gabrielle, making only a gesture of her sewing, looked down the long table at Reverend Mother.

Reverend Mother tapped her ring on the table for attention. It was the one time of day when everyone in the community had permission to talk, and sometimes it seemed that everyone spoke at once.

"Dear sisters in Christ," she said when it was quiet again, "we must tell you that there was another child, a little boy, who was taken from us at the railway station. We must pray that he is returned to our care. We have spoken to Monsignor La Roque, asking him to intercede on the child's behalf. But we must guard even at our own peril the lives of those given into our hands for safety. We welcome our sisters from the north, and embrace both them and their charges."

Gabrielle knew that she must speak to Reverend Mother about the Jewish couple at the first opportunity. After recreation, kneeling in turn for Reverend Mother's blessing, she asked if she might come to her. It was, strictly speaking, an infraction of the rule: she should have asked permission of the novice mistress.

Reverend Mother said, "With Sister's permission, you may come to our office before the great silence."

"But why do you come to us only now, Gabrielle?"

Gabrielle sat on the stool, shoulder-high to the wide desk on which stood only a pen and inkwell and an ivory crucifix. "Because, Reverend Mother, I did not think I should come at all. I tried not to think of them."

"But you can think of nothing else, is that it?"

"Yes, Reverend Mother. The harder I pray the more I think of them."

"Ah, child, child, Our Lord tests us in many ways, and the devil tempts us sometimes in equal measure. Where the Lord says be humble, the devil says be proud. Where the Lord says, Without Me you can do nothing, the devil says, You can do anything you want to do. Do you understand me?"

"I think so, Reverend Mother. I am trying to do the Lord's will."

"But first we must try to know Our Lord's will."

"Can we ever? I mean, can we be really sure?"

The older nun was silent for so long that Gabrielle dropped her eyes and murmured, "Excuse me, Reverend Mother."

"We can submit our own wills to the Lord's, beg His guidance, and then proceed according to the light He gives us."

Gabrielle thought again of how she had remembered the mill when they passed it. She told all this to Reverend Mother.

"Let me ask you, Sister: does it not seem strange to you

that these two people would have come to St. Hilaire with no hope of help except for their chance encounter with you?"

"Perhaps, Reverend Mother, they came with hope and lost it on the way."

Reverend Mother's eyebrows went up in spite of herself.

Gabrielle went on: "Tonight, in recreation, when you said we must guard even at our own peril the lives given into our hands, I knew I must come to you."

"I question that you are the guardian of these people's lives, Gabrielle, but you may tell me now what it is you feel we must do for them. That is why you have come to me, is it not?"

"Yes, Reverend Mother," she answered almost in a whisper. "The woman is ill and they are afraid to go to a doctor. If I could take Sister Agathe to her. . . ." Sister Agathe was the convent infirmarian.

"When?"

"Tonight—in the *camionnette*. In the daytime it would not be safe."

"And you think that you are safe in the nighttime?"

"I was not thinking of us," Gabrielle said, somewhat ashamed. Sister Agathe would become in a way her responsibility, and she had not had responsibility for the person of anyone since her father's death. For a moment her confidence wavered.

"But we *must* think of you," Reverend Mother said. "Are you not afraid after what we saw today?"

"Yes, Reverend Mother."

"What will happen if you are stopped by the military or the police?"

"Sister Agathe can wear her medical armband. And I shall pray that we are not stopped."

"So shall I," Reverend Mother said, getting up. "We must consult Sister Agathe. Then we shall decide."

7

THE PREFECT OF POLICE HAD NOT ENJOYED HIS SUPPER. NOT ONLY
had Maman overcooked the roast, but she had overseasoned it
to the purpose, he suspected, of his not being able to taste if
the meat were tainted. He still felt a certain distress in his
stomach. Nor was there bicarbonate in the house and Maman
refused to borrow in this neighborhood. But René actually
had photographed a wedding couple and he had probably received the loin of pork as compensation. Unless Maman had
lied to him about the price, and Moissac doubted that, René
had sold it to her much too cheaply. Why? He could have got
much more for it on the black market.

He sat in the garden. The night was warm and Maman
had heated the whole house with her oven. He pulled at his
pipe and listened to hear how far along she was by the clatter
of utensils in the kitchen, the gurgle in the drain. The moon
had risen, a day or two off full, and he found himself staring
at a ladder propped against the apple tree. It reminded him
of the times in his childhood when Maman had taken him
with her to the Convent of Ste. Geneviève where the nuns
permitted the poor of the town to gather the last of the plums
from the trees. And this reminded him of Reverend Mother
St. Charles and the position she had put him in at the station.
He had tried his best not to get involved, but the nun had
demanded his intervention. Afterwards Mittag had wanted to
know what made a young Jew different in his eyes from an
old Jew. The matter of Jewish refugees was one on which he
and the Gestapo had had no friction until today. He hoped
the issue was settled: a convent was no place for a boy
anyway.

He got up and went into the kitchen. The old lady was
hanging the last of her pots on the wall beside the stove.

"Put on your shawl, maman. We'll go down to Michelet and you can have a *glace*."

"I cannot walk, Théophile. I am too tired."

"But you can still go up a tree like a monkey."

She broke into a grin that showed every tooth left in her head. "How did you know that?"

"I know my maman. Come. We shall go in the car."

He drove first to Madame Fontaine's *pension* where the harvesters were being housed as they arrived. Madame herself, whom he had visited during the day, had been delighted when the syndicate chose her house: she had always protested it was not her fault that the Germans favored her premises and table. What could she do? Burn down her own house? Moissac was sympathetic. What could anyone do? The Germans had come. If the great French Army had not stopped them at the Seine, who had there been to stop them at the Garonne? But hearing the raucous singing when he cut the car motor, Moissac wondered if madame was still delighted. His own mother wanted to go in at once.

"No, maman, for shame."

"For shame," she mimicked.

One of his men on duty there came to the car window and saluted.

"What's going on in there?"

"*Vin ordinaire*, but a lot of it, *Monsieur le Préfet. Bonsoir,* madame."

"You are not to drink with them," Moissac warned his man.

"There are women?" Maman asked, for they were singing one of those wild Gascon songs where the high soprano takes off somewhat like a flute obbligato.

"Yes, madame."

Moissac felt the creep of the flesh at the back of his neck.

"She is a wild one, monsieur," the policeman said and rolled his eyes.

Moissac could feel the song in his very loins. "Keep them

off the streets," Moissac said, and started the car motor again.

Maman gave a little groan of disappointment.

He parked the Peugeot at the head of Rue de Michelet, and they descended the narrow street on foot. The clock in the *Hôtel de ville* struck nine. There was but one street lamp burning, and as well, Maman remarked, for it made her sad to see how badly the street had run down. The harnessmaker's shop was boarded up, Monsieur Garreau having died of pneumonia that spring and his son disappeared, Moissac thought, to the *Maquis*. There was a light in the back of the baker's shop. The baker was rolling his dough, his undershirt as grey as the walls of his shop.

"Let us stop, Théophile."

"No, maman. He will think we expect something without coupons."

"I do expect it. We are old friends. I remember the time you warned him of the complaints on his measure."

"He will not remember it now," Moissac said, and propelled her on.

Further down the street people sat in doorways, people Maman kept peering at, trying to remember, and the light as dim as her memory. *"Bonsoir, Monsieur le Préfet,* madame." There was no warmth in their greetings, but no particular hostility either. They believed of him on Michelet what they wanted to believe, and for the most part he did not want to hear it. Even the baker whom he had saved from arrest had told it around that Théophile Moissac had stolen sweets as a child: it was his conscience, not his heart, weighing the measure of compassion. That it was true only fed his melancholy.

Somewhere in one of the flats that protruded over the shops a child was crying. It was a rheumic cry, interrupted at intervals by a cough.

Maman stopped and put her hand to his arm. "That's the Lebel child."

"Maman, the youngest Lebel must now be sixteen or seventeen."

"I tell you I could recognize that crying anywhere. You wait and see, Théophile. It is Pierre and we'll find his mother drinking *anis* in Gaucher's."

"She will not be drinking *anis*," he said ridiculously as though nothing had changed except in that *anis* had become scarce. Then, he thought, how did Maman know we are going to Gaucher's? He had not told her, and it would have been many years since she had last stepped across the threshold of the bistro.

Maman stepped across it, however, as though not a page had turned in history nor she herself lost an inch of stature, and there, by the living God, at the end of the bar sat Madame Lebel, changed, but queerly, Moissac thought. She was not as old as he had remembered her.

Gaucher called out from behind the bar, *"Monsieur le Préfet,* we are honored!" It sounded more like a warning than a welcome.

Maman marched straight up to Madame Lebel. "You should be ashamed, madame. Little Pierre has the croup and he's crying again."

Madame Lebel looked at her, and Moissac at Madame Lebel more closely. She was a very young woman, ravished-looking, but young nonetheless. She said, "Madame, if you mean my brother Pierre, he is a thousand miles from here and if he is crying, it is of a *Boche* bullet, not the croup."

Maman drew back, her fingers plucking at her lip. Finally she said, "You are Marie Lebel's daughter?"

"I am."

"But there is a child crying," Maman said, indicating with a vague wave of her hand the direction from which presumably she had heard it.

"Most children do," the young woman said. "He will waken his father soon enough."

Maman looked around for her son. "Théophile, take me home. I have aged twenty years in five minutes."

"Sit down, maman." He pulled a chair out from the nearest table, then turned to Gaucher. "Do you have Armagnac, monsieur?"

"For *Monsieur le Préfet* we have Armagnac."

Men whose names Moissac had forgotten were playing cards at the side of the room. They did not look up. Maman sat staring at the doorway, badly shaken. She was old enough to die, Moissac thought. Then what would he do? Advertise? For a wife or for a mother? He looked around at the woman still sitting at the end of the bar.

"Madame, what are you drinking, may I ask?"

She looked at her empty glass. "Air," she said, "and anything you can put in it."

Gaucher, a dark man with a straggling mustache, communicated with Moissac by no more than an exchange of glances, the patois of any bar in the world. When he had uncorked the Armagnac, he poured the first of it into the glass of Madame Lebel's daughter and then brought the bottle and two glasses to Moissac's table.

Maman said peevishly, "You promised me a *glace*."

Gaucher said, "I am sorry, madame, but there is no more *glace* in St. Hilaire. The milk is only for the children and the very old."

Maman gave a cackle of laughter. "I am not old enough, monsieur?"

Gaucher, with a *savoir faire* Moissac would have sold his soul to possess, brushed the back of his hand against Madame Moissac's cheek, winked at her, and said, "Madame will never be that old."

Moissac said, "Bring a glass for yourself, Gaucher."

"No, *Monsieur le Préfet*, but I shall have a beer."

Maman sipped the Armagnac and made a wry face that changed suddenly to pleasure. Moissac turned in his chair. She had caught sight of an old friend. Standing in the doorway and spreading his arms to her as though they had not that morning bargained over a piece of a pig was René Labrière. He was only a few years older than Moissac but his hair was as white as fleece.

A small, wiry man, he pranced across the room to Maman and kissed her on both cheeks. "You have come home, Maman Moissac. It is a celebration."

"I have come home," she said, and then with a toss of her head: "But you are right—it is not to die! To die one lives among the rich and looks forward to an elegant funeral."

The old hypocrite, Moissac thought. Was it a game between them, this camaraderie? Maman's eyes were like live coals. The whole room had come to life, the card players abandoning their game and moving to the bar. Madame Lebel's daughter was fiddling with the radio.

To Moissac, René gave a curt but not unpleasant "*Bonsoir*, Théo."

Maman twisted around in her chair and demanded, "Gaucher, bring another glass."

"No, no, no," René protested without conviction. He greeted the other men while he pulled up a chair near Maman. His eyes caressed the bottle of Armagnac. "I had forgotten what she looked like." With a sigh and a wink at Moissac: "She is like a beautiful woman. The only difference is you know what she can do for you before you touch her, eh, Théo?"

Moissac did not want to hate him, he had never wanted to hate him.

Three more men drifted in. Gaucher drew beer for them. They had come off work from the power plant at the head of the dam. Madame Lebel's daughter settled for a program of flamenco music.

René said to one of the newcomers, "What happened up there tonight, Duroc? My whole studio became a darkroom."

Duroc shrugged. "They took another life today. The lights have a way of going out when that happens."

"I knew her," René said, looking mournfully into his

glass. "Once in a temper she cracked the skull of her own son. That did not make her a patriot." He sipped the brandy.

"The mayor himself came to the plant. He must think we are all *Maquis*." Duroc did not so much as glance at Moissac. "He was anxious to spread the word: the *Boche* who killed her is to be court martialed."

His companions made noises of derision.

Moissac felt uncomfortable in it, but to improve his own position in this company he said, "I was there, messieurs. The mayor exaggerates. The man is to be tried by court martial, which is a little different. Still, it is something that they even want to pacify us."

"They want the harvest," René said.

"And one way or another, my friend, they will have it."

The others murmured, *"Les bâtards,"* but they agreed with Moissac.

Maman said, "The harvesters have come again. Remember how it used to be when they came? Like a carnival, and we would take them in, up and down the street, for a few *sous* a night. Now they are quarantined at Madame Fontaine's."

The old mischief maker. "They are not quarantined, maman. I suspect they are drunk." To no one in particular he said, "She wanted me to bring them home with me."

He should not have baited her. She gave an arrogant little shrug of her shoulders. "It is a pity, but you have made us far too respectable for that."

Everyone laughed and René touched his glass to Maman's. She threw down the Armagnac in one swallow like medicine. While Moissac grew more and more morose, Maman grew garrulous and sentimental. She ridiculed her neighbors on the hill who would not scratch themselves in daylight. What, she wanted to know, had happened to Madame Lebel? Surely she would have known if she had died.

Madame Lebel was living on the farm now with her oldest son. Madame's daughter was married to Divenet, the plumber.

"That old man?" Maman blurted out, and then realizing the gaucheness of it herself, amended, "Ah well, they will not send *him* to a labor camp, eh?"

Moissac wished to God he had left her home.

The door opened and a young man entered, a stranger to all of them. He moved toward the bar like a man about to question Gaucher's license. He was tall, and while the grey-blue eyes rested on no one, Moissac had the feeling he had measured everyone in the room the moment he stepped into the bistro. Gestapo? It was Moissac's first thought, and he did not like being discovered by them in *Au Bon Coin,* pacification program or not. The whole atmosphere now reinforced his suspicion that Gaucher's was a meeting place for the Resistance. The man nodded to Maman, passing, and murmured, "*Bonsoir,* madame."

Maman twisted around in her chair and stared at the man's back, her mouth open, her tongue playing over the cracked lips as it sometimes did when she was about to speak but not quite sure of the words.

May she never find them, Moissac thought. "Come, maman," he said and got to his feet. "It is past our bedtime. Come."

She looked at him in sudden fury.

"We are going now!" he commanded, and she submitted.

"You will come and visit me in my studio," René said soothingly and held her chair. "I will take your picture."

Moissac called out, "I will take care of this, Gaucher."

"It is my pleasure, *Monsieur le Préfet.*"

René went as far as the door with them. The stranger did not look round, his back as stiff as armor.

Marc was badly shaken when he realized that he had walked into the prefect of police. It had been ordeal enough for him to confront again so many faces turned his way, and with the chance always that among them was the recognizing stranger.

"Yes, monsieur?" the barman said.

"Is it possible to have coffee, monsieur?"

"What passes for coffee in this country is possible, yes."

He could scarcely have gotten a more hostile answer. Then the little man who had gone to the door with the policeman and his mother came up and said, "The real question, monsieur, is: can you drink what passes for coffee in this country?"

Marc tried to smile, but he felt the effort. The white-haired man said, "Come, monsieur, have an Armagnac on the prefect of police."

The barman said, "When Moissac pays, then you can drink, René."

But Marc went to the table and sat down. "I will pay, monsieur."

René poured for Marc and himself, using the glasses that were already on the table. He watched Marc's hand as he reached for the glass. Marc willed himself to hold it steady. The little man's eyes followed the glass to his lips, and his expression saddened. He lifted his own glass. "Your health, monsieur," he said, but with a great weariness in his voice.

The barman brought a white mug with a brew as black as tar in it.

Marc thanked him and said, "I am looking for Monsieur Lapin."

Marc had the feeling that there was no one in the room who did not already know that, but the barman said, "I never heard of such a person." He went to the windows and closed the blinds. He fixed the night lock on the door. "It is closing time, messieurs, madame." He shook the crumbs from a couple of tablecloths while he waited, and put the cloths back on the tables.

Marc sipped the bitter brew. It had the taste of almonds in it.

"Why didn't you ask the prefect of police about this Monsieur Lapin?" René asked.

"I did not think he would know him," Marc said.

The men filed out one by one, some murmuring, *"Bonsoir,*

Gaucher." Gaucher returned to the bar. The woman there did
not move. Gaucher said, "Go home to your husband, madame.
Not every woman in St. Hilaire has one to go home to."

"Go to hell, Gaucher," she said, and getting off the stool
she pulled her skirts from between her buttocks.

Gaucher came round and got the bottle of Armagnac. He
went to the door after the woman and when she was gone
rechecked the lock and threw the inside bolt. He turned off
the lights, leaving only one small lamp burning behind the
bar. He waited. Marc went to the bar and paid him. The barman said, "Have you eaten, René?"

"Not enough."

"Who has? Come in when you are through." Gaucher disappeared into the kitchen, the door swinging closed behind
him.

Marc went back to the table. "You are Monsieur Lapin?"

"I may know his brother," René said, and Marc knew he
had made his contact.

Marc said, "I did not know he had a brother," the pre-
scribed answer.

René shook his hand with an attempted cordiality. Marc
understood. There would have been many others before him
and the Resistance man was having to operate under the nose
of the prefect of police. René said, "My name is René Labrière. I am a photographer. You may have seen my sign in
the window."

"Marc Daridan. I am an architect—or was about to
become one when the axe fell on Paris."

"Who sent you to Monsieur Lapin?"

" 'Richelieu.' "

"*Reseau Soleil?*"

Marc nodded.

"A dirty business," René said. "Only tonight I heard
'Richelieu' himself is on the run."

"I botched a job for them," Marc said.

René shrugged. "It happens."

Marc felt he had to tell the story to someone. He wanted

to justify himself; then it occurred to him that every man who came to Labrière would do the same thing. He waited.

René said, "If it is all over, tell me about it. Otherwise, I do not want to know."

"It is all over for everyone except me," Marc said. "Two months ago 'Richelieu' discovered that his *reseau* was being infiltrated by what is now known as the *Milice*."

Even as the trainman had, René said, "Fascist bastards."

" 'Richelieu' decided that I was the ideal person to join their corps, to recommend myself to their intelligence and find out who the infiltrator was. . . ."

René stopped him. "You were not a member of *Reseau Soleil?* No, no, of course not. Otherwise you could not have infiltrated the infiltrators."

"I was not even a member of the Resistance. I knew 'Richelieu' in . . . a different capacity." To the purpose of telling his story clearly Marc refrained from telling René then that his work up until the *Milice* accepted him had been with the Jewish refugee committee. Or *was* it to that purpose? He questioned himself even as he passed over the information.

"Go on," René said.

"The *Milice* needed a man like me. For one thing, I am fluent in German. I lived with them, ate with them, drank with them. I became an interpreter in their school for spies. I memorized thirty faces, finding a particular characteristic in each one—a scar—there were many scars, I can tell you—the shape of the head—the ears. It was the terror of my life that when the time came I might identify the wrong man."

"And did you?" René said. Then, "Forgive me. Tell it in your own way."

"There is no point in being melodramatic," Marc said. "When I was ready I contacted 'Richelieu.' The entire *Reseau Soleil* met in the basement of a burnt-out church. There was even a grave ready for the traitor. Almost the moment I walked in I was able to identify one of them as a member of the corps. But you see, there were two, and the second one got away before I saw his face."

"The *reseau* would have had to break up in any case," René said after a moment. "But you are a marked man, a particular *bête noir* to the *Milice*."

"A very particular *bête noir*, Monsieur Labrière. I am a Jew."

The little man did not conceal his surprise. Then he laughed aloud. "Excuse me, monsieur, but I will explain what I think is very funny. It occurred to me while you were talking why the prefect of police went out of here like a frightened rat when you came in. He would have thought you were Gestapo—it crossed my mind also—and for him to explain to his German colleagues why he was in such a place—very awkward. But here is the funny part: in St. Hilaire, we have always called Moissac the Jew. You know—his nose?" René described the nose with his forefinger, the historic caricature.

Marc managed a faint smile. "Why was he here, monsieur?"

"That is something Gaucher and I will have to ask ourselves, but it would have been better if he had not seen you. You want to reach the Spanish border, is that it?"

"Yes, monsieur."

"What kind of papers do you have?"

Marc showed him his I.D. card and Rachel's. "There are two of us, monsieur."

René took them to the light and studied them. He returned to the table. "Surely you have not traveled on these?"

"We traveled on the identity and permit of a man and wife named Belloir who are native to Fauré."

"And the Belloirs? What has become of them?"

"They will come soon. The permit is to travel for the harvest. Their papers are on the way back to them in Paris."

"A railway employee?"

"Yes."

"You are an honorable man to have returned the papers," René said.

Marc said nothing, but the phrase ran through his mind: So are we all honorable men.

"And your wife, monsieur? Where is she?"

Marc told him of the mill and how they had come to hide there.

"It was a chance to take, asking the nun. We also have a senior prelate in this town who thinks Vichy is the gateway to heaven."

"To have recommended such a place," Marc said, "she would have understood."

"We must hope so. Since you are there, go back and stay there. The prefect of police must not see your face again, not with these papers behind it." He gave them back to Marc. "I will come to you. Perhaps we can use the mill again if you are safe there."

Marc, with more than a little reluctance, asked, "Is there a doctor who would come? My wife has pain. I don't know what it is." He watched the lines in René's face harden. He expected it. He knew how he had felt himself under such circumstances.

"Is she pregnant?"

"We've only been married a week," Marc said.

"Congratulations. First there is the matter of identity papers. Doctors are cautious men . . . and we need them."

8

RUE LOUIS PASTEUR WAS DESERTED. NOT A LIGHT IN THE SHOPS, not even a stray cat to stalk its shadow in the moonlight. And with the darkness, an awful stillness prevailed. Marc could hear the rattle of the aspirin in the box in his pocket: it was the best he had been able to obtain for Rachel. The apothecary recommended that he consult a doctor. First the papers, then the doctor, Monsieur Lapin had said, and Marc had more deeply sympathized with him than with Rachel. He closed his hand around the aspirin: it would relieve the fever. That had been a shock to him. He had felt the sudden heat in her and thought it the flush of love at first, and was himself renewed until at last she had cried out. Anger should not follow love, but that was what he had been left with, anger with himself, with Rachel, with man's fate and its humiliations, the ingredients of being human and yet not human enough: to know, yet not to feel, which to him was worse by far then to feel and not to know.

He lingered cautiously before running down the ramp, and then again within the shell of stone before going up the steps. There, to the purpose of accustoming his eyes to the denser darkness, for only speckles of moonlight found their way through the turret windows, giving light no brighter, nor more constant, than the flickering of fireflies. He trod against the *camionnette* near the foot of the stairs and identified it by touch. The recognition set his heart pounding against his ribs. The police used such a vehicle. He waited, listening. Only the gentle sloshing of water in the cavernous well of the mill. He went up slowly, then hearing a moan from above, he abandoned all caution.

He could have cried out in relief, seeing the two nuns where he had expected the police, but the relief passed

58

quickly and a kind of outrage came over him, as though he
had discovered them in some ancient and obscene ritual with
Rachel their victim. She was stretched prone on the table, her
clothes parted breast to thighs. The nun in black bent over
her while the grey one held the candle. Brief as the association was—and reason banished it at once—it left him mute
and feeling separate even, or especially, from Rachel. He
approached them silently until the grey nun saw him and
made a little noise of alarm.

The black one did not lift her hand from where it rested
on Rachel's abdomen, the gold ring with its cross of Christ on
her finger glittering as with a life of its own. Go, he wanted to
say. Give her back to me and leave us. Instead he said what
they must have known far better than he knew: "My wife is
ill."

"Very ill, monsieur."

"I am grateful to you for coming." He said it: why or
how did not matter.

Rachel opened her eyes and found him. There was no
terror in them. She put out her hand to him. When he took it,
she said, "Oh, Marc, I am so sorry. I tried to make it go
away."

"I know."

The nun in black said, "It is necessary for madame to go
to a hospital, monsieur. The infection will spread quickly and
the appendix—who knows what will happen?" She pulled
Rachel's clothes down and took away her own black shawl
with which she had covered Rachel from her thighs down.

"How long do we have, Sister?"

"Only God can tell time under these circumstances, monsieur. She must go at once."

"She cannot."

"It will pass," Rachel said. "The pain will pass."

"I have brought you aspirin," Marc said.

"She has already had aspirin, monsieur. It cannot heal
and very soon it will not even help the pain. You must
understand."

"And so must you!" Marc said. Then, "Forgive me." He glanced at Gabrielle. "The grey sister will have told you we are Jews."

"They know, they know," Rachel said.

"It is why we came, monsieur," Gabrielle said. "Sister Agathe is our infirmarian."

Rachel was trying to get up. Agathe restrained her. "Better to lie where you are for now, madame."

"There must be something you can do for her," Marc said, and then, as though to persuade Rachel in their presence was the easier way to persuade them, he told her: "I have found Monsieur Lapin and he will come here. Soon we shall have new papers. . . ."

"How soon, Marc?"

"I do not know how soon! Perhaps tomorrow. How can I know except to beg him on my knees to make it soon?"

She smiled a little and squeezed his hand to quiet him. "Do not be so troubled. When they come, you must go on, Marc, and when I can I will come to you. I will find you. . . ."

"I will not go without you."

Her face seemed to stiffen like a plaster mask before his eyes. "Then I will die tonight. You have always said it is the only important choice we have."

"No, Rachel." He knelt down to be close to her. "The more important choice is to live."

"God in heaven," she cried, "why do you permit us to be so tortured?"

Sister Agathe paused in the turning down of her sleeves over the white cuffs of her undergarment. She looked at Gabrielle, being herself touched for the first time beyond the medical urgency of the situation. Gabrielle still held the candle, having nowhere safe to put it down. She knew well that Sister Agathe had taken every step reluctantly; nor had she spoken once to the novice except to give directions in the examination of the woman. God make her see, had been Gabrielle's constant prayer from the moment Reverend

Mother bade them go. That the woman should now join a kind of prayer to hers seemed an answer to her own.

"There has to be a way," Agathe said almost serenely, "and therefore we must find it."

Marc raised his head from where he had bowed it near Rachel's.

"You have identity papers?" she asked.

"We have our own, but they are passports to a concentration camp."

Agathe drew her dark brows together. "Is that worse than death, monsieur?"

"I have heard that it *is* death, but I would choose it if it were the only alternative."

"And the papers you are waiting for?"

"False papers which will say that we are merely French."

"No great honor under the circumstances," Agathe said so that Gabrielle knew she too had now embraced the spirit of Sister St. André. It made her bold enough to speak where she was not likely to in the presence of the older and professed nun. "If we took madame to the hospital ourselves, Sister, would they ask such questions?"

"To be admitted," Agathe said, "she must have identification. Otherwise they would ask more questions, and they would question us."

Gabrielle groped for her pocket and drew from it the folder with her own card of identity. What she really wanted to see was what an identity card looked like, what information it required. She had never used it, and her own feeling of identity was bound up entirely with the religious life and the habit of her order. Yet the instant she brought out the card she and the others, save Rachel, knew that they had found the way.

Without a word Agathe took the novice's card from her hand, and the candle, and going to Rachel, she held the card near her face. Rachel opened her eyes. The dark eyes dominated both the face and the picture of the nun. Marc knew that as a nun Rachel would have immediate and the best of care. In Sister Agathe, the caretaker of the sick, the urge to save a life grew very strong. Her bond and Marc's in this was immediate and fast. Both looked to Gabrielle.

It was to her as though a glaring light were shone upon her, blinding and numbing her. She put her hand to the crucifix beneath the cincture—and felt nothing inside her, and in her hand nothing but a piece of crossed wood with a smooth, cold metal figure on it. No new burst of courage came to her, no inner reassurance that the voice of God was speaking through her; only a deep and terrible sense of abandonment.

Marc, impatient as he was with all religion, nonetheless felt something of what it would mean to this protected child to shed the trappings of that protection. He thought then of what it would mean to Rachel to put on those trappings, Rachel, a child of that other religion. He turned his back on all of them and walked the length of the loft, away.

Gabrielle saw the woman's hand stretch out toward him and then fall limp at her side when he did not come back. She too felt abandoned, Gabrielle thought. "Is it possible, Sister?" she asked Agathe.

"If we make it so. I can take her in the *camionnette* and you will stay here in seclusion until I have spoken to Reverend Mother." She went to Marc. "You must explain to your wife what must be done. Do you have scissors?"

"Yes." He remembered having used them to make the blackout curtain.

"We must cut off her hair, monsieur."

In the remotest corner of the loft Gabrielle undressed in the ritualistic manner of her disrobing every night of her noviceship, removing first the white veil. The religious habit had become as protective of her as her skin, and for a moment, taking the crucifix from her cincture, she held it close to her as another woman might a lover's hand to her breast. She put it down carefully, removed the cincture, and unfastened the long grey robe. She tried desperately to think herself back in the cell at Ste. Geneviève.

Not until she had put on the clothes of the other woman did she remove the coif exposing her head in what seemed the ultimate nakedness. She huddled in the corner, sitting on the down-turned bucket, her hands covering her head. Sister Agathe came for her clothes and took them. Only once did Gabrielle look to the others, hearing the snip of the scissors and Rachel's protest. She remembered what might well have been her own last vanity, her long, dark hair. She yearned for it now as she had not since the first realization that it was gone forever if her vocation was a true one.

When the others had left—and they went without speaking to her—she came out to where the candle was burning. Another candle lay beside the glass in which it stood on the table. She looked down at the dark skirt which came to just below her knees, at the red silk blouse beneath which she could see the shape of her breasts, at her arms bare from the elbows, then down at the shoes, pumps with silver buckles. She stooped down and removed the shoes, setting them side by side beneath the table. She sat at the table and stared at the flickering candle. When she stared long enough it became a golden cross sometimes wavering in the draft, Christ stumbling on the way to Calvary. She put her arms on the table and her forehead on her arm and closed her eyes. She could see the afterglow of the candle and remembered the patterns and colors she had wrought from the darkness as a child by pressing her eyes tightly closed. She remembered the game she had played with her sister: "I see." I see lilac blossoms. . . . I see a kitten, his fur all ruffled. . . . He has a thousand eyes. . . . It's a peacock's feather. . . . It's the bottom of the pond where the frogs' eggs are. . . . It's God's eyes everywhere. . . .

Marc returned. "They are gone," he said when he had closed the door. "Do you know how far it is to the hospital?"

She could not speak at first. She shook her head and

when he came near and looked at her she covered her head
with her hands.

He crossed the room to the bedframe where his and
Rachel's valise was open, and took from it the blue scarf. He
brought it to the novice. She put it around her head and
knotted it under her chin.

"Thank you, monsieur."

"My name is Marc—though what it will be tomorrow,
God knows."

"I am Sister Gabrielle."

"Are you hungry . . . Sister?"

"No, thank you."

"Sleepy?"

"No."

She would not look at him. "Are you afraid?"

"A little, I think."

"Of me?"

She did not answer directly. "I've never been afraid this
way before, so I don't know."

He sat down at the table as far from her as possible and
turned the chair so that he would not be facing her. He tried
to think of things to say that might make his presence easier
to her—and hers more real to him. He had known many
waking nightmares, but none so unreal as seeing this strange
girl in the clothes of the woman he had known as he had
known no other woman. He said: "It has been so long since I
was not afraid I've forgotten what that was like."

Gabrielle stared at her hands. They looked large and raw
without the sleeves coming down to cover the big-boned
wrists, and the nails were dirty. She hid them against her
breast, folding her arms.

"Is it a good hospital?" Marc asked.

"I don't know. I don't seem to know anything now."

"Enough. You knew about this place, and to come back
and help us when no one else could."

"I didn't *know*. I prayed."

"It is a way of knowing," Marc said.

He got up and went to where the hair he had cut from Rachel's head was lying heaped on his white handkerchief, his only clean one. "There is a ritual in Orthodoxy—in Jewish tradition—in which a woman's hair is cut off at the time of her marriage."

Gabrielle wished he would not talk, not knowing how to answer him and unsure as well to what extent it was a violation of her rule to speak at all. The rule of silence prevailed within the convent from final meditation until after breakfast.

"She was very proud of her hair," Marc said.

"So was I once," Gabrielle said.

He did not answer, knowing perhaps, she thought, she should not have spoken that way. He seemed a wise man in the way he said things, different from such men as she remembered . . . except the *curé* in the village where she had grown up. She tried to stem the memory, but it came welling up: he had been her guide and counsel until one day, sitting opposite her in the cold little office off the abbey sacristy, he had got up and come to her, and lifting her chin with his forefinger, frowning until she was terrified of him, he had bent down and kissed her on the mouth. She reached now for the crucifix, forgetting it was no longer at her waist.

Marc folded the handkerchief over Rachel's hair and put it away in the side pocket of the valise. He set the valise on the floor and said, "You had better lie down here and rest even if you cannot sleep. I'll stretch out on the table. I would leave you alone if I could, but I must stay until a friend comes." He glanced at her. She was pale and immobile like a waxen doll. "Do you understand?"

She nodded. She did understand to some extent.

He came to the table. "If we put out the candle we can have some air in here. We can open the door." He gestured her toward the bed, and taking off his coat he carefully folded it and put it at one end of the table to serve him as a pillow. "There is no blanket, but the flour sacks will cover you."

"I would rather stay here, monsieur."

Marc shrugged and took his coat away. Glancing down, he saw Rachel's shoes on the floor beneath the table. "Don't the shoes fit you?"

Gabrielle looked down at them, not knowing what to say because she did not want to offend him. "They have silver buckles," she said.

To which he took offense anyway, or chose the biting retort to vent his diffuse anger. "There was a silver figure also on the cross my wife wore going out of here tonight, Sister."

Gabrielle bent down silently and put the shoes on her feet again.

9

MOISSAC WAS ON THE VERGE OF SLEEP WHEN THE TELEPHONE
rang. He had been several times only to come fully awake
again tormented by the recollection of one and then another
of the day's humiliations. He ran to the phone so that it would
not waken Maman.

It was the night man at the desk of the prefecture. A
woman identifying herself as a nun from Ste. Geneviève's had
phoned the hospital for an ambulance and the hospital had
phoned the prefecture.

"So?" Moissac said.

"She phoned from Place de Gare, *mon préfet*, a public
kiosk. It would seem she tried to take another nun to the
hospital in a *camionnette*."

"So?" Moissac snapped again.

"It is thought it might be a *Maquis* trap—to hijack the
ambulance."

"It is thought by whom?"

"By me, *mon préfet*." The answer was almost inaudible.

"It would be easier to hijack an elephant. Order the
ambulance to proceed and I shall go there myself."

Moissac, having to dress, arrived at the moment they
were lifting the stricken woman into the ambulance. He shone
his torch about trying to be useful. The sick one was very
young and a novice. He asked the older nun if there was any
way in which he could be of assistance.

"The *camionnette*, monsieur, we must not lose the *camionnette*."

He promised to have one of his men pick it up.

The ambulance driver said, "*Monsieur le Préfet*, we are
going to need Doctor Lauzin."

"I'll bring him at once."

"That will be the day," the driver said and closed the

ambulance door. Lauzin was the only really competent surgeon in St. Hilaire, and therefore the most independent.

Lauzin was also the town's only declared atheist. He
made it plain to Moissac on the way that he came because a
human being needed him; he was in no greater haste because
she wore a veil. Moissac hunched his shoulders and concentrated on the road. He had no wish to engage in an argument
his friend the monsignor had been pursuing for years to no
avail whatever.

"Eh, nothing to say in defense of your friends, Moissac?"

"They are good women." He remembered saying the very
words to the Gestapo that morning.

"Because they are chaste? Is that what makes them
good?"

Moissac knew he was being baited. "It must help," he
said.

"Help? *Mon Dieu*, what does it help?"

"*Mon docteur,* I am a policeman, not a theologian."

"A splendid distinction, Moissac, but I have never known
one who did not assume the prerogatives of the other."

In the hospital Rachel was taken directly to the surgery.
There was a moment, only a moment, in which Sister Agathe
was left alone with her. She leaned close to Rachel while she
untied the coif. "Sister Gabrielle?"

Rachel opened her eyes. Agathe nodded approval. "I will
answer their questions, do you understand?"

"Yes . . . Sister."

"We shall have you back with your husband in no time,"
she whispered, "but you must not betray us."

"I shall not betray you," Rachel said.

"I know that, my dear. It is only that in the fever you
might say something. You must think of yourself as Sister
Gabrielle, and a novice never speaks as long as there is a
superior present to speak for her."

A consumptive-looking orderly wearing a stained white
jacket that would have better become a butcher came in, clip-

board in hand, and asked to have the patient's identity card. Sister Agathe gave it to him. From it he took the statistics he needed, scarcely so much as glancing at the patient herself.

To Agathe he said, "You are the person responsible for—" he looked at the record, "—Sister Gabrielle's commitment to the hospital?"

"I am the infirmarian of the Convent of Ste. Geneviève."

"So that the patient's progress will be reported to you."

"To us, yes."

"And the hospital charges, Sister?"

Sister Agathe had not had so much as a *centime* in her hand in twenty years. "You will discuss that with Reverend Mother, please."

"It should have been discussed with Reverend Mother before you came," the man grumbled, his pen hovering over the blank place in the form.

Agathe said, lifting her chin: "You may put down 'pauper.'"

At the sound of the word Rachel opened her eyes.

"We *are* paupers. Poverty is one of our vows," Agathe said firmly.

The orderly shuffled out. Agathe drew her first easy breath in hours. She observed the room, so cheerless, the walls a bilious green, shelves stacked with aluminum and porcelain vessels. There was a rolling case of surgical instruments. The sterilizer looked like a fish aquarium. Several doctors' gowns hung on a rack, all of them having taken on the shape of the men who had worn them. The door to the operating room was open, a dark pit with the chrome of the equipment picking up glints of light like eyes in the night. She thought of her own infirmary, spotless white. And she thought of Reverend Mother who was to be wakened when she and Sister Gabrielle returned. She should telephone, but the very thought of trying to explain was more than she felt able to cope with at the moment.

A buxom and sullen nurse came, her eyes puffy from lack of sleep. She proceeded to prepare by turns the patient and

the operating room. Agathe, despite her anxiety, was fasci-
nated to see the equipment. After taking Rachel's tempera-
ture, the nurse read it and handed it to Agathe. It registered
almost forty degrees. She brought a hospital gown and left
Agathe to undress the sick woman.

The moment Dr. Lauzin entered the room Sister Agathe
felt confident. He went to the patient even as he removed his
coat, dropping the coat on the floor when the nurse failed to
take it in time. With two fingers he parted one of Rachel's
eyelids. She opened her eyes. He continued to study the eye-
ball. Then he stood back and looked down at her. "Well,
well," he said, "we shall have to see what's inside you to stir
up all this trouble in the middle of the night."

Agathe liked him, particularly when he turned to her and
asked, "Are you competent to assist me, Sister?"

"I've had nurse's training and I am in the habit of doing
what I'm told," she said.

"That is a habit to which our regular staff is not particularly addicted. Good."

She watched him explore the abdomen with fingers far
more efficient than her own. "Is there a matter of permission
to be got for the operation?"

She said, "I ought to telephone Reverend Mother in any
case."

"Then do so at once, madame. I shall want you in the
surgery in a quarter of an hour."

Sister Agathe went down to the admissions office to put
through the phone call to the convent. Sitting in the dingy
room with the orderly was the prefect of police. Moissac rose
as the nun entered.

Reverend Mother came to the phone almost at once. She
had been waiting for over three hours. It was five minutes
past one.

"We are at the hospital, Reverend Mother," Agathe said.
"I am needed to assist the surgeon." Then, because within the
hearing of the orderly and the prefect of police she could not
otherwise explain, she added: "Sister is very ill."

There was a brief silence before Reverend Mother said, "I see."

Moissac, coming close to the nun, said, "Excuse me, Sister, but if she wishes to come here I will bring her at once."

Sister Agathe told this to Reverend Mother.

"Perhaps it is best," Reverend Mother said. "I shall be waiting for him."

10

REVEREND MOTHER HAD LONG SINCE SENT THE PORTRESS TO BED, taking up the vigil herself. With the striking of midnight she had commenced to read her next day's office. Then when Sister Agathe called she took her breviary to her cell and got her shawl. As soon as she saw the lights of Moissac's car, she picked up the key from the portress' desk and went out, letting the great door lock behind her.

Moissac ran around the car but by the time he reached her, the nun had opened the front door and climbed in next to the driver's seat. It disconcerted him that she should choose to sit there instead of in the back. Proximity made deference difficult. In fact, proximity made all his relationships difficult.

Reverend Mother gathered the folds of her habit around her ankles and said that it was kind of him to come for her, and at so late an hour.

"It is my duty as well as my honor, Reverend Mother." At the wheel of the car again, and careful in shifting gears not to touch her, he said, "It would have been better to have called for the ambulance straight away."

Reverend Mother did not say anything, weighing his words in the context of Sister Agathe's cryptic message on the phone. She had assumed Agathe to have meant to convey that it was the woman they had visited who was now in the hospital surgery. But that Agathe wished Reverend Mother herself to come suggested an involvement Agathe and Gabrielle could no longer deal with themselves. Something else then crossed her mind: if Agathe was required to assist in the surgery, why had not Sister Gabrielle been the one to telephone?

"Mind," Moissac added, "I would not presume to reprimand. I greatly admire such independence. And may I say

72

now, Reverend Mother, I am sorry I was not able to do anything about the Jewish boy."

Reverend Mother said nothing. He had called the boy
"Jewish." But that she had not been able to do anything for
the child herself was at the root of her being on her present
mission.

"What most people don't understand," Moissac said, "is
that in wartime it is the obligation of some of us to remain at
our posts no matter what our personal sentiments may be."

It did not quite follow, what he had said, and she felt
rather than understood his urgency to justify himself. But why
with her? "We must do our duty as God gives us light to see
it," she said.

"Exactly, Reverend Mother. I am no soldier. I could not
pass muster for the last war, much less this one."

"One heard that the war would be over now for France,"
she said, "but it would seem we are only beginning to suffer
it. Do you think we shall be bombed as they were in the
north?"

Moissac slowed down a little, the better to talk with her.
After all, there would be nothing she could do at the hospital
until after the nun was operated on. "Pardon me, Reverend
Mother?"

She repeated the question, and told him of the devasta-
tion Sister St. André had described.

"That is the Allies. They will not forgive us for saving
France."

"And do you believe, *Monsieur le Préfet,* that France is
saved?"

"The Germans love France. *They* will not destroy it.
After all, they too are a Christian nation."

"It is sometimes difficult to believe. We saw a woman
killed today in her own field."

"Their examples are ruthless. It is true. One woman's
death may save many, but mind, I do not condone it."

"We hear of the atrocities, the concentration camps."

"Much is rumor, I am convinced," he said.

"And the persecution of the Jews?"

Moissac shrugged. "We too have persecuted them, Reverend Mother. It is their fate. There are the ruins of a synagogue in St. Hilaire, but even before the war a handful of Jews were all that were left. No more."

Reverend Mother said nothing for a few moments, giving herself over to thoughts of the two nuns she had permitted an errand of mercy which had carried them far beyond the necessity she had envisioned. If they had confided in Moissac, she was reasonably sure he would now have told her so. Or he would not have spoken so of the Jews. But how had they managed without it?

Moissac, choosing the road that approached the hospital from the side of the town away from the canal, had done so in order that they would pass the checkpoint where the Occupation officers queried all who entered St. Hilaire. He drew up at the gate presently and touched the car horn. A German soldier came from the gatehouse and peered in at them.

"Prefect of police." Moissac identified only himself.

The soldier saluted sharply and the gate was raised at once.

Moissac, driving on, confided to the nun, "You see, Reverend Mother, I consider every such salute collected from them a mark of French independence."

The unfortunate man, she thought, trying so desperately to justify himself, to reconcile with his conscience what she supposed would have to be called his cowardice. She remembered then the wayside crosses she and Gabrielle had seen memorializing those who not merely did not condone, but had given their lives in opposition.

"The monsignor was saying at dinner the other night," Moissac went on, "that if the Germans stay long enough in France we shall civilize them."

Reverend Mother found Moissac's insinuation of the monsignor's views to bolster his own offensive, and she now suspected that neither he nor the monsignor had lifted a finger on behalf of the child. She said, "But you have already called them a civilized nation, *Monsieur le Préfet.*"

"Begging your pardon, I called them a Christian nation, Reverend Mother."

"Ah, yes," she said, "I see the distinction."

Moissac glanced at her out of the side of his eye. He could see nothing but the tilt of her nose profiled behind the black cambric, but the tone of irony was unmistakable. The monsignor, on another occasion, had remarked in Moissac's presence on the preference of the Sisters of Ste. Geneviève for the Jesuits over other orders of the priesthood. It gave them a certain independence, not to say arrogance, which he thought unbecoming in any women, much less in a religious community. Moissac at the time had felt flattered that the monsignor would speak so frankly in his presence. He now felt justified in delivering a little lecture.

"The nun was obviously ill, of course," he said, "but at a time when any irregularity arouses suspicion . . . what I mean to say, Reverend Mother, the summoning of an ambulance to a street corner after curfew, and on behalf of a sister. . . . " He was making a mess of it, his confidence diminishing with every word. "If you had called me I would have brought Dr. Lauzin to the convent. It would all have been so much more . . . dignified." He was shocked with himself for having said it.

But Reverend Mother was not attending him at all by then. Her mind stayed with that first sentence: *The nun was obviously ill* . . . That, and a new understanding of Agathe's message could mean but one thing: the Jewish woman had been admitted to the hospital as a nun.

"As it was," Moissac went on miserably, building on the very premise he had himself dismissed, "it was suspected that the *Maquis* was trying to decoy an ambulance. They've done it before, using it then to transport explosives."

"How daring of them," she murmured.

"You are very unwise, if I may say so, Reverend Mother, to voice such sentiments. With me you are safe, but the Gestapo is everywhere. With them even I am not safe."

"I admire courage," she said.

Moissac construed the remark to his own needs, and therefore confessed himself humbly: "I do not have as much of it as I should like, but we must make do with what God gives us."

Reverend Mother concealed her astonishment. This man, she realized, could justify anything. Knowing his own weakness, he called on God, not for strength but to justify the weakness. One could be sorry for him, but one ought not to be. Truly, one ought not to be.

11

NEITHER MARC NOR GABRIELLE SLEPT, BUT THEY WERE LONG SI-
lent each of them turning within for a more familiar compan-
ionship. Once during the early hours a barge passed on the
canal and afterwards the waves slapped in measured strokes
against the foundation. Even the candle trembled. Marc looked
to the flame across the room. Like the breath of life it wavered.
The image was so immediate in its association he groaned aloud.

Gabrielle raised her head, hearing him, and tried to think
of some thing she might say in comfort. She could think of
nothing. Her thoughts kept turning back to the illness of her
father and the long vigils she and her sister had kept by turns
at his bedside. She could see again the room, the uneven
whitewashed walls yellowing with dampness, the windows
looking out on the plains he loved. She felt again the longing
for them which had almost overwhelmed her in the early days
of her noviceship when, alone in her cell, try as she might to
banish them, they prevailed. She had confessed herself time
and again of the distraction, and on the advice of her confessor she had tried to use the memory, converting the golden
plain to the desert where Jesus was thrice tempted and thrice
repelled the devil. But for her they remained the plains of
Agenais where, on the most vivid of days, she had gone out
and gathered red poppies to brighten her father's sickroom.

She bowed her head and tried again to pray.

The candle sputtered at the wick's end and went out.
"No!" Marc cried out.

Gabrielle continued to pray, now for the Jewish woman.

Marc got up and groped his way to the table. He found
another candle and lighted it. "That will do us until dawn," he
said. "If dawn ever comes."

Gabrielle glanced up at him, her eyes wide and dark like

those of a cornered animal. Her lips continued to move faintly.

"Are you praying for her?"

"Yes, monsieur."

"I wish I could." He turned away. There was no place for either of them to hide. The room had become small and tight, it seemed, where when Rachel was with him it had been too large and they had hovered close to one another.

"Sometimes that is all God expects," the novice said quietly.

"What God expects." Marc weighed the words, not in mockery, but with a removed kind of wonder that the simple of heart could conjure a personal God responsive to their mere wish to have Him respond. He came back and sat down at the table. He covered his face with his hands.

Gabrielle, to brook the despair she felt to have come on him, said, "Where will you go, monsieur, when you are able to travel again?"

"I don't know. First to wherever we can go, but some day to Palestine."

"It is far away."

"Not as far as Paris is for us now."

"I do not understand."

"I only mean that we can't go back there."

"Do you wish to?"

"No. And that is the truth." He put his hands, a cradle behind his head. "I must learn first to make your kind of peace with myself."

She glanced at him and away, not understanding.

"You are more Christian than you are French. Is it not so?"

"I am not Joan of Arc but I am French," she said with a spirit that surprised him. Her eyes flashed as she spoke, then were lowered, and the color came to her cheeks. He had thought, insofar as he had ever thought about nuns at all, that they would be the runts of the litter, so to speak, the daughters least likely to find husbands, the shy, the crippled, the ugly ones.

"Forgive me," he said. "I presumed into an area I do not understand."

"What do you not understand, monsieur?"

"The . . . business of being a nun." He simply could not be reverent about it.

She puzzled the word for a moment. "But you see, we do not engage in business. All nuns take a vow of poverty."

Again he marveled at the simplicity, the directness, and what he could only call the openness. It stirred in him a feeling he did not want now that it was incumbent on him to seek his own safety, a kind of protectiveness. "What else do you vow to?" he said, more to reinforce his own skepticism than to bait her.

"Chastity and obedience."

The abnegation of everything that gave life meaning. "Suppose," Marc said, "you were commanded to do something you considered wrong. Would you obey?"

"I would not be so commanded."

"How can you be sure? Are your superiors saints?"

"They are holy women—or want to be. They are wiser than we are."

"How do you know?"

"I have faith in them, monsieur. We are not compelled to take vows when the time comes. I shall become a nun if I am worthy and because I wish to be one. I wish to serve God."

"Not your fellow man? It seems to me they need your service more."

She did not answer.

"Then you are here tonight in the service of God?"

"Yes. I pray that it is so."

"And in obedience to whom?"

"Reverend Mother consented," Gabrielle said.

"Did she also consent to . . . ?" Marc, by plucking at his own clothes, indicated the exchange of garments.

"No, monsieur. I do not know if she would have consented. It may be that I have sinned. It may be I am sinning in talking now, for we have a rule of silence through the night."

Marc did not say anything for a few minutes. The enumeration of sins was beyond his understanding or wish to understand. He looked at his watch. It was almost two o'clock. In bringing food and charcoal he had planned to boil water and do such cooking as was to be done in the dead of night. He set about it then, Gabrielle occasionally glancing at him, unable to entirely suppress her curiosity. He set half a loaf of bread and a square of cheese on the table, adding then a few plums over which he poured water when it boiled.

"Rachel and I decided that we would eat at night and fast in the daytime," he said. "It is safer having the fire now."

"I understand."

He was afraid that she would refuse to eat, and somehow that would have hurt him in a way he did not now want to be hurt. Nor did he want to hurt her, absurd though he thought the affectations of the life she had chosen. The fact remained, he reminded himself, she had chosen it: she had made that point very clear.

He said what he hoped would be the most conciliatory of words to her: "You may bless the food if you wish, Sister."

Gabrielle had indeed resolved to eat nothing, although the gnawing of hunger came with the sight of the bread; she had thought of Sister Ursula and her craving for food. Tentatively, following the practice of Reverend Mother at the refectory table, she made the sign of the cross with her thumb, just touching the crust of the loaf. She looked up at Marc, his scowl not quite banished before she caught it.

"Divide it," he said, "and let us eat."

"I am not permitted to eat in public, monsieur."

"I won't look at you. There are times when rules, even religious ones, must be suspended. Who knows when we'll have the chance to eat again? Eat and give thanks."

"Thank you, monsieur," she said almost in a whisper, and broke the bread in two.

Marc cut the cheese with his pocket knife, the only utensil in the loft being one spoon.

They had not finished eating when, without sound or signal, René eased the door open and entered. Marc's first warning came from Gabrielle who faced the door. "Monsieur Marc . . . . "

Marc swung around, by instinct opening the larger blade of his knife. "It is a friend," he said to Gabrielle.

René seemed more interested in the room itself than in its occupants. He ran his hand almost lovingly over the door and its latch as he closed it, for no light whatever had escaped. He crossed to the boarded window, the blackout further reinforced by the heavy serge. Finally he turned to Marc and Gabrielle, nodding to the woman and mumbling, "Madame," by way of greeting. "I cannot believe it," he said to Marc. "To have come from Paris and found a place like this in St. Hilaire. The nun must be a worker of miracles."

Gabrielle and Marc exchanged the briefest of glances. Neither of them spoke.

"Or in the employ of the enemy," René added, seating himself at the table. "It is a *cul de sac*." He shrugged. "But so is a hole in the ground." He looked from Marc to Gabrielle. "Madame is feeling better?"

Gabrielle hesitated, hoping Marc would explain. He was silent and she said, "I am well, monsieur."

René said, "I am relieved to hear it. God knows, it will be difficult enough to get Marc Daridan out of the country without an ailing wife."

"My wife goes with me."

"Oh, indeed she does. In fact it occurs to me that she becomes a part of your next disguise. Forgive me, but am I right that in getting married you omitted the civil ceremony?"

"You are right."

"So neither the government nor the *Milice* has a record of it. What name did you use as a member of the *Milice?*"

"Claude Renard."

"The fox," René repeated. "How interesting: the fox and the rabbit. We are two different men, eh, monsieur?"

Marc sensed a kind of judgment in René's comparison. "Yes," he said.

"Let me have your identity cards." While René brought out his knife and tested the sharpness of the blade with his thumb, he said: "What do you think, madame—can a rabbit save a fox?"

Gabrielle was about to say she did not understand, but she did understand the question if not what was said before it. "If the fox is in a trap, yes, monsieur."

"Good! I hope you are right." René moved the candle closer to himself. His hand trembled with an almost palsied shake until the instant the blade made contact with the card. Then it steadied and he probed the edges of one picture, then the other. The sweat stood on his forehead, his face as rigid as his hand.

Gabrielle could not help watching him. She and Marc exchanged one brief glance. He nodded encouragement to her. Instinctively, and from René's words about the ailing wife, she understood Marc's reluctance to tell this man how ill his wife actually was. She thought of leaving the table lest the man look at her and compare her face with that in the photograph. But she was constricted in her feeling of nakedness. She simply braced herself to endure and stared at the hands at work. Then briefly she saw the woman's picture: she was wearing a scarf, probably the one she now wore herself.

The pictures removed, René stood up and took off his coat. He folded it back to expose the inside of the shoulder and inserted the two photographs in a slit in the padding.

"You will have duplicates, monsieur."

"Yes."

"Let me have them. You will need work papers, a military history, God knows. I am still amazed that you sent back the other papers."

Marc was angered, but he did his best to conceal it.

René tried to amend. "After all, you have done your best for us, and what is France doing for you?"

"I don't consider honor a matter of choice," Marc said coldly.

"So little really is," René said with a sigh. "I have been thinking about your predicament: if you can identify thirty members of the *Milice,* thirty members of the *Milice* can also identify you. Is it not so?"

"Twenty-nine," Marc said. "One was killed and buried on the spot because I could and did identify him."

"Oh, yes. They will want you badly."

Marc gave him the pictures he had removed in the train from the Belloirs' I.D. cards, René slid them into the lining of the other shoulder pad and put the coat on again.

"These people from Fauré, Belloir, did you know them well?"

"Only what we had to know. There was so little time."

"And do you know the village?"

"No."

"Let me tell you, monsieur, if all of France was like Fauré there would not be a German on our soil today."

"I can believe it. It was no small thing the Belloirs did for Rachel and me. Now they are holed into a Paris cellar until they get their papers back."

René put his knife in his pocket. "Stir up the coals and burn your cards, monsieur. For a while you will be Monsieur-Madame Nobody—on your honeymoon at the top of the world. Do you have food?"

"For how long?"

René shrugged. "Why do you care? When does a bride and groom have such privacy in times like these? Let me tell you, my friend, I envy you."

Marc forced a smile. He needed all the time he could have here now for Rachel's recovery.

"Let me have your ration cards," René said.

Mark went to the valise to get them and René gave his undivided attention to Gabrielle. "Stand up, if you please, madame."

With the stiffness of a doll, Gabrielle got to her feet.

René went close to her. He put his hand on her shoulder; his fingers probed the muscle of her forearm. Gabrielle clamped her lips in silent terror.

Marc looked around. "What are you doing?"

René laughed softly. "Believe me, monsieur, it is an innocent appraisal. Madame is as strong as an ox. Good."

As Marc returned Gabrielle pleaded with him with her eyes. Her look was that of one at the stake. "Do not touch her again, monsieur."

René pulled himself up to his full height, not much above that of Gabrielle. His eyes blazed in sudden anger. "If I touched her, it is to save her life, not to violate her. How do I pass you from here? As Parisian intelligentsia? Students perhaps of . . . what is it that Jews study?" His voice was staccato with derision.

"I am sorry," Marc said.

"So am I, monsieur. You speak of honor, but you live on pride. Look at your hands, monsieur, and get them dirty, for it is the work of a laborer you will have to do to pass in this part of the country."

"I am strong," Marc said, "but my wife is not." It was useless to protest on any other point.

"Again may I correct you? There is a tradition in our province of the strength of the women of France and I say thank God for it."

"Amen," Marc said. "Amen, amen."

Gabrielle said to René, "Do not be angry with him, monsieur. I am not angry with you."

"Nor am I," Marc said. "You have misunderstood."

René ruffled his shoulders. "I hope that is so. You, monsieur, have the arrogance to pass for a German, but your wife has Jewish eyes."

Oh, Christ, Marc thought: this was another kind of night-mare, reinforcing those before.

René, his anger spent, turned to Gabrielle and with ridiculous gallantry, bowed as he explained: "Which is to say, madame, that they are very beautiful." He tore the coupons from the ration books. "So many books and so little rations."

Marc noticed that his hands were trembling again. He went to the valise and brought the bottle of cognac. René drank like a man in deep need. He pocketed the coupons. "If I am caught with these, they will think I am about my more respectable commerce, a far safer occupation, let me tell you—the black market." He handed the covers of the books to Marc and told him to burn them as well. He was ready to go. "To survive: sometimes I wonder if it is so goddamned important."

"Having been born, it is," Marc said, "but I consider that to have been no great luck."

Gabrielle clung to the table's edge, her knuckles white, and then sank down in the chair.

René said, "You are afraid, madame. So am I. Let me be truthful. I was angry because I could afford to be angry with you. With the police, with our enemies, I am all smiles and bows and scrapings. If they trust me it is because they think I do not have the guts to resist them. And maybe they will soon be right. I have chosen my own cover name: I am a rabbit."

At the door René and Marc shook hands. Marc came back to where Gabrielle sat, now utterly withdrawn. "Thank you, my kind friend."

She covered her face with her hands and wept silently.

12

REVEREND MOTHER ASSURED THE PREFECT OF POLICE THAT IT WAS
not necessary for him to wait for her, but he insisted. Borrow-
ing a week-old copy of *Paris-Soir* from the orderly, he seated
himself and pretended not to listen while the hospital man
drew from the nun further information on Sister Gabrielle.
The novice's parents were dead, her nearest of kin a sister
now married and living in Marseille. Reverend Mother did
not hesitate: to do so would serve no purpose, for she saw
Sister Gabrielle's card of identity attached to the admission file.
When she said that the hospital might bill the Convent of Ste.
Geneviève for the patient's care, the dour little clerk com-
pleted the form and cheered up considerably. He himself conducted Reverend Mother along the dim corridor. The ward
doors were open, emitting the smells and sounds of the restive
sick. A statue of Our Lady of Perpetual Help stood vigil, a
candle flickering at her feet. At a *prie-Dieu* alongside the
shrine an old man knelt in his bathrobe, bare from the knees
down, the toes of one foot folded beneath those of the other.

The orderly opened the last door. It was to a room no
larger than a nun's cell and equally austere. "It is the only
private room. The Germans have the second floor, you see."

Reverend Mother's eyes were drawn to Gabrielle's habit,
the veil, the coif, all neatly folded in the proper order. "Thank
you," she said. "I shall wait here until they come."

After he was gone a muted bell sounded twice. Reverend
Mother looked at her pocket watch. Two o'clock. Another
hour had passed before she heard the shuffling of feet and the
squeaking wheels of the carrier.

Dr. Lauzin and Sister Agathe accompanied the patient
and assisted the nurse in lifting her onto the bed. The woman

86

was beginning to regain consciousness. It was across her prone figure that Reverend Mother's and Agathe's eyes met, Reverend Mother seeking to reassure the tired and now somewhat frightened infirmarian. Only with the emergency passed was Agathe beginning to comprehend the responsibility she had assumed without even seeking permission. She sighed deeply at Reverend Mother's calm and compassionate gaze.

"So! You will sleep well, *ma soeur*," Dr. Lauzin declared, offering his hand in congratulations to Agathe. He was plainly pleased with himself and his assistant. Sister Agathe allowed her hand to be shaken. Indeed, sharing in his exhilaration, she would have danced around the room with him.

Reverend Mother studied the pale young face moving from side to side on the pillow. Her head was covered with a white handkerchief which was fastened beneath her chin. Choppy strands of black hair showed at the temples. The woman opened her eyes. Her lips parted and then shaped a name she did not speak aloud.

"This is Reverend Mother St. Charles," Agathe said clearly. The introduction was to the doctor, but her intent was also to register the presence with Rachel.

Dr. Lauzin said, "Let me tell you, madame, I have never been so ably assisted. The sister belongs in the surgery."

"It is kind of you to say so," Reverend Mother said. "How long must the patient remain in the hospital, *Monsieur le Docteur?*"

"It will depend. A healthy girl, but we had work to do in there, let me tell you. If I may say so, madame, your charges would be better off making known their discomforts. This could not have come on without warning. Suppose I had been out of town? You might have lost her. Very bad." He patted Rachel's shoulder. "You'll be fine now. A good sleep and tomorrow will be better."

"I'm sorry to have been so much trouble," Rachel said, turning her head toward Agathe.

"It is all right, Sister."

"How long, *Monsieur le Docteur?*" Reverend Mother repeated.

"A week perhaps. I'll look in tomorrow. We shall know better then. Now for her a strong sedative and we can all go home to bed."

"May I stay with her, Reverend Mother?" Agathe asked.

"It is not necessary," Lauzin said. He went on confidentially: "The staff is competent enough—and very touchy. Take my advice. Visit, but don't stay. She will get better care that way."

Again Rachel spoke. "I will be fine, Sister."

"We shall make arrangements," Reverend Mother said. "You are not to worry." Then, since the doctor had reached the door and was instructing the nurse, Reverend Mother ventured a further assurance: "You will find the Convent of Ste. Geneviève an excellent place to recuperate. Do you understand?"

"Yes . . . Sister."

"Reverend Mother," the nun corrected, but kindly and only to the purpose of proper identification. Saying it, she laid her hand on Rachel's. The sick woman pulled the nun's hand to her pillow and brushed it with her dry lips.

The doctor turned back to Sister Agathe. "I will not say it was a pleasure, *ma soeur,* but it was a privilege. *Au revoir.*"

When he was gone and before the nurse returned, Sister Agathe began to explain. Reverend Mother stayed her, inquiring with words she chose carefully: "Is Sister Gabrielle secure?"

Rachel unexpectedly responded, "I am secure."

"Yes, my dear, you are," Reverend Mother said, but her eyes demanded an answer of Agathe.

"Yes, Reverend Mother, as secure as *he* is. But he is a man."

"That is not my meaning," Reverend Mother said briskly.

Agathe colored. She said, "She will have no identity card now except. . . . " She nodded at Rachel.

"Then we must assume she is secure for the present."

Another admission was taking place when the nuns reached the hospital entrance. A night-worker at the power station had badly cut his hand. He was hiding it from himself under his arm, but the blood was seeping through. When he glanced down and saw the red crawling stain, he crumpled to the floor at Reverend Mother's feet.

Dr. Lauzin took off his coat again. "Get him up to the surgery. I'll have a look at it."

Sister Agathe half hoped he would ask her to assist him again, but he did not, and Moissac steered the nuns out of the building.

In the car Sister Agathe remembered the *camionnette*. Moissac had forgotten about it although he assured the nun otherwise. He drove past the railway station and stopped at the kiosk alongside which the *camionnette* still stood. Moissac called the prefecture from the public phone.

From habit of conservation he had turned off the motor and the car lights. He was about to leave the kiosk when a man on foot turned into the street a few yards away. It would have been impossible for him not to recognize René, his mane of hair as vivid as a white flag. Moissac waited. The nuns were silent. René, seeing the car, hesitated a moment and then came on, supposing the car to have broken down there. Moissac took his pocket flash out and waited in the kiosk, his finger on the switch. When René was abreast of him he stepped out and flashed the light in the little man's face.

René brought up his hand hard so that the beam of light shot upward into Moissac's own face for an instant. "You are a bastard, Théo." He covered his shock with bravura.

"A man on the streets after curfew—I can be forgiven precautions."

"I've been visiting a sick friend," Rene said.

"Have you? So have I, my friend. I am driving Reverend Mother home from the hospital. Come with me and we can talk afterwards." He moved to the car and opened the door for René.

"It is late, Théo. I am too tired."

"Nonsense. I should arrest you for violating curfew."

René, looking in at the nuns as he climbed into the car, remembered having called Moissac a bastard. "Excuse me, Sisters. I did not know you were in the car."

"Where does your sick friend live?" Moissac asked, starting the car motor.

"It is old Brie at the end of Louis Pasteur. He had the priest tonight." All this was so: René had covered his presence in the neighborhood with a late visit to the Brie home.

"It is time for him to die," Moissac said. "He must be eighty." He thought of Maman and fell silent for the rest of the way to the convent. No one else spoke either.

He returned to St. Hilaire by way of the checkpoint again. Once more the German sentry saluted and permitted him to pass without questioning either him or his passenger.

René thought how different it would have been for him alone, the questioning, the search. "Makes you proud to be a Frenchman, doesn't it, Théo?"

Moissac ignored the shaft. "Who was the stranger who came into Gaucher's as Maman and I were leaving?"

René gave a snort of laughter. "I was about to ask you the same thing."

"What did he want?"

"Coffee. At least that's what he asked for. It was Gaucher's and my idea that he was Gestapo."

Even as Moissac had himself suspected.

"But if you say he was not, *Monsieur le Préfet,* who can say who he was?"

"I did not say so. They do not report to me."

René said nothing.

"Nor I to them unless I have to. Gaucher should be more careful."

"Of what?"

"His place is suspect. It is on the Gestapo's list."

"I shall tell him you said so, Théo."

"I know you will. That is why I'm telling you. Théophile Moissac is not the bastard you all think he is."

"I shall tell him that also."

13

THE NIGHT NURSE, SUMMONED AGAIN TO THE SURGERY FOR AN
emergency, went in the middle of preparing the injection Dr.
Lauzin had ordered for Rachel. In great pain and craving
water, Rachel fought crying out for as long as she could. Then
the subconscious prevailed.

The old man praying before Our Lady of Perpetual Help
heard her cries. He made his way to her bedside.

"Water . . . Please, water."

He hobbled down the hall to his own ward and got the
glass from his bedside table. He borrowed the tube from the
glass of the sleeping man in the next bed and brought Rachel
the relief she craved. He supported her head while she
drained the glass. He felt much better himself for having per-
formed the charity and went back to bed knowing that he
would sleep at last.

Within a few minutes Rachel was nauseated. She managed to edge herself to the side of the bed, but retching
violently and now delirious, she flung herself from the bed.
The wound opened.

At ten minutes to eight that morning Reverend Mother
was summoned again to the hospital, but by the time she
arrived the patient had died.

14

"NOW I HAVE THOUGHT OF WHAT MAY HAVE HAPPENED." MARC
sat up and swung his feet to the floor. When dawn had come
up full he had blown out the candle and removed the blackout curtain, letting in such light as could at least make
shadows. These he had watched crossing the roofbeams as the
traffic wakened in the street below. "Rachel has converted,"
he said with a mock heartiness. "She has run away from me to
the convent, and when she is well again she will seek the veil.
Is that what you call it, seeking the veil?" He stretched to his
full height, stood on tiptoe, and touched the beams. The
tension broke for the moment.

"No."

"Taking the veil. That's it, isn't it?"

"You are not serious?" Gabrielle said.

"No. I am not serious."

The silence again, the stifling silence, more suffocating for
the medley of noises drifting up from Rue Louis Pasteur.
Gabrielle continued to gaze through a large knothole that
itself was the shape of an eye.

"What do you see, friend-sister?" Through the night he
had tried many ways of addressing her, none of them comfortable.

"I am not looking to see. I am watching particularly."

"Ah, but you are seeing nonetheless. Close your eyes. You
are able to tell me several things that have passed. Is that not
so?"

She closed her eyes. "A chestnut horse like Poirot; Père
Duloc with the children for First Communion instruction. And
some soldiers. I did not want to see them, but it was all
right."

"It was all right," Marc repeated.

"I mean I thought of something else—of other soldiers."

"Is that what it's like, being a nun—always thinking of something else?"

"Something else than what, monsieur?"

Marc threw up his hands. "It was you who said you thought of something else, seeing the soldiers."

"I thought of the soldiers at Calvary, and then of the soldiers burning Joan of Arc."

"They merely lit the fagots. It was the Inquisition that decreed her death."

"They didn't have to light the fagots," Gabrielle said.

Marc cocked his head and looked at her, trying to make her return his gaze. She would not. "What about your vow of obedience? A soldier takes it too, you know."

She thought about that for a moment. "Maybe he did not want to be a soldier."

"In which case would the vow not count?"

"I don't know. I only know I want to be a nun."

Marc sat down at the table and then got up immediately, exploding: "Christ! Why don't they come and tell us something? Why don't they come for you?"

"They will when it is time. Or I shall go."

"You cannot!" Marc said irrationally. "Not until Rachel returns. For her sake, not for mine. Oh, yes, for mine as well," he amended. "I want to live and I'm afraid to risk the daylight. Before Rachel I risked it many times. Now I no longer want to risk it. Love should not make cowards of us, little child of God."

"It isn't cowardly to want to live." Gabrielle gave up her vigil and returned to the table.

"I suppose not—no more than it is brave to want to die."

"Please don't talk about death any more," she said, and then, "unless you want to."

"All right, I won't. In the concentration camps, I've heard, they don't speak of death at all."

"We speak often of it, but as a friend," she said.

"So I have observed," Marc said cuttingly, after which neither of them spoke again for a long while.

Gabrielle had commenced praying the hours past with the six o'clock striking of the Angelus bell. Although she prayed silently, the pantomine accompanying it set Marc's nerves on edge, the breast thumping, the up and down on the knees, the signing of the cross. He tried to counterpoint it in his mind with such ritual as he remembered from his childhood, his grandfather touching the *mezuzah* at the door, the philacteries the old man strapped upon his arm, and sitting *sheva* himself when the old man died. His skinny buttocks numb, then prickly, and his neck prickly with the wailing of his grandmother in the other room, and the sing-song prayers of the *minyan* he had put on his shoes and gone from the house leaving one place vacant out of eight. "I do not believe," he said when his father had come after him. "Neither do I, my son, but it is our tradition, and without it we shall lose our Jewishness."

Marc removed a board from the window to the north, one that he could replace before dark, and took a book to the light. After reading for a little while he sought again to make up to Gabrielle for his harshness. "Shall I read aloud to you? I'm afraid you'll find it inappropriate—Stendhal's letters—but it's the only book I have."

"No, thank you, monsieur."

"If I could go out now and bring you a book, what would you want it to be?"

"Please do not make fun of me, monsieur."

"That is far from my intentions. You must have had a favorite subject in school."

"History."

"It was one of mine—and of Stendhal's, I should suppose by this. He was very silly about important people."

"I love best the stories about the saints who did things, you know, like St. Ignatius Loyola who was a soldier first."

"You're rather fond of soldiers, aren't you?"

"I'm not! I don't mean to be. I don't think I am."

"But the Crusades and all that—they were admirable, weren't they?"

"Oh, yes."

He went back to his reading. She sensed just by something lingering in the air that he did not believe they were admirable at all. So she sat, her head bowed down and tried to remember the reasons she believed in them: it came down really to the rescue of the hallowed places from the heathen Turks, the Holy Sepulchre, Jerusalem, the Holy City: it was much easier to think of Jesus Himself than of the Crusaders about whom she had never really thought at all, the entrance to the city on Palm Sunday with all the people coming out to follow Him, the children running after the donkey and His reaching down to them. His blessing of everybody, His touching of the unclean lepers. He was not afraid ever, except in the Garden when He was alone and foresaw Calvary while the disciples slept. And when He woke them, He did not want them to be afraid either. . . . Even when He arose from the dead and reappeared to them: Be not afraid. . . .

It was the tolling of the bells of St. Hilaire that broke her meditation. As she listened there was a pause. Then commenced the solemn peal of the passing bell. She marked each stroke with her fingers on the table while she whispered, *Requiescat in pace.* There seemed a sudden silence everywhere, then in the stillness the metallic clatter of horses' hooves in the street below. She went to the window and stood on tiptoe the better to see down through the small opening. Two horses, black ribbons flowing from their harness, drew the carriage on which the coffin rode, high and solitary. The driver walked alongside the horses, and behind the carriage Reverend Mother and Sister Agathe walked, their black beads in hand. Behind them a few people of the town followed, the women cowled in their shawls, the men bareheaded, and old Father Duloc had come out from St. Sébastien's with the processional cross.

Everything blurred for an instant for Gabriel. She cried out, "Monsieur Marc!"

Marc came, throwing the book on the table. He stared at her and she gestured that he must look out. The sound he made when he saw the procession was like the moan of a wounded animal. He moved his head one way, then another, trying to see better. Then with his bare hands he ripped the board from the frame.

Gabrielle looked out with him. A platoon of German soldiers, approaching, quick-stepped to the side of the street, turned about-face, and remained at attention while the carriage passed. Marc covered his mouth with his hands.

"Poor man, poor man," Gabrielle said. She lifted her hand but she could not touch him.

The soldiers resumed their march toward the station. Marc drew back from the window. He looked about him, bewildered, at Gabrielle as though he did not know her, then toward the door.

"You must not go out, monsieur. It will not help."

He turned back to the window. The procession was leaving Rue Louis Pasteur. A moment later it disappeared from sight.

"What will it not help?" he said, scarcely audible.

There was no sign now on the street to show that the procession had passed at all. The blacksmith had gone back to his forge. A gendarme was pumping up his bicycle tire while two children watched. Then one of them skipped away. The bells of St. Hilaire had been silent for some moments, but in the distance the convent bell had taken up the tolling.

Gabrielle made the sign of the cross and began to herself, "Out of the depths have I cried unto Thee, O Lord, Lord hear my voice. . . ."

"Do not pray for her. Please."

"I must pray, and God can make it fitting."

Marc kept shaking his head. Then he asked, "Where are they taking her?"

"To the Convent of Ste. Geneviève."

"Let us go then."

"No, monsieur. It is not safe."

"It is absurd to say now what is safe."

Gabrielle tried to think of a way to persuade him. "It is not safe for me," she said.

Marc was too distraught even to try to understand. He looked back and, seeing the board dangling, tried to put it in its place again. The nails were bent. He let it fall. "It does not matter."

"It does matter, believe me, monsieur. But it is better that we stay away from the window until it is dark. Someone might see you trying to fix it now."

"So much the better." After a moment he looked up at her. "Did you recognize the sisters?"

"Yes, monsieur."

"It happened?" He gestured vaguely toward the street. "It was not . . . I am not dreaming?"

"No, monsieur."

"During the night I kept thinking every once in a while, I'll wake up."

"I saw the procession as you did, Monsieur Marc, and I heard the passing bell. It tolled nineteen strokes."

He seemed about to smile. "But Rachel was only eighteen, friend-sister."

Gabrielle said nothing.

Slowly he understood. "You are nineteen?"

"Yes."

"And it is you they are mourning?"

"I think it is so, yes, monsieur."

He leaned his head back, twisting it, his hand at his neck. The numbness was going away. "Let them mourn for a little while. I shall go out then and tell the truth."

"Those who matter know the truth, monsieur."

"I need to know it, and I shall only know it when I have told it myself. My wife is dead. My wife—the word was not even real to me yet, the newness of it."

He sat down on the bench and Gabrielle, for the first time moving toward instead of away from him, sat opposite. For a long time he stared at the opening in the back window he had made to read by. "I want to think of you, friend-sister, and I cannot. I want to think of her and I cannot. Only of myself, of the uselessness, the absurdity of being me. The Resistance man that was here last night was right about the pride. Before . . . I got into trouble . . . I'm going to tell you something about Rachel in a minute, but this comes first . . . before I got into trouble, I used to think about going out into the streets in Paris, particularly I wanted to go into the Champs-Elysée where the Germans promenade, and I wanted to say to everybody, I am a Jew. But that was because I did not want to be a Jew. It was not that I was ashamed of it: there were many of us at the University who felt this way: it was a matter of getting rid of something old in ourselves so that we could be what we are, what we would become, aware only of self. It was not that we denied the blood of our forefathers, only its relevance to what we are. Then came the Nazis and the only relevance to them was the very thing we had cast off. Now it has become the only relevance to us. Do you understand?"

"I am trying to, monsieur. I think I do a little."

"To talk, to be alive, what is it?" He looked at his hands and turned them over, then back and over again. Then, "What is more beautiful than a child skipping down the street?"

"Please, monsieur, go on. I would like to know about you." This was not entirely so, but she wanted him to keep on talking for his own sake.

"I could have left France long ago, but I didn't want to. Many times I could have gone, because with the Occupation I went to work with an organization to try to get all the Jews out of the country before it was too late. I had friends in the Resistance who helped us. It was a mission of mercy, wouldn't you say, to get them out? And yet I hated every man I saw across the border safely. Why? Because I felt in my heart that

Frenchmen despised him, and despising him, despised me. I would not go myself. And when one of the Resistance leaders in Paris asked me to do a most dangerous assignment—to pretend I was a Nazi and get certain information for them—I embraced the opportunity. To prove what? That I was not a Jew? Or that I was?

"Afterwards, when I had failed my mission and the Nazis wanted me so that I had to run for my life, I said all this to Rachel one night, hiding with her. And she said to me, 'But Marc, you *are* a Jew.' And suddenly I understood: until I became a Jew, I could not be anything else.

"It was time for Rachel to go also from Paris. She knew Hebrew and Yiddish and there was getting to be a legend about her, for she had persuaded many people out who would rather have died where they were than start again another exodus. We were married—a week ago today, I think. And we would have gone to Palestine. Or tried to. I told you that, I think."

Gabrielle nodded.

"I wonder if we would have made it. I wonder if Rachel is right, if there will be a Jewish nation. I am not convinced; but I have come to think that only when there is such a nation, could I be a Frenchman again."

"But would you want to be, monsieur?"

"That is what Rachel said, shall we want to? I hated her for saying it. I was not ready yet. And when I started to run, I kept thinking: they will shoot me in the back and it will be said that like all Jews I had to be shot in the back. Now I will stop running and meet them in the face."

After a moment Gabrielle said, "You wish to be a martyr, but it cannot happen."

Marc looked at her. Her eyes remained fixed on her hands where they were folded before her on the table.

"To be a martyr," she went on carefully, "you have to believe."

"And don't you have to want to live?"

"I think that is so, monsieur, yes."

"Then it is simple—I do not want to be a martyr."

"Then why do you want to die?"

"Because life is meaningless unless we give it meaning, and I have none to give it now. But you are right, to die meaningfully one must also believe. Rachel believed. I only pretended."

"And to believe we must love, I think," she said.

Marc did not answer. He tried to think of love, of Rachel and his feeling for her which was as close as he had come to love.

Gabrielle said, "When I was preparing to enter the novitiate Reverend Mother wrote something in my retreat book which I memorized. Let me say it for you. 'God gives us love, something to love He lends us, and when love has grown to fullness, that on which it throve falls off, and love is left alone.' "

"I shall have to think about that," Marc said. "I shall have to think about it to try to understand it—and I will try because I know you would not have said it unless it had deep meaning for you. But I suspect it will be difficult without God."

"God is love, monsieur."

15

REVEREND MOTHER DIRECTED THAT THE COFFIN BE PLACED IN THE vestibule outside the chapel's great doors. Father Duloc who had followed the hearse all the way up the road remained at her request. He was an old man now and given more and more to the company of the children to whom in spirit, Reverend Mother felt, he had always been very close. He was the confessor of the lay nuns, but much loved by all the community. As on innumerable other occasions, for he was always hungry, Reverend Mother sent him to Sister Barbara in the kitchen. She then summoned the community to the common room.

The absence of Sister Gabrielle from her appointed place and duties had been observed, and when Reverend Mother and Sister Agathe had left the convent on receiving a call from the hospital, a prayerful vigil had commenced. Whispered rumors had spread, the worst of them seeming confirmed with the coming of the funeral cortege. Reverend Mother was aware of the sounds of sniffling as the nuns waited in silence for her sign to be seated.

"Dear sisters in Christ," Reverend Mother commenced, looking down the two long rows of solemn faces which at this table were so often mirthful, "our beloved foundress, the blessed Marie d'Étienne, once said, 'We shall not always be wise, for even the Mother of Christ could not always understand His ways. Therefore does humility the more become us.' Sister Gabrielle is not dead. But she gave her identity to a Jewish woman in order that the woman might enter the hospital, and in the expectation that this would save her life. We consented, or would have consented, had word of the emergency been able to reach us. We do not wish to burden you with more than you need to know, for it may happen that the police or the Occupation authorities will question us. We shall try in every way to spare you such distraction, but we must all be prepared."

The redoubtable St. André gave a nod of approval. It required an act of will on the part of Reverend Mother to control her irritation. "The Jewish woman died this morning, but her husband is still alive and in hiding. So we shall bury this unfortunate woman in a nun's grave until such less troubled time when her people may claim her as their own. Her death has been publicly registered as Sister Marie Gabrielle."

Certain of the novices bowed their heads as though at word of the death of one of them.

"I am sure Sister Gabrielle will return to us as soon as it is safe to do so. Whether or not this is so, our rules of silence and seclusion henceforth rigidly prevail. We shall not any of us again leave these walls by our own consent unless it is not to return."

The older nuns who sat closest to her as in counsel nodded approval of this stricter construction of the rule. She would have to go far down the table to find a member of the community who would have countenanced Gabrielle's mission in the first place. She considered her admission the humbling of herself before them: the manner of it, however, needed to be consistent with the maintenance of discipline among the entire community. "We wish now to consult our historian on the manner most fitting to the burial of someone of the Jewish faith."

The convent historian, Sister St. Jérôme, sat in silence for a minute or two. Her scholarship in Greek and Latin was greater than in Hebrew, but her knowledge of the Old Testament was fair. "May we speak, Reverend Mother?"

"We have so requested. I should say that Father Duloc is with us and I am sure he will assist in such manner as we wish. It will be well for the people to see a priest present, and we have set the hour for burial at twelve today."

"Then I should suggest the reading of certain of the Psalms which I shall mark for Father in the Psaltery."

The old priest squinted and twisted his head with the glare of sunlight on the illuminated pages. The wind from the plains billowed his surplice and bent the tall grass round the gravestones which themselves had bent before the wind, as had also the gnarled trees by the fence. It was among these trees that twenty or so of the townspeople stood in silent attendance. They had come up the hill with the tolling of the convent bell, but not many had come, for there had been one funeral in the town that morning, that of the woman killed by the German soldier. There was also a rumor among those who had come that the novice had died of a mysterious disease which accounted for the early burial. If Father Duloc stumbled in the intonation of the Latin phrases that were unfamiliar to him, no one knew: he would have stumbled now and then on familiar ones as well.

> . . . God hath spoken in his holiness.
> I will rejoice, and I will divide Sichem, and I will mete out the vale of tabernacles.
> Galaad is mine; and Manassas is mine; and Ephraim the protection of my head.
> Judah is my kind: Moab the pot of my hope.
> Over Edom I will stretch out my shoe: the aliens are become my friends.
> Who will bring me into the strong city? who will lead me into Edom?
> Wilt not thou, O God, who has cast us off? and will not thou, O God, go forth with our armies?
> O grant us help from trouble: for vain is the help of man.
> Through God we shall do mightily: and he will bring our enemies to nothing.

Father Duloc threw a handful of dust on the coffin. Reverend Mother threw a handful also. The community, as one voice, said three times: *"Requiescat in pace."*

In the wake of Reverend Mother and Father Duloc the nuns filed back toward the cloister, leaving only two novices to spade the earth over the shallow grave. The mourners outside the fence began their trek back into the town, stopping to pray for a moment at the roadside place where the other

woman had died. The scythe still stood to mark it. Overnight
throughout St. Hilaire, crude drawings of the scythe had appeared, chalked on walls, smeared in mud on the public
noticeboard the Germans had erected outside the *Hôtel de
ville*.

Moissac, returning with Maman to where he had parked
the car near the convent gate, saw that someone had traced a
scythe in the dust on the Peugeot door. He opened the door
quickly so that Maman should not see and demand to know
what it meant. She had eyes like a ferret, but at that moment
she had chosen to head toward the convent. He caught her
arm and moved her on to the car.

"Shall we not pay our condolences to Reverend Mother?"
She would not let him go to a funeral without her.

"No. I have already done so."

"Did we know the girl?"

"No, maman."

"They have so many strangers now," she complained as
he tucked her skirts in round her legs. "I used to know every
nun by name. Do you remember when we came for the plums
at the end of the picking, Théophile?"

"I remember."

He turned the car around and drove down the hill onto
the highway. The first of the walking mourners had reached
the site of the scythe. They did not raise their heads when he
passed.

Maman twisted around in her seat to see what they were
looking at. "What's that, Théophile?"

"It is where the woman was shot yesterday. She was a
crazy woman, but they will make a martyr of her."

"Couldn't we stop?"

"For what?"

"To pray for the repose of her soul."

"We can go to the cathedral chapel later. You can light a
candle for her."

"But no one will know."

"God will know," he said.

16

"WHEN YOU ARE GONE," MARC SAID, "THEN I WILL KNOW THAT SHE is gone as well."

"I cannot go until dark, monsieur."

"I know. And when it is dark I will go with you for I want to see her grave. Then I will believe it. I will bury her hair as well and then there will be nothing to show that she walked the earth at all."

"You will know it, monsieur, and the people she helped."

"Why do they live—men, women we had to coax, threaten, beg to save themselves? Why? Why should I live and Rachel die at eighteen years of age?"

"She had faith, monsieur. She would not have been afraid to die."

"That is romantic, friend-sister. If she was not afraid it was because she did not believe she was going to die. Do you tell me you are not afraid to die?"

"I do not know. You are right. I do not know what it is to die because the one death I think so much about means life. Christ died to save men from eternal death."

"Eternal death," Marc repeated. "Christ died to save men. . . ." He let the words trail off hoping to catch an association the promise of which, if he could but catch it, seemed relevant. He had it then. He began to hum softly. Then: "'Mine eyes have seen the glory of the coming of the Lord. He hath trampled out the vintage where the grapes of wrath are stored.' It is an American song. I've forgotten. . . ." Then he had that too: "'As He died to make men holy, let us die to make men free, His truth goes marching on.'"

"It is very beautiful."

"What does it mean? Mine eyes have not seen the glory.

No Jew's have. We are still waiting for the Messiah."

"But He has come, monsieur, and He was Jewish."

Marc laughed aloud at the folksiness of it, the kind of confident persuasiveness that was meant to help him understand. "Forgive me, little sister. I cannot explain, but it is quite pointless, this conversation."

"I know, monsieur, and it is wrong of me to speak."

"If I converted to the faith, would that make it right for you to have spoken?"

She said nothing.

"Well?"

"You are mocking."

"Do you realize, sister, that every time I ask a question you cannot or do not wish to answer, you say that I am mocking you? I am not. I could wish that I believed as you do, that I believed a flight of angels waited on Rachel to take her home to Abraham's bosom—for she was good, if kindness is the measure of good and I feel it may be the only measure—I could wish I so believed, but I cannot."

"It is enough to wish."

"No. It is not enough to wish: that's much too simple and utterly futile. I wish Rachel were still alive and in the clothes you wear. But one must somehow act, do, and wishing is not action. Prayer is not action." He paused, remembering something strikingly close to the mood and the feeling of that moment. "Last night. . . ." He repeated the words marveling that so little time could encompass so much change. "Last night when Rachel lit the candle she said the prayer and I responded, just saying, Amen. And then I tried to make it seem of no importance, that I really was not participating. Tradition, I said, and Rachel said, It is enough.

"And that is how we'd have gone on, wandering until we reached wherever we were to go, she with faith and I dogging along in the tracks left by tradition. Which in itself is strange for me. If I believe in anything it is only the now, the existence within the moment. But to live, a man must have a place. Isn't it strange? For all the slaughtered Jews in history there was place enough to bury them, but for the living, not a place at all."

He was touching on something that had disturbed Gabrielle during the night: there had come to her mind with great vividness the face and gestures of a nun who had once taught her Christian doctrine. She remembered the nun's saying with a kind of spitting zeal, for the spittle gathered in the corners of her mouth when she was excited, "And from that day forward, the Jews were condemned to wander the face of the earth forever, a cursed race with no country of their own."

"There has to be a place," Marc said. "If graves can be carved from the earth, why not a country? Will you say Amen to that, little sister?"

"If it is God's will," Gabrielle murmured.

"Be damned to you and the will of God," Marc said, and went from her as far as the confines of the loft would allow. In a little while he came back. "I'm sorry I said that. I forget that to you all good things are done by the will of God."

"And some bad things, monsieur, though it must grieve Him."

Marc studied her face in the shadows: he thought she had aged overnight, but so had he. "There is this we both believe in, friend-sister, our freedom to choose. However narrow the alternatives may seem, there are choices to be made."

"You will go on, monsieur?"

"It is my duty."

Her eyes seemed very bright in their brief meeting with his. She bowed her head.

"You are giving thanks for that?"

"Yes, Monsieur Marc." She did not look up.

"Amen," he said and reached out his hand, intending just to touch hers where they were folded upon one another on the table. She snatched them away and buried them in her lap.

"I am sorry, monsieur. I know you did not mean evil."

"What man thinks he does in his heart? Yet evil is done night and day. I am very tired. I'm going to lie down and try

to sleep now. Yesterday. . . ." He turned and looked at the
bed in the corner beneath the eaves. "We have no choice of
yesterdays, that's certain. But if I had, it would have been just
as it was for Rachel and me for a few hours yesterday. And
for that, little Sister Gabrielle, I am profoundly grateful to
you."

Gabrielle turned the chair so that its back would be
toward him when he lay upon the bed. For a few minutes,
discovering the sheen of a spider's web in a shaft of light near
the rafters, she was caught again in the daydreams of her
childhood. She remembered catching grasshoppers and holding them until they spilled their amber liquid; she remembered burrowing into the haycock where the setting chicken
had concealed her eggs, and the wild strawberries of May she
also remembered. Then came that loveliest of all her memo-
ries, the herding of the cows and her most particular friend
among them: she had sometimes lain crouched against the
bulging warm belly protected there from the wind, and she
had played her fingers over the silken hair in the hollow
above the udder, and over the veins that rose like map mark-
ings in the udder itself which, as the day went on, filled mi-
raculously with milk until by sundown it was spilling from the
teats onto the back of her hand, and she had known then that
it was time to go.

Gabrielle was recalled from her reverie by a sound from
the bed. Marc lay face down trying to stifle in his arm the
choking sobs: tears had come at last. In her own throat she
could feel them too, salt and sear. A man's crying was too terrible: she remembered her father's when her mother died.
Her mother she could not remember at all, only the high bed
and its whiteness, and her sister following the priest with a
candle, and most strongly, the horny palm of her father's
hand as he led her into the room.

At six o'clock she said again the Angelus, and toward
sundown, vespers. Marc slept for several hours, but even
when he wakened they spoke no more until darkness came
and the street fell silent. He straightened the nails in the

board and put it back in place. Then, dropping the black
curtain, he lit the candle and got Rachel's shawl from the
valise. "You will feel better wearing this tonight," he said.
"Afterwards you can give it to the poor."

They walked along the canal wall and out of the town by
the road the procession had gone that morning. The hour was
early, but the travelers few. Their one encounter with a vehicle was with a truckload of singing soldiers. Caught in the
approaching headlights, Marc and Gabrielle merely stood
aside.

"*Gute Nacht*," the men called out and kept on singing.

"What has gone wrong with them?" Marc said. "From
Brahms to the *Horst Wessel*. It would be ridiculous if it were
not so terrible."

Gabrielle offered up the pain from the shoes which did
not fit her, but when she realized that she might blister her
feet she took off the shoes and went on barefoot.

They moved from the road to the path that climbed up
through the grove of wind-bent trees, even as the townspeople had approached the nuns' cemetery that day noon.

"There is an iron fence," Gabrielle said.

Marc had already seen it in the moonlight. "There would
be only one new grave?"

"Yes, monsieur."

He stopped among the trees. "I will be able to find it
myself, then. Go, kind and gentle friend, back to the life you
have chosen."

"It is better that I wait until you go."

Marc swung himself up and then vaulted over the fence.
He waited hunched in the grass, and listened. There might
have been peace the world over for all the sounds in that
silvery moonlight: crickets and a distant owl hallowing the
moon. Gabrielle followed Marc moving alongside the fence.
When he stooped down and sifted the fresh earth through his
hands, she knelt and, blessing herself, prayed for the repose of
the girl she was finding it hard now herself to believe dead.

Watching Marc dig a little furrow and empty into it Rachel's
hair, she thought about the word husband, *mari,* and bride,
and why it seemed appropriate to call a nun the bride of Christ:
truly a marriage sanctified in heaven and the only one beyond
death's touching.

Marc straightened up and stood at the graveside and
looked up at the stars. He pointed his finger at one; then
another, and another yet of them to the number of seven and
called himself the eighth.

> *"Yis -go-dal v'yis-ka-dash sh'may rabo*
> *B'olmo dee-vro hiir usay, v'yamleeh malhusay . . ."*

And on he went, saying into the night all of *kaddish* that
remained with him of childhood's rote: "Magnified and sanctified be his great name throughout the world which he hath
created according to his will. May he establish his kingdom
during the days of your life and during the life of all the
house of Israel, speedily, yea, soon; and say ye, Amen . . ."

There was the slightest turn of his body with the last
words, and behind him, hearing the word, Gabrielle repeated
the amen.

As Marc climbed over the fence and dropped to Gabrielle's side he saw the man coming out of the woods. He
caught Gabrielle's arm and turned her around so that they
would confront him together. René took off the beret, identifying himself by the white hair, but he said bitingly as he
came up, "And where from here, monsieur—madame?"

Neither of them could speak for a second or two. Then
Marc said, "It is Monsieur Labrière."

"Fortunate, is it not? Perhaps I am too cautious. I was
waiting in the mill, taking no chance of leading anyone up to
you, when down the steps you came like a pair of babes on
their way to their grandmother's."

"My circumstance has changed since our last meeting,
monsieur," Marc said.

"I have figured that out for myself. A Jewish lady does

not kneel and make the sign of the cross when she prays, even at the grave of a nun. And it so happened, the prefect of police picked me up last night when he was bringing two nuns back here from the hospital. But you should not have deceived me, monsieur, that this young lady was your wife."

"We did not know then that my wife would die."

"I understand, but you should not have deceived me all the same, for now we could be in a fine mess. This morning I contacted our people in Fauré and arranged that you should keep the Belloirs' identities a few days longer. You are to join the harvesters tonight. We have fixed up papers that should be safe enough for that and the arrangement is made with the syndicate. You will be on your way well ahead of the Belloirs' return. In three days' time you will see the mountains, and some of them in Spain."

"I am ready now," Marc said.

"And you, madame?"

Gabrielle drew back a step, not sure of what he meant.

"She will go back to the convent from here," Marc said.

René shook his head. "That is what I thought you had in mind. No, monsieur. It will not work. They are expecting a man and wife, Jean and Marie Belloir. You have one work permit between you, don't you understand? It gives you the added cover of the wife. Do you think it is easy to pass someone with your history?"

"I am grateful, Monsieur Labrière, but it is simple. The harvesters are not going to wait for workers who do not show up. They will go out on schedule, and if you cannot provide me with other papers, I will leave St. Hilaire without them."

"How far will you go, do you think? A man without an I.D. card, especially you, will not be long in getting your own back, and after it a bullet. It is a quick death, the firing squad, if that is what you wish."

"You are cruel, monsieur," Gabrielle said.

"If I am cruel it is to save his life, and if you are kind you will stay with him. I did not mistake you last night, my little peasant sister. You are no stranger to the harvest."

"It is so," she said.

"The gentleman-architect will not know a binder from a *gazogène*. If you have stayed the night with him, you can stay a few nights more."

"Why do you insist, monsieur?" Marc said.

"Because it is a workable escape, if you will help it work."

Gabrielle walked toward the fence, going apart from them. Why there was such stillness except for their voices, she did not know. The convent was in utter darkness. Not even the portress' light was burning. It was as though everyone had gone away.

"I cannot ask it of the girl," Marc said.

"If I were you, I would beg it of her. If I can tell her for a farm girl, a nun will know her for a nun, and we do not lack for convents in this part of France. When you are gone, she will not have far to go alone."

Finally the men stopped talking. She could not pray, only the whispered, Thy will be done. She went back to where they waited. "I will go with Monsieur Marc."

"There, monsieur. I have told you, it is the women of France who have the courage." To Gabrielle, René said, "From here on you will call him Jean, and no more Monsieurs. And you are Marie, Marie Belloir. You will go back to the loft, sign your papers, and get your baggage. I have left two blankets for you. It will be a cold winter for me also if you do not make it. You will go at once to seventeen, Rue de Marseille, Madame Fontaine's. . . ."

While he instructed them, he worked an envelope from what Marc thought was an elastic truss. "Do you have money, monsieur?"

"How much do you want?"

"Not a *centime,* but I have given you the name of a mountain guide. He will expect a great deal of money and you had better give it to him. It would be a great shame to escape the *Boches* and fall victim to a smuggler's knife."

"I have money," Marc said.

René said, "Come, Madame Belloir."

They sat upon the ground among the trees, the three of them, for a few minutes while Marc and Gabrielle rehearsed the things they needed to know by rote.

"It is possible," René said then, "that you will encounter again our prefect of police and he will remember you from *Au Bon Coin*. You will say you came that night looking for the harvesters: they used to stay in Michelet—when all of us were innocent. This morning you will say, you saw the prefect of agriculture. Then you went home to bring your wife, home being the village of Fauré."

"I understand," Marc said.

"Moissac may be a patriot, but I doubt it. He is what the wind tells him to be, blowing him from place to place. *Mon Dieu!* I have just thought of something: did you deceive me with the photos of your wife?"

"When I gave them to you, it was necessary that her photos be on the documents."

"It disturbs me," René said. "I did not properly observe."

"There was a certain resemblance," Marc said, and though instinct told him not to, he nonetheless added: "The Jewish eyes, I suppose."

René let a second or two pass before he said, "You do not have enough enemies, monsieur?"

"You are right. It was unnecessary for me to have said that."

"But then again, it is not necessary that we be friends. What is necessary is that madame come to my shop—Number 12, Rue de Michelet—very early in the morning. There is no time now so we must chance the pictures. But tomorrow madame's portrait must be her own. There is risk enough for everybody without that. Madame?"

Gabrielle finally answered. "Yes, monsieur?"

"Your left hand, please. Hold it out."

Gabrielle obeyed.

"You must wear a wedding ring."

"We can say that she lost it," Marc said.

"Monsieur, there are things you will say which truth would only burden. Do you have your wife's ring?"

"Yes."

"Give it to madame and allow her the delicacy of explaining to her heart."

Marc took the ring from his coin pocket and gave it into Gabrielle's hand.

I am the betrothed of Christ, she said, but to herself only, and she slipped the ring on her own finger.

17

IT WAS ALMOST TEN WHEN THEY APPROACHED RUE DE MARSEILLE just above the Old Town. They carried a blanket apiece, and Marc the valise.

"Marie, Marie, Marie," he said.

"It is not so difficult for me. After all, I am Sister Marie Gabrielle."

"And I am Jean. Come," he whispered, "let me hear you call me Jean."

"Jean . . . I had an Uncle Jean," she said as in sudden discovery.

Marc said, "I don't think you had better call me uncle."

He saw a little flash of her white teeth, the momentarily irrepressible smile.

The lights were on full in Number 17. Men's laughter crashed the stillness. It had been so long since Marc had heard it, ringing, hearty, unbrooked, that he moistened his lips with a kind of appetite. Gabrielle hung back. He wanted to give her his hand, to take her arm, something to temper the strangeness. It would have harmed more than helped.

He ventured, "They won't pay us much attention."

"I'm fine," she said. "It's only that there are sounds I am not used to any more."

Two policemen drew themselves up as the travelers approached. There was the fragrance of wine in their manners and on their breath. Marc identified himself as a harvester and offered their identity cards. The examination was cursory.

"Go in, monsieur, before the feast is over." The officer opened the door for them and pulled the bell cord that hung alongside it.

Marc's quick impression was of a bordel although his experience of such was meager—the faded plushness that had never been quite elegant, the worn stair carpeting, the beaded curtains between the vestibule and a sitting room from be-yond which came the talk and laughter, the tinkle of silver, the clatter of plates. Even the vestibule was redolent with the smell of roasted fowl and the pangs of a long hunger con-stricted his stomach. He was wrong about the bordel, he told himself at once, and the impression was typical of a Parisian venturing in a provincial *pension.* It was a new world to him as well as to Gabrielle. If it had been Rachel beside him, and there were times he almost believed it was and all the rest a dream, he would have said that this was the true beginning of their journey. He kept watching Gabrielle, the flight of her eyes at each new sound, the bird-like alertness.

A face as comic as a pantomimist's poked through the beaded curtains. His nose was red and his black hair tousled. "You are the Belloirs, no? You are not hungry? Come quickly, now." He groped at the curtains, parting them in strands.

But at that moment Madame Fontaine herself came out from another door, this one onto the *petit salon,* where Marc saw briefly, as though glimpsing a room-within-room painting, the masters of the feast, the men of property, whose lands would yield the harvest.

"You are late, monsieur, madame." She asked for their I.D. cards. She was an ample, florid woman, her bosom all but overflowing the bodice. Gabrielle's eyes were briefly cap-tive to it. The color rose in her face as she realized and looked away.

"We have walked a long way," Marc said.

"Then you will eat. Everyone eats tonight!" She took their cards, and held Marc's briefly under the light. To learn his profession, he realized. She said, "You will be busy. They need a doctor in attendance, that crew." She locked their cards in a drawer with numerous others. "Please sign the registry, monsieur, and go in to dinner." She raised her voice to the comic one, who lingered, draping himself with the strands of beads in the archway: "Monsieur Jacques! Take madame in."

To Marc: *"Monsieur le docteur* and madame will have a room to themselves, at the top of the stairs, the third floor. For now, leave your luggage here by the desk."

For the first time Marc realized the possible implications of carrying a medical student's identification on such a project. He did not correct madame's *"le docteur"* however, cherishing for Gabrielle what privacy the room at the top might provide. He hastened to catch up with her where she was being propelled—carried would almost have been the word —by the tall, gangling man with the sadly comic face. They reached the long table together, where all faces turned to them. The tall one introduced himself, but by one name only: "I am Jacques."

Marc shook hands with him. "I am Jean, my wife is Marie."

And pointing one by one around the table, Jacques introduced as motley a crowd as Marc had ever met: some there were who looked to be gypsies, but that was a kind of prejudice on his part. Nor should he have had anything against gypsies. After all, they ranked almost as high with Nazidom as Jews, but he tended to take everyone with a Spanish cast—Gascon, Basque, Languedoc—for gypsies; and there was also in his view of such countrymen the awareness of class: these were working people; even the students, mostly from Toulouse, were the sons of peasants—and the daughters. The names he might remember, given time: Philomène, a woman well over forty with great strong shoulders and a laugh that quivered the glassware; it was she Marc had walked beside, escaping the station with some of these very people; she winked at him, but said nothing of that encounter; there was Artur, a dwarf, who seemed to be proud to be one, for he hopped down from the chair and came to shake hands, and he only a head above the table; Antoine and Michelle, lovers, Marc pegged them at once, volunteering for these two weeks under the stars together. . . . In time, given time, he would learn all their names. Given time: it was the byword of the refugee. He and Gabrielle took their places at the table. Madame's serving girl brought them soup, thick bean soup with shreds of meat in it.

Marc inhaled the aroma, then took a spoonful. He turned to Gabrielle: "Bless the food, Marie, for it is good."

Gabrielle gave thanks. He had made it easier for her to eat. She spoke not a word aloud and kept her eyes cast down.

The women opposite, Philomène and Céleste, who called herself an actress so that Jacques had introduced her as Céleste, the actress, nudged one another, watching Gabrielle. They mistook her carefulness in eating for the discrimination of class, Marc thought, which in combination with his blue-eyed fairness—from his Polish grandmother, he'd been told —and his over-refined features, could make their lot among this crowd a hard one. Add to that his own ineptitude with the pitchfork. Their harvest journey was going to be something short of a honeymoon. The irony of this comparison made him draw his lips into a tight smile. His eyes met Philomène's. She smiled back at him and her chest rose with the sudden intake of her breath.

A man must use the talents he had. Marc said, "You are an actress, *mam'selle?*"

She shook her head.

Céleste said, "I am the actress."

"And yet a harvester?" Marc said, giving Céleste his attention.

"My mother has a farm and I was raised on it. I am between engagements and it is healthful to follow the harvest."

And there are more men among us than women, Marc thought, but he nodded agreement and turned again to Philomène. "Then you sing?"

"How did you know?"

He made a gesture using his own chest, to indicate awareness of her splendid bosom. She lifted her wine glass to

him and, about to drink, slopped a few drops on that ample
bosom. The man next to her laughed aloud. She flipped the
last of the wine into his face. The dwarf clapped his hands
for joy.

Jacques cried out, "What a waste of wine!" but he was
between Philomène and the man, Félix, in one long stride, the
wine carafe in hand. He refilled both their glasses—and in-
sured the peace.

One of the students at the end of the table tuned his
guitar.

Madame Fontaine brought a large wheel of cheese and
quartered it at the table. Her red-faced helper, who did
everything at a trot, brought Marc and Gabrielle a platter
of roasted fowl, understandably now in shreds and pieces,
but who could care? and potatoes. Jacques filled their
glasses.

"Give up the harvest, Jacques. You must stay and be my
host," madame said.

"Alas, I have signed a contract," Jacques said, "but I shall
remember in the fall."

Marc passed the cheese. It went hand to hand, no plate,
each taking his own knife to carve a piece for himself. Marc
sipped the wine. It was not bad, though he would venture to
say they were drinking better in the *petit salon*. His first
hunger tempered, he sat back and looked over Madame Fontaine's decor. A Moorish influence: the heavy use of timber,
archways, the graceful iron sconces on the wall. The door of
several carved panels separated this large room from the
smaller dining salon which he had seen from the vestibule. He
would have liked to see that setting again; and as though to
oblige him, a moment or two later a man slid open the door
and came in.

Jacques lifted his glass to the gentleman and said, "Monsieur Dorget, the minister of agriculture."

The man, dressed in a dinner jacket that no longer could
meet across his cummerbund, held up his hand in demur.
"Please, please. It is trouble enough to be prefect of the de-

partment." He was a shy-looking, if burly, man. He stood for a second or two, his finger to his lip as he thoughtfully looked around the table. "You have not starved either, I see." Then, indicating with his finger—just a flick of it to Marc: "Monsieur Belloir."

Marc rose from his chair and went to the man. The prefect of agriculture offered his hand, and although they had not met before, he said, "It is nice to see you again. I am glad you and madame are able to complete our group." He addressed the others then also: "We'll make a good team, is that not so?"

It was an invitation to come alive, to volatility. The response pleased him, a vigorous assent.

Under its cover he said to Marc, "You have your work permit, yours and madame's?"

"Yes, monsieur."

And to the others again: "Didn't I hear a guitar? Our hosts wouldn't mind a serenade. I think you'll agree, they deserve it."

Marc was able once again to observe the other dining party, all of the guests in dinner jackets, save one in the purple garb of the Church, substantial men, high-complexioned now. The table shone with silver, and the glassware had its own song. The wine was in bottles and not in carafes, and there was fruit piled high—Spanish oranges, the apples and plums of Agenais. One knew this feast to be traditional, and indeed it was not hard to transpose these very men with their counterparts in a group portrait hanging over the buffet, seventeenth-century men in ruffs and doublets with their broad-brimmed hats somewhat askew.

Again the dwarf was clapping his hands.

"I knew I was wise to sign him on," the prefect said and nodded to Marc to return to his place.

Gabrielle glanced up at him.

"It will be fine," he said, "but you must eat more than that."

"Couldn't we take it with us?"

Marc laughed aloud. "Yes, inside us," he said, and set to his own food with a will.

The guitarist gave one loud strum. But instead of making music, he said defiantly, "I do not play for Vichy."

The government official, not a large man in any flamboyant way, ambled the length of the table and stood, his arms folded, looking down at the youth. "Play for yourself, my young fool. Or else do not play ever. If Vichy is listening, so much the better that they hear only music."

Meanwhile Jacques had begun to snap his fingers, rhythms Marc associated with Spain more than France. Softly Jacques whistled a beguiling tune to coax the others, and because the dwarf broke the rhythm with his off-beat clapping, one and then another of the men strengthened it, tapping on the table. Philomène began to hum, then one man and another to sing. The guitarist was left to catch up.

Madame Fontaine and Monsieur Dorget opened the panel doors, making the two rooms one. At the master of the feast's behest she brought the bowls of fruit to the workers' table. The gentlemen had reached Armagnac and cigars.

"How old is this tradition?" Marc asked the man beside him. He realized at once he should not have asked such a question, posing as a native of a village twenty kilometers away. But the man misunderstood him with the singing, or perhaps because of his accent. The response was as though he had himself told something. "I know," the man shouted, nodding.

Gabrielle said, "Very old. It might even once have been a pagan feast, a sacrifice to the gods. Now it is in honor of the Blessed Virgin, to pray for good weather and a bounteous harvest."

The words, Marc thought, must come from a patterned prayer: she would not have used such a word as "bounteous" otherwise. This, and seeing at the right hand of the master of the feast, a purpled prelate, somehow reminded Marc of who he was, or rather, by his own calculation, of who he was not.

"Do you not drink wine?" he said, for her glass remained full.

"Water, monsieur, but I do not need any."

"What is my name?" Marc whispered.

"Yes, yes," she said. "I knew the moment I said it."

"The priest in the next room—or is it a bishop?—will he recognize you if he sees you closely?" Marc spoke leaning close to her ear and then turning his head that she might speak into his.

For the first time Gabrielle looked directly into the *petit salon*. She had been aware of it on the edge of her vision, but made a little discipline of denying her curiosity. "It is Monsignor La Roque. He will not look at us that closely, never fear."

The way she said it and the blush that followed closely on the words told Marc much about the monsignor, and something also about Gabrielle. But then he would not have expected a rubber stamp to do what she had done.

The song was about a drummer boy on his way to serve in King Louis's war. Jacques displayed an intriguing talent: he could whistle two notes at once, and with a sharp sweetness that resembled the sound of a flute. He grinned and bowed afterwards, and pointed to the space between his front teeth.

The guitarist stroked the strings, and choosing his moment, sounded a tremolo. His fellow students called out for everyone to listen to "Our Jules." Jules tossed back his hair and began to sing. His was a small voice but that somehow added to the poignancy of the song: "These mountains so high keep me from seeing my love. . . ." Marc, his wine glass in hand, sat back and thought of the mountains into which he must vanish some few days hence, and of Rachel. "If I knew where to find her, I would pass over water and have no fear of drowning," the song went on. Marc tried to distract himself, looking into the other room. The man of the Church cared about neither song nor singer obviously: he talked

throughout and the undertone of his voice annoyed Marc. He
would have liked to tell him to be silent. He thought then
how, given back the security he once knew, he would have
enjoyed baiting the ascetic prelate. And there was something
in him now that made him want to parade Gabrielle before
his eyes. To what purpose? She knew what the man was like.
Indeed was not his own hatred of the monsignor—and it was
that somehow—based on her character of him? There is a
cruel streak in you, Daridan, that mark of the beast in every
man, however pale in some. No more than a jeweled cross
could make a saint of the cleric in the other room, did persecution assure the innocence of its victim: it assured only the
guilt of the persecutor.

Moissac lingered in the vestibule for a few moments before making known his presence. He listened to the singing.
He wanted to hear again the song called *Bigarren Kalez-Kale*
which had troubled him so marvelously last night. He had
learned from one of his men that the high whirring falsetto in
the refrain was meant to convey the whinnying of mountain
horses. This only provoked Moissac more, for to him there
was nothing more exciting than a mare in heat and a stallion
about to mount her. Tonight he wanted to see the woman
whose voice could melt the marrow in his bones. But he did
not propose to play the swain, assuredly not before the most
influential men of the countryside. He had dressed carefully in
his Sunday suit; carefully but casually. He purposely put on a
mended collar; with neither airs nor groveling, he played that
which he profoundly wished to be, a man in command of
himself. Fearful of being discovered alone and without purpose in the vestibule, he touched the bell alongside the registry, and while he waited glanced at the names in the book.
The last signed in, Jean Belloir—for himself and madame—
had a signature worthy of a more distinguished document
than Madame Fontaine's guest book.

Madame came through the door of the *petit salon* leaving
it open on a scene that filled Moissac with longing: men of

property enjoying one another's company and the pleasures of their wealth.

Madame brought out the identity cards for what Moissac knew she wanted to be a routine check. She would not like so important a room of guests disturbed. "Take your work into the parlor, *Monsieur le Préfet*," she said. "I will bring you coffee and Armagnac."

"Coffee?"

"And I will tell your friend, the monsignor, that you are here."

"Did he speak of me?"

"You will be very comfortable there, and you will be able to see what is going on. They will dance perhaps tonight, and I will be grateful that you are here."

She went off instantly, closing the door between him and his betters, and having answered none of his questions. It did not matter. It was enough that she knew him and the monsignor to be friends. He had not himself told her so. He groped his way through the beaded curtains and settled in a chair where he could observe the harvesters' table without himself being noticed. It was a great shame that he would soon have to see their work papers also, and therefore interrupt the festivities. He heard it then, the beginning of the song he craved to hear again. He moved swiftly nearer the door, the better to find among those at the table the songbird: she must not be too young, he thought, nor yet too old, and then he cursed himself for such a thought at all.

His eyes fell first on the face of Gabrielle: she too had been caught by the wild vigor of the song. Her eyes had shot up and her lips parted in the excitement. Moissac thought he had never seen anything so beautiful in his life. At first he thought it was she who was singing, but he knew almost instantly that it could not be: there was such innocence in the face—a purity, he could think of no other word; then, when the eyes lowered demurely he felt a gallantry come upon him, a touch in his own soul of the chivalry he so much admired. It was only then that he looked to see who was beside her. He had to move a little to see around Jacques' great tousled head. He saw Marc as the latter leaned close to Gabielle to tell her what he had just learned of the origins of the street song. Moissac remembered at once where he had seen him.

Was it possible that the Gestapo was infiltrating the harvesters? But of course he did not know the man was Gestapo: that René had told him he also thought so was proof of nothing. He watched the couple so absorbed in one another that he had to assume they were together, and instinctively he thought the man must fit the signature he had observed in madame's book. He had forgotten the name, but he could find it from the signature on the identity card. They were registered as monsieur and madame: he remembered that. He lingered a little longer to watch them. This man could not be Gestapo and have this girl for wife: on that Moissac would stake his job.

The song ended and he had scarcely heard it. The harvesters were pushing away from the table and some of them moving chairs. Soon the table was pushed to the wall. In the room beyond he saw the monsignor rise in purple-sashed splendor. Would he come to speak to his friend, perhaps to take him in among the gentlemen? Moissac hastened to the table with the lamp on it in order to be busy and began his search for the I.D. card of the stranger he had first seen at Gaucher's. Belloir. He had just found the card when Madame Fontaine returned and threw on the wall switch, lighting up the room like a circus tent. Now everyone could see him.

Madame Fontaine said, "The master of the fête requests that you join the gentlemen, *Monsieur le Préfet.*"

Moissac no longer minded the light. He gave back into her hands the identity cards to be put away again for the present.

If the master, who was actually the president of the Farmers' Syndicate, had sent for him, it was the prefect of agriculture who came to shake his hand and find a place for him. Moissac, flattered though he was, soon felt isolated and gauche, and at the sound of the castenets clacking, he longed to be among the workers: he envied all and was at ease with none. The monsignor returned, having gone where all men must at the end of the wine. He gave Moissac the curtest of nods. Among themselves the *châtelains* were commenting freely but with shocking intimacy on the women in the other room. By the time the dancing started Moissac was sweating with discomfort.

The young people wanted jazz. Something with "hot licks." Marc said the words in English and translated them for Gabrielle. She shook her head, not understanding. Madame Fontaine promised jazz recordings later: she had three Benny Goodman records belonging to her son. But first that night tradition must be obliged. "Where are you from?" she demanded of one and then another, until she had appointed the leadership of a half-dozen dances. That the appointees protested ignorance of the dance did not matter. Madame would lead herself if need be: in truth, she was enjoying herself, but in deeper truth she was determined that the syndicate would dine with her again next year.

With the word, tradition, Marc again fell into a reverie that he did not escape even as the dancing started, a *farandole* with Madame Fontaine taking Jacques to the center of the room. Madame's helpers came from the kitchen and in no time paired off with some of the extra men. Soon all the women were dancing save Gabrielle. Marc, suddenly aware of it, wondered what he should do if one of the old boys decided to come down below the salt and ask her to dance. Small chance, he thought, glancing in at them. But he discovered then the prefect of police. And the prefect had discovered him: no question of that. He sat like a crooked-beaked eagle staring in from under half-closed eyelids. Marc would have liked to dance, tired though he was, anything to get out from under that hooded scrutiny, to stop calling attention.

We ought to dance: he thought of the words, but he did not say them, for he watched with an awed knowingness when the dwarf climbed down from his chair. He came strutting and took up a sadly ridiculous stance in front of

Gabrielle. He bowed until his head nearly touched her knees and then asked her to dance.

Gabrielle rose and took the little man's hands in hers so lightly their fingers scarcely touched, and then they danced, arms length apart, and something of Gabrielle's barefooted improvisation. Rachel's shoes sat under the vacant chair. It was a clown's dance, no, a child's dance, with the playful strides of the polka turning, and at no change at all in the music, into a mockingly solemn minuet. They were not long dancing apart in a little square all their own until Jacques and madame fell in behind them, urging them to lead and the rest to follow. Gabrielle demurred, shaking her head, but the dwarf clung to her hands, and Jacques and madame turned leaders, the dance becoming a quickstep, a procession of all the couples around the room, then into the parlor, the vestibule, and back by way of the *petit salon*, the *châtelains* cheering them on and slapping at the behinds of the passing girls.

Moissac moved in to sit beside Marc. "Your wife is a kind woman, monsieur. Or don't you dance?"

"I am a kind man: I don't dance," Marc said.

Moissac touched the buckled shoes with his own square-toed brogue. He bent down and picked up one of the shoes. "She must have the smallest feet in the world."

Gabrielle did not, which was the trouble. Marc said nothing. The police prefect held the shoe as though it were a wounded bird, and examined it, label, size, and leather.

The dancers came rollicking back and madame, seeing Moissac, spun Jacques away from her so that, let unexpectedly loose, he went sliding and tumbling across the room. Madame, a-glisten with sweat, caught up Moissac and pulled him into the dance. Marc wondered if she meant to relieve him of the policeman's questions. The questions would come. And Moissac had been carried off with the shoe which Marc saw him stuff in his pocket. Marc looked for Gabrielle. Artur, seeing his friend Jacques on all fours, let go Gabrielle's hands and ran to him. Jacques, however, avoided the dwarf and sprang to the side of Gabrielle.

He circled her, snapping his fingers, stomping his feet, and every time she made to escape him—she did not want to run, she tried to get away without more calling of attention to herself—he caught a bit of her clothing and pulled her back. The other dancers slackened their pace, and soon stood watching, beating time.

"*Bourrée—bourrée!*" Jacques demanded of the guitarist, pounding out its rhythm with his heels. Everyone picked it up.

Gabrielle did not want to feel that rhythm, but she felt it nonetheless, growing stronger and stronger, as much of a pulse as her own heartbeat. Jacques caught her hands, probing with his fingers for them where she had hidden them close to her waist; he mistook her wild look for the dance's excitement and wet his own lips. He crossed her hands with his and spun her round and round. Philomène began to sing, but it was more like the piercing cry of bagpipes, akin in tune to the song that brought Moissac running. And he came now. Marc watched him, the policeman's hand in his pocket where the shoe was. The dwarf jumped up and down for attention, Jacques' or Gabrielle's, and getting nothing from them or the crowd pressing round but the cries of Go away! Sit down! or, worse, Go lie down! he ran sobbing from the room. The gentlemen rose in their chairs, the better to see. The air crackled with the staccato snapping of fingers, the accented strum of the guitar. There was something in the room, Marc felt, on the point of explosion.

Jacques quickened the tempo, whirling again. Everyone shouted approval. Gabrielle tried to pull back, but swinging around, her weight and his in their hands, the harder she pulled, the quicker her feet: they took to the dance with a will of their own.

Marc looked from her to Moissac. He stood with the shoe in his hand, close to his belly, stroking it like something alive.

Marc wanted to shout. The monsignor had come to the door
with the master of the feast; he stood clasping his own arms,
his thumbs beating a slow tempo of disapproval. A cry burst
from someone, and Marc looked back to the dancers. Gabrielle gave such a wrench to break her hands free from Jacques'
hold that she slipped, her feet shooting out in front of her.
She fell on her back, and Jacques, off-balance too, tried to
lunge past her. That Marc would say. He tried; but fell short,
his long body collapsing on hers. He put one hand to the back
of his head, the clown, and wiggled his fingers. His audience
shrieked with delight.

Marc, sick with whatever had frozen him in the chair,
forced himself into action. He strode across the room and
caught Jacques by the collar. He pulled him up to his knees.
Jacques made to collapse again on the girl. The crowd
howled. Marc thrust him away, and, again the clown, Jacques
propelled himself on his knees, helter-skelter away, bringing
laughter from the women. Then without breaking motion, he
climbed to his feet and, arms and legs flailing, found his way
to Céleste; he whirled her around and into the parlor. Gabrielle rolled over, the impulse to hide her shame. Marc bent
down and pulled her up. Then he lifted her in his arms and
carried her to the side of the room. The women cooed their
mockery.

Gabrielle struggled to be free of his arms, beating at him.
He would have liked at that moment to beat her, the anger in
him fierce at her, at himself, at all. He put her down hard on
her feet.

"Give her some wine, monsieur. Make her drink the
wine." It was the female of the pair Marc had pegged as
lovers. She came smiling and fawning and brought a goblet in
which the wine sloshed over the brim. The other women
pressed in upon them. Why? Marc wondered; it was as though
out of some primitive motive they wanted to crush her, to
overwhelm her with the thrust of their own sexuality. Gabrielle's eyes were frantic. Marc thought she would scream.

But Gabrielle took the glass in her hands, steadier now

than Marc's own. She put it to her lips and, eyes closed, drained it even to the dregs.

"EEEeeeee!" the woman gave a high squeal of pleasure. "She's a Gascon sure!" And the pressure of the women round them eased off.

Marc caught the glass from Gabrielle's hand when she might have dropped it. "We'll go out now," he shouted, close to her face. "It's too much and I will not have it at all. No more."

Gabrielle leaned, one hand on the back of the chair, half-laughing, half-crying. She shook her head that it was not necessary that they go. The music subsided with a crash, Jacques and his partner having careened into the table where the guitarist had perched himself. They all went down together, the musician holding the guitar high over his head to protect it.

Gabrielle tried to compose herself by taking long, deep breaths that she almost choked on. The room was a whirling panorama of faces: not one would stay still in her mind's eye, not even Marc's, where the veins in his forehead seemed to be crawling like worms. She covered her own face with one hand, holding still to the chair for support. Slowly the composure came. Opening her eyes she saw first her own breasts where the blouse V'd at her bosom. She gathered it tighter. The dizziness passed. "It's so much noise," she said. "I'd forgotten."

"If you can make it, let us go," Marc said.

"I'm going to be all right, Jean. I promise you."

"And I promise you," Marc said. He picked up the shoe still on the floor, and then saw the other where the policeman had set it on the table and fled the room. He left Gabrielle's side to get it. It was only out of the corner of his eye that he saw the dwarf dash back into the room, screaming at the top of his lungs for attention. The revelers gathered around him. Marc, both shoes in hand, hoped to escape during the dwarf's distraction. But what Artur brandished in the air for attention was a bottle of cognac. It came, Marc realized, from his valise

which the dwarf held hanging open in his other hand. Before
Marc could reach him, he had plunged his hand into the
valise again and brought out the silk nightgown, the one bit
of trousseau Rachel had managed before they left Paris.

"Are you a bride?" The woman lifted Gabrielle's chin
with her finger.

Gabrielle did not deny it.

"A bride, a bride!" The words rang round the room, an
explanation at last for everything, the girl's shyness, the man's
hauteur. The revelry now could start in good earnest, with
dances that everyone knew. The women pressed in on Marc, a
sea of billowing flesh.

Marc grabbed the valise, but the runt skittered between
the women and reached Gabrielle where, like a grotesque at
the feet of a princess, he groveled on his knees, offering the
silken gown, playing with it sensuously all the while in his
upraised hands.

Gabrielle drew back against the wall until she could go
no further. Utterly desperate, she cried out, "Monsignor!"

Monsignor La Roque stood with his arms folded, gazing
with disdain on the entire scene. The *châtelains* had drawn
back into a tighter little circle of their own. The monsignor
turned to the prefect of police who seemed to be looking
himself for a place to hide, and said with mock formality,
"Monsieur Moissac, it would seem the damsel is in distress."

Moissac charged toward Gabrielle. He put his foot to
Artur's backside and sent the dwarf sprawling. He gazed at
the girl until she opened her eyes. Then he lowered his, letting the heavy lids fall to where he could not be seen gazing
at her breast. For only a moment; he looked then to the bare
feet, feet he would have caressed as he had the shoe. When
the husband came, Moissac went from the room, by way this
time of the parlor, for he wanted no more traffic that night
with the aristocracy. Trying to get back to the vestibule,
which was where he belonged, where he should have attended to his duty in the first place and then departed, he had
to fumble his way through the blasted beads. A strand caught

in the buttons of his coat sleeve; he caught it and pulled it
from the valance and then from his cuff, taking the button
also. He stuffed the lot in his pocket, and went to madame's
desk bell which he rang until she came and unlocked the
drawer with the I.D. cards.

Marc, having the valise and the nightgown, and moving
into the vestibule with Gabrielle, saw Moissac at the desk. He
took Gabrielle upstairs directly.

Moissac had wanted to question Belloir. A number of
things had got beyond his control, and now the prefect of
agriculture came up and asked for a ride as far as the *Granges
Vieilles* where he was to stay. Moissac put off until the next
day the checking of papers.

Marc watched from the small third-floor balcony that
bellied out over the street. The smell of charcoal wafted up
from the *gazogènes* awaiting three of the guests. He listened
the cars out of hearing and the revelers into their beds. He
heard the last clatter of dishes and madame throw the bolt on
her vestibule door. All became darkness below which did but
make the sky seem brighter. Finally he went indoors.

He knocked softly and opened the door. He was sure that
he would find Sister Gabrielle billeted on the floor. It startled
him nonetheless to see her prone, face down, her forehead to
the bare boards, she still fully clothed and her arms outstretched in the shape of the cross. She did not speak. Nor did
he. He turned out the light, removed his shoes and jacket
only, and lay down upon the bed. Sleep was sudden and
deep.

18

HIS MOTHER WAS WAITING UP FOR MOISSAC, HER HEAD SWATHED in a nightcap which made him think of a bonnetted infant, its face puckered up to cry. She turned off the radio.

Moissac did not want to talk. "Leave it on, maman. I haven't heard the news all day."

"Lies," she said. "One thing one day, another the next." She switched on the radio again and took his coat from him.

He went to the sink and while he turned up his cuffs and drew a basin of water, he watched her reflection in the window. She was straightening the coat on the hanger when she discovered the bulge in the pocket, the string of glass beads he had torn from Madame Fontaine's doorway. She put her hand in the pocket and pulled them out, the loose beads scattering over the floor.

"Put them in a dish, maman. I'll have to take them back to Madame Fontaine."

He could not hear what she was saying until he turned off the radio. "Now, what did you say?"

"I said, what else was she wearing?"

Moissac described the curtain of beads in the *pension* vestibule and how he had caught the strand in the button of his sleeve. He showed her where the button was now missing. It was ridiculous, but the more he explained, the guiltier he felt. "Believe me, maman, if she had been wearing them, I would not have come home with them in my pocket."

"Did that woman sing again tonight?"

"Everybody sang. I will tell you about it in the morning."

"I wouldn't think of asking," she said. She got the clock from the window-sill and wound it.

"Maman, was René here tonight?"

She paused, her hand on the door to her bedroom. She was deciding whether or not to lie to him, Moissac thought. But why would she lie? "No," she said.

Moissac dried his hands and wiped his face on the towel. "What do you talk about, the two of you?"

She shrugged. "The Michelet gossip."

"You'd think he would have told you then about Madame Lebel's daughter marrying old Divenet."

"I may have forgotten. Don't try to trick me, Théophile. I am not one of your refugees or black-marketeers."

"Do you talk about the refugees?"

"We talk about you," she said impatiently. "You forget that I like to talk about you and the way you've come up from the days in Michelet."

"I came up, maman, because my predecessor was recalled to military service and then preferred de Gaulle's exile to the prefecture of St. Hilaire. René knows that and so do you."

"What are you trying to say, Théophile?"

"I am saying that if René pretends to admire me it is only because he wants information about the police."

"What could I tell him? We are never that serious anyway. He flirts with me. You saw it last night."

"Yes, I did."

"I see," she said. "Why would a man flirt with an old thing like me? Is that it?"

That was it, but even in his present mood he could not say so. "I do not like to be spied upon and I feel that's what René is doing."

"I shall tell him not to come any more," she said and went into the bedroom.

A few minutes later, in bathrobe and pajamas, Moissac took his rosary and went into her room. She was buried deep under the quilt with only her face and the brown, twisted fingers showing. The bed seemed larger even than it had seemed to him as a child when she would take him into it and warm his cold backside against her. "It is ridiculous for us to quarrel about René, maman."

"That's not what's ridiculous," she said. "It's the way you always bring him up when there is something else that you don't want to talk about."

He got her rosary from the bedside table and handed it to her. He made one more effort to placate her. "I will tell you about the harvest feast in the morning. The monsignor sent you his blessing, by the way."

"The monsignor sent me his blessing," she repeated, weighing the words. "Did I raise you to be so crooked, so sly, my son? Or is it because you're a policeman?"

"You're criticizing me for your own faults, maman."

"Am I? Maybe I am. It is better than criticizing you for your father's. It is strange to see a son grow older than his father. He would have looked just like you, Théophile." She gave a dry little laugh. "It's no wonder I get my generations mixed up."

"Goodnight, maman."

"We haven't said our prayers yet."

"I think I'll say mine in bed tonight."

She held her arms up to him. He bent and kissed her cheek. He could smell the age of her through the lavender. She touched his nose with her finger. "Just like his," she said.

19

SHE HAD DREAMED DURING THE NIGHT OF HER FATHER, AND IT WAS a dream of waking: he had come into her cell and covered her with a quilt and he had touched her cheek with his fingers so that, waking within the dream, she had caught his hand and kissed it, but never looked up at him, even as the child awakening to the presence of love sinks back toward sleep holding fast that love until it too becomes a part of sleep and sleep itself but love's prolonging. The first few seconds of real awakening that morning were a kind of ecstasy to Gabrielle, the dream so sweet and vividly remembered, and its having seemed in no way strange that her father should have entered the convent cell.

Then within the compass of her gaze, the silver-buckled shoes, the bedpost, the chamber pot, the woolly field of dust beneath the bed brought back reality far stranger than the dream. There was a blanket warm upon her back. She sat up and gathered it around her. Her whole body ached and the prayer it prompted was from childhood. . . . Oh, Jesus, through the immaculate heart of Mary, I offer Thee all my prayers, works and sufferings of this day. . . .

She was alone in the room; the bed had been straightened: she knew he had slept on it, having heard the creaking of the springs when he lay down last night. He had left his watch on the dresser. It was half-past seven. She listened to see if the watch was running; she could not remember ever having slept into that hour in the morning. At home—the word seemed not quite right now, having a diffuse feeling, neither farm nor convent—oh, but yes, the convent: she was able to summon its presence almost instantly—she would have finished in the scullery and answered the matins bell: *Venite, exultemus* . . . "Come, let us praise the Lord with joy. . . ."

With joy, with joy, with joy. She repeated the words again and again, for her own sense of joy at the moment was not diminished.

On the washstand she found a square of soap and, by the cup of fresh water, Marc's tube of toothpaste where he had left it. She squeezed some on the corner of the towel and rubbed her teeth and gums. She put the latch on the door and washed thoroughly, even her head. Marc had put out all Rachel's things on the chair, one change only, except for two sweaters. Gabrielle chose the one that seemed likely to cover the most of her, a dark blue with a turtleneck collar; when she put it on, however, and especially because she wore Rachel's brassiere which was tight on her, her breasts stood out like bishops' mitres. No amount of stretching seemed to remedy the situation. Finally, she took off the brassiere and bound herself round with the second of Rachel's scarves. Throughout she was aware of the mirror over the dresser, but avoided it steadfastly, catching only the glimpse of her arm motion as she passed to and fro.

Marc knocked on the door and identified himself: Jean. She opened it and for a moment he stood, his eyes wide as though he were seeing a stranger—or perhaps Rachel, she thought, turning immediately away.

"I have brought you breakfast," he said. "It is real coffee."

"Thank you . . . Jean."

He set the tray with the bread and preserve and coffee on the dresser. "You slept well?"

"Yes."

"And you had good dreams." He watched her in the mirror.

"How did you know that?"

"You smiled."

"You must not look at me," she said. Then realizing he had covered her, she added, "But I thank you for the blanket."

"It was nothing," he said, but time and again since dawn

when he had awakened and covered her with the blanket he
had gone over in his mind the way she looked, the little smile
and the pursing of her lips. He had lain awake himself then,
wondering what the tenderness meant that it evoked in him.
He had turned his thoughts to Rachel, but he had turned
them, they had not flown there, and he had remembered
chiding Gabrielle in the early hours of their vigil together: Is
that what it's like, being a nun, to always think of something
else?

He went to the door and looked into the hallway, for he
had come upstairs to discover the dwarf trying to see through
the keyhole. He did not tell Gabrielle, he just made sure the
small one had not returned.

"Please have your breakfast while the coffee is hot. I shall
not watch you."

"It's all right. I ate among the others, and I drank wine
last night."

"Was that a sin? I forced you to it if it was. Therefore the
sin was mine."

"I don't know. So much is new."

"Only the wine is old," he said.

"What do you mean?"

He shrugged. "I don't know exactly, but I was thinking
that if there is such a thing as sin, we have found new ways
of doing it in our time."

"Do you not believe in sin?" Gabrielle sipped her coffee.

"I do not believe in rewards for good deeds and punish-
ment for bad, let's put it that way. I see no scale of balance in
this world, and nothing in it argues for me for another world
just to sum things up. Is it wrong of me to talk this way to
you?"

"What is 'wrong' to you, monsieur?"

He smiled. "Jean. You must remember! It is a good question, Marie. Dishonesty with oneself: I guess that's the best
way of putting it."

"So," she said, with a kind of belligerence that delighted
him, "dishonesty with others does not matter."

"I did not say that. I only say that unless one is honest entirely with oneself, there can be no honesty with others either. One's first obligation is to oneself."

"Of course. One must save one's own soul. We believe in the same thing."

"Perhaps we do. Now. Marie, Marie, Marie. We must find a way to get you out of here quickly." He gave her their work papers on which his and Rachel's photographs appeared side by side, and her I.D. card which he had insisted Madame Fontaine return so that his wife could go out to do some necessary shopping. "Do not smile for the photographer. Try to look as serious as Rachel was on the day that likeness was taken."

Gabrielle licked her fingers and turned the card to where she could see it better. "What do you think was on her mind when it was taken?"

Marc was slow to answer. "Actually, she was very happy, I think." He returned to the issue at hand. "The machinery will go out first. They say now we'll be here till noon, but I'm sure we'll have a processing of some sort, either the Germans or the police. I will try to make friends while you're gone."

"Just do not make enemies," she said, remembering René.

Marc grinned. There was in every woman something of the wife even if she were the bride of Christ. "I'll remember that."

Gabrielle's face was on fire. "Forgive me, monsieur. It was wrong of me to have spoken so."

He wanted to take her by the elbows and shake her. Instead he delivered a short lecture: "It was right. You spoke the truth of my nature, and therefore for my own good. It was right . . . Marie."

"Yes . . . Jean."

"Now you must be prepared if you are questioned about visiting a photographer's shop: you will say that your twenty-first birthday is a few weeks off—it says so on your I.D.

card—and you want to have a likeness to send to your parents
in Marseille. It is believable, don't you think?"

She nodded. "And I have a sister living in Marseille."

"And there is something you must purchase while you're
in the neighborhood of shops, something you would call
decent in which to sleep."

"I will wear my same clothes at night," she said.

"No, that will not do." He gave her money and the
clothes ration book that René had given him. "Something less
than a tent that will nonetheless satisfy your modesty." He
turned from her and stared out the window. "I don't know
how to say this to you, gentle friend, but if you find yourself
in deeper trouble than you can manage, surrender to the
police and tell them who you are. Then say nothing more until
they bring you to the Reverend Mother of your convent."

"It is possible she would not accept me now."

"She would be a great fool not to, and I do not think that
of her," Marc said.

Gabrielle slipped out of the *pension* a few minutes later.
The only attention paid her came from Jacques, who was
propped against a tree in the sun, his beret over his eyes but
not so far over them as to shut out that which he wished to
see. He whistled softly as she passed which in turn brought
the policeman at the gate to attention. The policeman saluted,
bending to be closer to *la petite mariée*, the little bride, as she
had been spoken of that morning, and would probably be
called henceforth among the workers.

She walked with an air of confidence as Marc had bade
her, and with Rachel's pouch handbag swinging from her
wrist she became aware of giving pleasure to those who saw
her. Men made way for her to pass. Shopkeepers called out
greetings. The giving of such pleasure might not be a sin, but
the awareness of giving it was a lack of discipline to say the
least. This sunniness, as it was called when she was a child,
was a part of her from birth, and the nuns had carefully

nurtured the joy while tamping down the exuberance. It troubled her also that she was no longer so much afraid of being in the street alone and unprotected by the religious habit, but what that was really was the relief of being away from Marc and the pretense of an intimacy she tried not to think about, while at the same time knowing that the very purpose for which she was there would succeed only if she made the pretend-life seem real to the others. Now, alone, no matter what she wore, she was herself in God, and by some act of mortification she could atone for vanity, for pride, and perhaps lay up a little strength against temptation. She walked imagining herself in the boned stays of the convent corset, in the chafing coarseness of its linens, and in the concentrated heat of the serge habit. She could almost feel the starched binder around her head, and as in the days when she had suffered headaches from it, she wondered again if it was not intended to suggest to those who followed Christ the thorns with which His head was crowned.

Her world was all so terribly upside down: here she was conjuring a headache whereas the true act of piety would be to accept the headache one could not avoid, and seek through it some small understanding of Christ's sufferings and their meaning. But she had not achieved this piety. The trouble had always been that the worse the headache, the less the understanding. But that was because she had not advanced very far in the religious experience yet.

She went by way of the railway station and followed Marc's directions from there. But when she reached Number 12, Rue de Michelet, the shop was closed, the shades drawn. The confidence that had brought her boldly to the door fell off at once. She tapped on the window most tentatively, not wanting to call the attention of the passers-by. All the benevolence she had felt in the people she had met seemed to have vanished: now they were hostile strangers. Her suffering was brief but a grave lesson. Almost as soon as she knocked René came to the door and opened it to her. Then he raised the shade.

"You are late, madame, but it did not matter. There were no other customers."

"If there had been customers I would have said what my husband told me to say." Gabrielle spoke with a deliberateness that made it seem by rote. And rote it was, her having particularly rehearsed the words "my husband." "For my twenty-first birthday I wish to have a photograph to send my parents in Marseille."

René nodded and rubbed his hands together. "We shall take that picture first. It is my pleasure to serve you, madame," he said with some cheer. He expected to be paid for the photographs.

He led her through a neat but shabby shop, past the counter with its samples of his portraits. "Weddings and First Communions, what would I do without them?" He posed her first in a chair against a courtyard backdrop, draping her round with black velvet and insisting that for the portrait she must remove the scarf from her head. "We must be as authentic as we can. For your parents you would want as chic a picture as possible. Yes?"

She said nothing, removing the scarf.

René straightened her shaggy hair with his fingers. By her stiffness he might be applying a match to it. "Weddings and First Communions," he repeated, hoping to relax her, "it would seem to me the occasion would be its own celebration and therefore memorable. The taking of a photograph should be an event in itself."

Quickly then, having glanced again at the identity shot he would be replacing, René bade her put on the scarf and stand against a silvery screen. "I will need an hour, and as steady a hand as I can manage." He took her to the front of the shop. "It is better that I lock the door so that no one walks in on me. Come back when you see that the door is open."

"Yes, monsieur."

Gabrielle walked along Rue de Michelet until she came to a shop advertising dresses and lingerie. A bell rang as she

opened the door. A mannequin stood, hand extended; a sign
propped in the fingers told the price and the number of ration
tickets. Gabrielle was a second or two realizing that it was not
a person but a dummy on which hung what seemed to her an
enormously expensive dress. A woman came from the cur-
tained room at the back.

"It is beautiful, is it not, mam'selle?" She corrected herself: "Madame." She had seen the ring on Gabrielle's finger.
She calculated the customer to be a girl from the countryside,
newly come in town to work, conscripted perhaps to the box
factory. She would have ration coupons galore. "It is worth
every coupon in your book. What else do you need if you
have a dress like that? You could go all week in your shift and
wear that on Sunday and be the envy of every woman in
church. . . . "

Gabrielle listened without understanding. Or, more precisely, she could have understood without listening. She did not
like the sales person. With her cheeks rouged and her lips
painted, the woman was as false as the dummy. When she
finally paused, Gabrielle said, "I would like to buy a nightgown, madame. It must be cheap and large and have long
sleeves."

The woman batted her eyes, to what purpose Gabrielle
had no idea. "It is a gift perhaps for someone older?"

"Do you have such a garment, madame?"

"I do not know that such a garment exists. Perhaps if
madame would tell me how much she wishes to pay . . . "

"I have enough money," Gabrielle said. She had no
notion in the world how much money a nightgown should
cost, but Marc had given her five hundred francs and that
seemed a lot of money indeed. She did not intend to spend
half of it.

On the hunch that this was a strange, shy girl who had
been married off to an old man with money—and who in such
bloom would not under the circumstances conceal herself as
much as possible?—the proprietress ventured: "I have remem-

bered something that might just suit madame. Please be
seated for a few minutes."

"I must hurry," Gabrielle said, wanting only to be out of
the shop as quickly as possible.

"Believe me, madame, he will have a glass of wine and
forget the time." She laid her hand with the painted nails on
Gabrielle's arm. Gabrielle felt her muscles grow taut but she
did not pull away from the touch. She smiled as falsely as the
woman. And when the woman left her, Gabrielle said, "Forgive me, Lord, but it will help me save his money and he
needs it."

She sat down and calmly watched the shopkeeper go to
the cupboard at the back wall and fumble through the
garments stacked there. It was essential to the bargain, Gabrielle felt, that she not take her eyes off the woman, that she
advance the position she had established by the fact that she
had money. And that became something too that she wanted
to think about later: there was in this a personal lesson for her
on the merits of poverty, and the reason therefore it was part
of religious commitment.

The woman brought a large white, if yellowing, garment
and shook it out of its folds. It was a beachrobe left from the
happier days when the better class of people from St. Hilaire
went to the sea in August. Gabrielle was satisfied in the
roughness of the towelcloth and the fact that it buttoned from
throat to toe. The woman held up the dolman sleeves and
Gabrielle was reminded of angel costumes in school pageants.
The woman began to unbutton it. "You will see in the mirror
how becoming it is, madame. Beautiful lines, and white. It is
very chaste, no?"

"I will take it," Gabrielle said and rose from the chair.

Without batting an eye this time, the woman said, "Very
good, madame. I will even find a box to put it in. That will be
four hundred francs, madame."

Gabrielle said, and with aplomb equal to the shopkeeper's, "I will not take it, madame. The price is too much."

"Then I will sell it to you at a loss, madame, for I shall never have a customer to whom it is more becoming. Three hundred and fifty."

"I will pay you two hundred."

"*Mon Dieu!* Madame would like me to make her a gift of it!"

Gabrielle smiled. "That would be very kind."

"Two hundred and fifty. You have your ration book?" She chipped the words with the precision of a stone cutter, and Gabrielle thought that would be the substance of which her heart was made.

Only after she had left the store and made a further purchase at the chemist's shop did she contemplate the possible lack of charity in her own judgment of the woman. She would have to deal with her conscience later in that matter. Passing the photography shop, the blind on its door still drawn, she went on to the church of St. Sébastien near the railway station.

St. Sébastien was not among her favorite saints although she could not say why. She had never thought about him very much, and he should have been among those she admired because he was a soldier—if Marc had been right about her fondness for soldiers. Monsieur Daridan was not necessarily right: he only sounded as though he ought to be.

She tried to think of St. Sébastien and not Marc Daridan. It was not the saint's nakedness that offended her, she was sure. Her dearest images of Christ were quite as naked. And Christ's wounds, and those of the saints who suffered the stigmata—particularly St. Francis and Ste. Catherine of Sienna—were dear to her. She could put her lips to such wounds. Why not then the wounds of St. Sébastien, the arrow wounds of persecution?

Seeking to know more of the saint whom she seemed deliberately not to have known, she went to the literature rack in the church vestibule. She took a faded pamphlet of Sébastien's life to where the light was best and read about the martyr who was twice left for dead and twice, once after death, attended by devout and kindly women to whose compassion his helplessness—and yet his dignity—recommended him. She thought at once of Daridan, and was almost as quickly stricken with the knowledge that under the guise of pious pursuit, the devil had presented her with temptation beyond any she had hitherto experienced.

She fled the chapel as though it were a charnel house. She would have walked on her knees, but the shoes gave pain enough for her to contemplate. To concentrate on pain until it came near pleasure allowed her to empty her mind of everything else, to open it once more, she begged, to a true and reassuring vision of the will of God. What came riding hard upon her thoughts was the wish for flight: he, the man she now feared to call by name even in her own thoughts, he had said that if she were in trouble to go back. . . . He had not quite said that, but everything within her said it now. The very clopping of the hooves of a carter's horse rang out on the cobbles, "Go back, go back, go back." And then at the head of Rue de Michelet she saw Father Duloc, the old priest, bringing back his flock of children from their morning trip to the infirmary. She had only to cross the street, confront him and make him see who she was, and he would take her home. But as she stood on the verge of running to him, a motorcycled patrol of helmeted Germans passed between them, six of them, before which the people in the street gave way, the repeated acceleration of the motors like the roar of beasts at their heels.

She turned back into Rue de Michelet, and when she reached it, she found the door to René's shop open. His face was tense and his hand shaking as he gave over to her the identity card and the envelope with the Belloir work papers. "You have no sense of time, madame. Let me tell you, it is a terrible thing to do to someone whose life is balanced in the scale by time. Give me eighty francs and go from here now. Godspeed to the Jew. He will need it if he counts on you to tell time for him."

"Thank you, monsieur," she said and opened the string purse.

René went to the door with her more to the purpose of getting her out quickly than anything else. Thus he saw Moissac park the Peugeot across the street a few seconds before Moissac saw him and Gabrielle.

"Sweet Jesus," René said. "Listen to me carefully, madame. The prefect of police is across the street. We shall tell the same story if we are questioned: when you return from the harvesting, I will have the photograph ready. Forget the money for now."

Again Gabrielle said, "Thank you, monsieur." Nothing more.

René watched her up the street and he prayed, although he knew that it was cowardly of him to do so, that Moissac would follow her. But the prefect came across the street and stood, without acknowledging René's greeting, staring after the girl. The eyelids drooped down a little, concealing something, René thought. And knowing Moissac, he could suppose there was but one thing he would conceal in such a manner. René kept breathing deeply while yet holding his shoulders rigid. A few seconds more and he would be in control of himself.

Reaching the top of Michelet, the girl looked back as she was about to turn out of sight. She waved. René waved back and called out, "Good harvesting," although she was probably beyond hearing. It did not matter: the masque was for Moissac's benefit.

"So you know her?" Moissac said.

"I have just taken her photograph. Very soon now she will turn twenty-one years old, and oh, my friend, I wish that I were twenty-two."

"You know her husband also?" Moissac said.

"No, I think not."

"Let us go in your shop and see if you can't remember him."

It was almost noon when Gabrielle got back to Madame Fontaine's. Suitcases and sleeping bags lined the walk and already from the upstairs windows bolsters and quilts had been hung out to air. A group of the men were at *boules* in the garden. Marc turned from watching them as she came up the walk. He did not come to her at once, but the players teased him all the same for having worried. The legend of bride and groom persisted.

The women were sitting, most of them crosslegged on the floor of the veranda, and one of them was selecting cards from a deck. Gabrielle wanted to slip by them. Oddly, it seemed to her, she was more afraid of the women than of the men. It was their voices probably. She could not get used to women speaking loudly. She had almost made it to the door when one of them arched her back like a dancer and with her outstretched hand caught Gabrielle's ankle.

"Come and sit down and I'll tell your fortune," the card dealer said. "Michèle, let her go. She looks like a doe with its leg in a trap."

"It's all right," Gabrielle said, and briefly smiled at her captor who released her hold, and with the sinuous movement of a snake—or again a dancer—writhed slowly into a sitting position, her blouse falling low beneath her shoulders and lower still to her breasts. Why she could not stop looking at her Gabrielle did not know: the other women seemed to think nothing of it at all.

"Sit down, my dear. A bride's fortune is always happy. You do not need to be afraid."

Gabrielle shook her head. Marc came up and put his arm around her. It was an iron band meant to sustain her. She permitted herself to be drawn against him, for all of the women now were looking at them.

"Why don't you tell *my* fortune, madame?" Marc said.

"*Mon Dieu*, what I would tell you, monsieur, my husband would burn the cards."

Gabrielle was able to interpret the laughter more quickly

than the words themselves. Her eyes darted at the fortune
teller: again it was shock she had not been able to conceal in
time, but now the woman chose to interpret that glance to her
own suspicions.

"Yes, my dear, my *husband*. Did you think you're the
only one married? You're a little too good for us, aren't you?
A little too good to be true." She threw down the cards. "I
would rather tell the fortune of the bow-legged dwarf."

Gabrielle felt the pound of Marc's heartbeat against her
arm. She pushed away from him and thrust the handbag and
box into his hands. She turned to the fortune teller. "Please,
madame, do tell my fortune. It is not so that I have such
thoughts of you as you say. I cannot help what I am—but I
am not what you say."

It was not a very clear speech, but the earnestness of it
even the fortune teller could not deny. Gabrielle pulled the
scarf from around her head and sat down, also crosslegged,
among the women. She pulled her skirt over her knees; it was
full enough to touch the floor. The fortune teller raked in the
cards, looking at Gabrielle all the while. "*Mon Dieu,* where did
you get that haircut?"

"My husband cut it."

"With his teeth?"

The others laughed and Gabrielle forced herself to join
in. Philomène put her arm around Gabrielle's shoulders. "We
were all brides once, and it was the only time we were as
beautiful as you."

"Thank you," Gabrielle whispered. She could feel her
color, the blood warm in her cheeks.

But before the cards were dealt Madame Fontaine announced lunch, the last meal she would have to serve them,
thank God, and Gabrielle was spared a public fortune. Marc
held his hand out to her when she started to get up. She pretended not to see it. He touched her arm anyway when they
started indoors. "You were a long time."

"I almost went home," she said.

"I kept thinking all morning that it would have been

better to chance things as they were than for you to have gone out into the town alone."

"It was better that I went alone. It is easier to get used to the difference that way."

"Nothing went wrong?"

"I do not know for sure. I have the papers, but the prefect of police came as I was leaving. Monsieur René would have told him I was there to have a photograph made for my parents. And he did take such a photograph."

Marc did not speak of it but as they took their places at the great long table with its four tureens of soup, he thought further about Monsieur Lapin who confessed to having chosen his own cover name. He was startled out of a grim reverie when Jacques, who had spent much of the morning trying to amend for last night's wildness, banged his fork against his glass.

"Bread, soup, and wine, my friends. We should give thanks. Young Jean Belloir, will you say a blessing for us all?"

Marc hesitated in his demur. The only ruse he could think of was to propose that since it was Jacques' idea, it should be Jacques' privilege.

But Gabrielle spoke out almost instantly: "In our house I say the blessing. Jean does not go to church. . . . " She made the sign of the cross as did everyone at the table except Marc. "Bless us, oh Lord, in these Thy gifts which we are about to receive from Thy bounty."

All said, "Amen."

Marc bowed his head.

20

MOISSAC HAD NOT EXPECTED SUCH LUCK AS TO COME ON THE LITTLE
Madame Belloir leaving René's studio. It justified his feeling
that there was a connection between Belloir and René. He
was more certain of it, aware of the little man's struggle with
his nerves. It was this that decided him to tackle René now,
regretfully abandoning the opportunity to intercept madame
and talk with her alone.

"You know her husband also, the stranger at Gaucher's."

René denied it. Actually, he was denying knowing that
the man who had come into Gaucher's was Belloir. Sitting on
the stool behind his counter while Moissac occupied the one
easy chair in the studio, René said, "Why should the name
Belloir mean anything to me? The man was looking for the
harvesters. Didn't Maman say herself that they used to gather
in Michelet?"

"You forget, René: when we spoke about him, you said
you thought the man might be Gestapo."

"Would that have prevented him from looking for the
harvesters? I should think the Gestapo might be very interested in a crowd like that. I've heard there's a dwarf among
them. The Germans will say, French decadence."

He had underestimated René's cleverness. He said, "He is
no one's pet, the dwarf. And he deserves the worst that could
happen to him."

René avoided moistening his lips although they were dry
as dust, and not to break a life-time pattern, he had to continue baiting this left-over bully from youth. "I would think
the worst has already happened to him, being a dwarf. It is
worse than a gypsy, as bad as a Jew."

Moissac said, "Do you know the Belloir family in Fauré?"

"No. Should I know them?"

"Have you been in Fauré during the last few days?"

"It is a cursed village."

"That does not answer my question, René."

"No, *Monsieur le Préfet.*"

Moissac changed his tack. "What did you think of the little lady?"

"She is charming, but stiff as marble."

"Could I see the picture, René?" Moissac got up from the chair.

"I have not printed it yet. If you wish to see that it exists. . . . "

"Why should I doubt that it exists? But why did she come to you, I wonder. You are not the only photographer in St. Hilaire."

"I am the only photographer with a sign in the window of *Au Bon Coin*. Perhaps the husband saw it. I do not know. Madame came in this morning and said she wished to have a portrait done for her twenty-first birthday, to send to her parents in Marseille."

"Did she pay you?"

"A deposit." There was not a *centime* in the till. "Do you need money, Théo?"

"No, I do not need money. What will you do with the photograph when it is ready?"

"She will pick it up on her return from the harvesting."

Moissac made a noise in his throat: it was meant to convey his skepticism. He looked at his watch. If the train was late he would go directly to Madame Fontaine's. He picked up the telephone on the counter. It was dead.

"I am sorry, Théo, but I have been ruled a non-essential business. They will be taking out the instrument to give to an essential German."

It was unwise of them, Moissac thought as he drove to the station. A telephone was a device which could be listened in on. But of course, René also would know that.

More and more he realized, seeing the troops in the railway yard, it was becoming a garrison. Which left the prefect of police with very little to do there: illegal travelers would be advised against the terminal. There was no train yet so he went on to Madame Fontaine's. He knew that he would not hold up the processing of the harvesters: the Agricultural Department had cleared their working papers. As for the Belloirs, he wanted to pursue them at his own pace, his own discretion, and he wanted to derive what pleasure was to be gained from the association.

He began the checking out of the harvesters while they were all together at the luncheon table. During the routine processing of the Belloirs he brought up the matter of the photograph, commenting on the miserable likeness of her I.D. shot. "Even René could do better than that."

Madame made no response. Under the pretense of scratching his nose with the back of his hand, he sniffed at the card. The smell of perfume or face powder was pungent. Nonetheless a little smell of what?—something chemical clung to it. Also, Madame wore no makeup.

Belloir was looking annoyed, as though it was improper for Moissac to examine his wife's papers. Moissac shifted the cards, Monsieur Belloir's now on top. "Now, monsieur takes an excellent photo."

"I am vain. I make the photographer work." Marc held out his hand for the papers.

Moissac ignored the hand, and for the moment, the impertinence. He addressed himself entirely to the wife: "I hope my friend, Monsieur Labrière, has done better for you. Is it a long time since your parents have seen you?"

Marc answered: "Since she came to me in Paris, well over a year ago."

"That *is* a long time," Moissac said as though madame had answered for herself.

She smiled, the white teeth gleaming briefly. It was a smile that went through him to the bone. He stamped the work papers, and scratched his initials beneath the stamp. He gave the papers to Marc and spoke to her at the same time: "Where do they live, madame?"

"In Marseille," she said after a brief hesitation her husband did not try to bridge.

"And the address?"

Now without hesitation: "Fourteen, Rue Paradis."

"And your father's name?"

"Cassin."

"Thank you, madame, monsieur." He moved on.

Gabrielle had done splendidly, Marc thought. The address he assumed to be that of her sister, but Madame Belloir's parents were named Cassin. It would take time to sort out the discrepancy if the prefect checked it at all.

Moissac moved through the rest quickly. Not until he reached the dwarf did he hesitate. "What makes you so valuable to this enterprise?"

"They hired me, monsieur." Artur looked around for acclaim of his wit. There was none.

Moissac folded his arms and addressed them all: "Now. Who will speak for you? To whom do I give your pass for the checkpoints?"

"To Monsieur Belloir," Jacques said instantly. No one questioned his choice.

Moissac gave into Marc's hands the general *Ausweis* provided for the group by Colonel von Weber. He cleared his throat and made a little speech: "No more inspections unless you get into trouble. Bon voyage and a safe harvest. I hope you won't need the services of the apprentice doctor." He began to feel expansive, having the attention of them all. "Come back to St. Hilaire and sing for us before you break up." He looked from one of the women to the other. "Which of you is the songbird?"

"Philomène," they all responded.

Philomène shook her head. Her cheeks were the color of ripe apples.

"You sing like a lark, mam'selle."

Philomène gave a throaty laugh. There was a lot to her, Moissac thought, and she had been in many beds and maybe a few wagons. It would be an interesting caravan to follow, the threshers going out from St. Hilaire within the hour. He almost wished himself a natural partner to their labors. A natural partner: he contemplated the words sardonically as he went out. Then he set his mind to the quickest way by which he could get to Fauré and back.

Having persuaded Von Weber's aid to provide him with a tankful of gasoline that he might travel on a security mission, he drove the Peugeot to Fauré.

He reached the village as the markets were closing. He got no welcome, driving a gasoline-propelled car, but the citizens would give no stranger welcome there. Fauré had been the scene two weeks past of three reprisal killings in the square: citizens chosen at random to atone the death of a German soldier sniped at in a convoy. Three crosses of freshly stripped oak had been erected there. Moissac removed his hat, passing. If it impressed anyone, he saw no sign of it in the women covering their stalls. Moissac went along to the post office on foot and asked for the address of Jean Belloir.

The postmaster removed his glasses. "It is in Paris, monsieur. Shall I look it up for you?"

"Please do."

The man went mumbling to himself and presently returned with a piece of paper on which he had written a Fifth-*Arondissement* address.

Moissac thanked him. "I understand they have come home on a holiday."

"If you say so, monsieur. They would not come to see me."

"But you would have heard. It is only a village," Moissac persisted. He did not identify himself.

"A moment, monsieur. I shall inquire." The postmaster went to the table in the back of the room where the clerk was franking letters. Their exchange of words was inaudible to Moissac. The postmaster returned. "They will perhaps have come. There were letters."

The clerk meanwhile abruptly left his work unfinished, and went out the back door.

"Their address in Fauré, please." Moissac showed his identification.

The postmaster put away his glasses and came from behind the partition, all at a pace Moissac felt was designed to delay him. The man took him by the arm to the door, and on the street directed him the way to the Belloir farm by the shortest route. It was the longest route, Moissac was sure, but he thanked him and walked back across the square to his car, half-expecting his tires to have been deflated.

When he reached the crossroads outside the village, he wondered if he had not been entirely misdirected. He began counting off the farms. Within the kilometer he slowed down, about to overtake a cyclist. He remembered the postal clerk. The rider waved him on. Moissac passed him. He could not be sure, the man in cap and goggles. Moissac resumed his counting of the farms, keeping the cyclist in mirror view. On the far side of a hill he lost him. He stopped and waited. When the rider did not come he turned around and drove back. Not another vehicle was in sight, but a golden dust hovered over the courtyard of the nearest farm.

A flock of geese set up a great noise when he drove into the yard. They retreated before the Peugeot and returned to attack when he parked. The gander nipped at his legs as soon as he closed the car door behind him.

The half-door to the cottage was open, revealing the kitchen-sitting room, neat and comfortable-looking with a cabinet of books on one side and a cupboard of dishes on the other. A letter lay on the plate at the head of the table which was set for the evening meal. He could smell the soup where it simmered far back on the stove. From where he stood, too, he could see what he took to be a wedding picture among others on the mantle.

No one came when he called out. The gander stabbed at his ankles, drawing blood, he was sure. He lifted the door-latch and went in, calling out again to announce what he was doing. The letter was addressed to M. Jacques Jean Belloir, and it was postmarked Paris. The date of postmark was not clear. Nor could he read anything within the envelope even though he held it to the sun. He put it back on the plate and went to the mantle where he studied the picture of the bridal couple. If they were Jean and Marie Belloir the couple in St. Hilaire were not. He looked for the photographer's imprint, thinking of René. The picture had been taken in Paris. Who then was the couple with the harvesting corps?

He took the broom from the side of the hearth and went outdoors, wielding it as a shield between himself and the gander who ran alongside him as he approached the barn, thrusting again and again its long neck obscenely. To take an axe to that neck would have been a pleasure. Passing through the barn arcade between the grain bins and the washup room, he closed a gate between himself and the angry fowl, and left the broom in the barn. The broom fell and when he bent down to pick it up he saw the bicycle, the back wheel just showing inside the grain room.

He followed the lane with its fresh wagon tracks until he came to the field where two men and three women were working. One of the men stood with the horses while the other repaired an ancient binder. The women were cocking the grain, one gathering it and tying it into sheaves where the binder had failed to tie it. It was a very old man that held the horses, the one at the machine was roughly his own age. He worked on until Moissac came up to him.

"Monsieur Belloir?"

The man straightened up. "I am."

Moissac identified himself. "I wish to inquire as to the whereabouts of your son, Jean, and his wife."

"Why, monsieur? What have they done?"

Moissac watched the others come up, three generations of family he thought. "I have reason to believe there is a couple traveling under their identity in St. Hilaire."

"But, *Monsieur le Préfet*, my son and daughter-in-law are in St. Hilaire. They went up by foot last night."

Moissac looked from one stolid face to the other. Nothing. "It is so, monsieur?"

"Unless something happened to them on the way and that is what you have come to tell us."

Moissac, remembering the cyclist, was on the verge of anger he could not afford. "Then, may I ask, who are the handsome bridal pair on your mantle?"

Belloir straightened his back again. His shoulders tended to hunch. "It is very like the Germans, monsieur, to enter a house without cause or permit. I did not think it of a Frenchman."

"God Almighty, Belloir. Your bloody goose drove me in. He has my trousers in ribbons."

For the first time Belloir showed that he could smile. "He is supposed to keep people out, not to drive them in, but my apologies, monsieur. The couple you ask about: they are my brother's son and his wife. He went down to Paris with Jean, but now he is in a work camp."

Moissac was helpless to contradict him. Yet the very ease with which Belloir told it made him suspect. "When did your son return from Paris?"

"Three days ago, is it? We are proud of him, monsieur. It is not every family in the canton who will have a doctor of their own."

"It seems to me remarkable," Moissac said, "that in so rich a farming area your son would volunteer to harvest the crops of strangers."

"I do not question my son's intentions, monsieur, any more than I would question his honor. We did not need him. As you see, we did not plant more this year than we could reap ourselves. Jean's permit to travel was to take part in the harvest. That is what he is doing."

Moissac knew he was bested for the moment. He thought of the letter lying on the plate in the house. He also thought of a fat goose to take home to Maman. Reluctantly he put the goose out of mind. "Thank you, monsieur. I will not keep you from your work any longer."

"I will walk up with you," Belloir said. "The binder is fixed. Papa can run it."

"It is not necessary."

"You will need protection from Hercule."

Since he was to have the man's conduct whether or not he wanted it, Moissac said, "My mother is fond of goose. I would like to buy one if it is possible."

"I will sell you one cheaply if you will take a message to my son."

"A pleasure, monsieur," Moissac said.

The gate he had closed was open and the bicycle was gone. Belloir picked up a long pole with a hook on its end. He asked: "Is there a particular one in the flock you fancy, monsieur?"

"As long as it is not Hercule."

Again Belloir allowed his craggy face to break with a smile. "Please wait in the house, monsieur. You must dress the bird yourself, but I will bind the neck and wrap it."

Moissac reached the house just ahead of the gander. The gander then took after Belloir as the man moved into the screaming flock with his leg hook. Moissac had never heard such noise. He turned from it, trying to stop the sound in his ears. He went to the table intending to examine the letter more closely. It had been removed.

21

ALL MARC'S FEARS OF WIELDING THE PITCHFORK, AND HE HAD come to understand why it was represented as the devil's weapon, proved without foundation. By sundown he was swinging along from one grain cock to the next and pitching the sheaves onto the wagon rack with a rhythm some farmers never achieved: of this Gabrielle assured him. He hoisted the stone jug to his shoulder and drank deeply of the cool well water. He poured some into Gabrielle's hands and she drank it from them. But turning them up for the water she revealed blisters that matched his own. Most of the harvesters had them, having come back to the fields after a long absence. He passed the jug on and stood gazing down the broad, clean field which lay like a golden sheet under the pearly sky. He could feel where the afternoon sun had stung his forehead and cheeks, and his lips were salt with the sweat of the day. At long, long last he had rid his nostrils of the reek of Paris cellars.

"So much sky," he said, arching his neck to see more, ever more of it, and feeling with the arch the promise of a stiffness in his back and shoulders.

So much sky: Gabrielle had thought that very thing the day she drove Poirot out through the convent gates to meet the train in St. Hilaire. She turned from the sunset to the opposite horizon where the pearl was deepening into blue. A funnel of smoke going up from the threshing machine, so far off they could hardly hear its sound, shimmered in the last of the sun's rays: it was spangled with bits of chaff like a shower of sparks.

"Look. It is so beautiful."

Marc looked to where she pointed. "Like a comet in the

daytime. I saw a comet once. My father took me to the observatory, but I can't remember which comet it was."

"Where is he? Your father, I mean."

"He's in America. But my mother—I do not know. My father left in time and my mother was to join him, but the Germans came too soon. It was the same with Rachel's family; all except her were taken. She was in school at the time. Afterwards her teacher found a hiding place for her."

"Some of you will be together again—in the Holy Land."

"That would be fine," Marc said with something less than conviction.

"Do you not love your parents?"

"I love them." Again the tentativeness. He did not want to lie, but neither was he likely to be able to explain that what he felt was duty, and even that did not seem to relate to family or to have any emotional components to it. It was simply that he had chosen to live and the family relationship was part of what survived in the choice. Someday perhaps he would feel some deeper attachment to people; it might come with a deeper sense of self—if that came ever.

"Perhaps I will be a pioneer," he said, wanting to give Gabrielle the satisfaction she deserved.

She smiled. "You will be a farmer because you *are* a farmer today."

"Thank you."

"I do not tease you," she said. "When you are working in the earth you will know what it is to love it, to love animals, to love God."

"I will know what it is to love, isn't that it?"

Suddenly she was shy of him again. "Yes, monsieur."

"Jean," he said and wagged a finger at her. He pointed to where the horse-drawn rack was coming for them, picking up Jacques and Philomène, Thérèse and Philippe first. The latter two, Marc had learned, had closed their grocery shop to return to the land for this little while. There was among all the older members of the group the sadness of having, by necessity or folly, given up their birthright to the land. "You make earth sound so beautiful," Marc said, "I could almost forget how terrible it has become in the custody of man."

Again she had to sort his meaning from his words. She almost always liked the words.

Jacques offered a hand to each of them down from the rack.

"We're full of blisters," Marc said, and to Gabrielle: "Turn around, your back to the wagon." She obeyed. He put his hands to her waist and lifted her up. She went stiff, but she did not reject him.

"Wouldn't it be grand to go swimming?" Jacques said, "or to lie down in a trough of water. Preferably with a woman." He nudged Philomène, whose long legs were swinging from the rack. "Have you ever made love under water?"

"Do you take me for a guppy, dear?"

"A mermaid, a beautiful mermaid who I'd like to meet at sea during my next voyage."

Gabrielle tried not to listen.

"Are you a sailor?" Marc asked him.

"I was. I gave up the farm for the sea, but now where is there a ship for a man to sail on out of France, except to Bocheland? And I'll not go there if I can help it."

"That's where my husband is," Philomène said, "so just shut up."

"Sorry, my dear. There is no safe conversation." He leaned forward to look past Marc. "How is the bride?"

"You know," Marc said, "we've been married over a year." The Belloirs had. "I don't know how you got onto the bride and groom business."

"Well, if I'd had to guess at the matter, I'd have said you weren't married at all."

"Marie living in sin?" Philomène crowed. Her voice penetrated Gabrielle's wall of protection.

"You're right, you're right," Jacques said.

Thérèse leaned across her husband who had stretched

out between her and Gabrielle. "Where were you married? Monsieur comes from Paris. I can tell by his accent, but not madame."

"We were married in Paris," Marc said. "To what church did we go after the courthouse? They are all the same to me."

"Ste. Geneviève," Gabrielle said, "the patron saint of Paris. She saved the people from the Huns fifteen hundred years ago."

Jacques heaved a great sigh. "It is too bad she died so soon."

Everyone laughed and then fell silent. A couple of minutes later Jacques spoke again. "They say Mussolini is out of a job."

Philippe sat up, wriggling his hips to get more comfortable. "He has no need to worry. Pétain will make him premier of France."

In the courtyard the threshing machine was still going, two wagonloads of sheaves left. The chaff swirled about like yellow snow, and a great mountain of straw was yet to be bailed. Artur, almost black with grease, jumped up and down on the platform, waving to them. It had come as a surprise to Marc that the dwarf was a fine mechanic; as Jacques said, the only really necessary man on the team. Along the platform, bag after bag of oats was being sewn up by a woman of the farm.

They all washed at the pump and Marc treated with salve and bandaged the worst of the blistered hands. That much medicine he was competent to practice.

A thick soup and good wine along with the best bread Marc had had since the beginning of war were served them by lantern light in the courtyard, and after it a pudding with a treat of treats, thick cream. The *châtelain* himself came round and bade them eat well. He was a different man in jodhpurs than in dress suit. He sat among the workers and drank the wine he served them.

Jules tuned his guitar and strummed a melancholy impro-

visation. The lovers, Antoine and Michèle, kissed uninhibit-
edly. Marc glanced at Gabrielle and caught the flutter of her
eyelashes as she closed out the lovers. She missed very little,
he thought, swiftly taking in that which she proposed there-
after not to see or hear. Was it perhaps the sweeter for the
briefness of the savoring? But that was not the point. The
point was complete denial. Such a shame, the waste. Philomène began to sing. Nobody really wanted to sing at first, but
she had an *agent provocateur* of a voice: you wanted to pitch
in to help get the tune to wherever it was she was trying to
take it. The music might be melancholic but the theme was
militant. Marc had heard it before, but he could not remember where. Suddenly Antoine sang out, words different from
those of Philomène. He had a fine tenor voice that nobody
had heard till then. Philomène and the rest faded their voices
down to a hum.

Marc was not likely to forget that moment: this frail man
whom only in the field had he observed to be lame, sitting
upright, his hands clasped between his knees, rocking himself
slowly while he sang, and for the moment entirely separate
from the woman.

> "Si me quieres escribir
> Ya sabes mi paradero. . . ."

Marc recognized it as an anti-Fascist song of the Spanish
War. Antoine's eyes shone with a wistful zeal, and the lamp-
light caught the changes in a face that was alternately old and
young. He was singing of what would have been a sadly
glorious time of his life. Marc thought about what it meant to
survive, defeated. Men always expected victory, though not a
one existed to whom defeat was not ultimately inevitable.
Thus, he mused, the myth of heaven. Resurrection. Immortal-
ity. The final justice.

The women picked up the rhythm with the faintest clacking of castanets. The song was familiar to most of them as a
Spanish folk song. He heard Gabrielle humming. He wanted
to go closer, the better to hear, but he dared not, knowing she

---

would stop. It was a high, sweet sound. Philomène, also hearing it, coaxed with her hands. Gabrielle parted her lips to smile and the voice escaped. There was to the sound such poignancy and—the word he was so loathe to use—purity, that he was swept into that feeling of protectiveness again. She did not need his protection. He needed hers, and more than protection. What he was taking from her was her sense of purpose for him. All day, whenever they had rested together, she would ask about the place where he would go, the kind of soil, what it grew, the people, the language. It was a pure and unironical truth that telling her he found more purpose of his own than he had had even with Rachel. Much more. Rachel had conjured for him. Now he was the conjurer, and he was beginning to believe in his own magic.

The Spanish song ended and Antoine fell back, his head finding the lap of the waiting woman. Marc was filled with a great sadness for them, the homeless lovers, their haven in wandering. Almost without intent, he began himself to sing, a wordless song to which the sound *tum-bah* set the rhythm, and which everyone took up and repeated while he went on with the melodic chant. Again, the song came from his student days, from a singer he had all but forgotten though the melody had haunted him and he sang with the fervor of one who wishes to believe but cannot. Everyone wanted to know the song's origin, particularly Jules who proposed to know it before he went to sleep that night.

"All I know," Marc said, "it is Palestinean. Arabic perhaps, possibly Hebraic."

"Ay, ay, ay," Jacques said. "It is sad enough for that."

The *châtelain* arose from the circle. "I bid you goodnight, friends, and an early departure in the morning. You have worked well and I have no complaint. Sing now, if that is your pleasure, but for God's sake, remember, a German patrol passes this way three times a night."

There was no more singing. They would travel with the dawn wherever possible during the harvest, and the dew would be dry in the fields when they reached them. Those with sleeping bags unfolded them in the open courtyard. The *châtelain* locked the gates to the yard himself.

Those with blankets, Gabrielle and Marc among them, went into the loft where the fresh straw was still settling. The darkness, relieved only by the shafts of moonlight, made separation easy. From the moment they left the others, Gabrielle began her night's silence. She heard him speak, but did not answer and he did not speak again.

She lay down with the new robe over her, but she had not undressed. She fought sleep, a harsh battle, sometimes having to dig her nails into her flesh. Finally, catching herself dozing, she managed to come wide awake only by irritating the blisters on her hands. The novice mistress would not approve: it was sinful to inflict self-injury. Wearily, she wondered if choosing among sins for the lesser of them was not in itself a sin, and then she wondered further if this very thought about the choices was not temptation: a new way of the devil's, bidding her to sleep. And there was something further yet to be said for sleep: no matter how evil the dreams, one did not have to answer for them unless one dwelt upon them, waking.

When there was all of the stillness she expected of the night, accustoming herself to the whispers of the settling straw, she got up, left the white robe where she had lain, and went to a place where the boards were bare not far from the loft door. There she knelt and devised an hour of prayer and meditation, or as close to an hour as she could estimate, based on as many of Christ's miracles as she could remember. Sounds intruded and were banished: the night-baying of a dog; someone's snoring and spittle-spewing which sounded like the wash of the river repeating itself on the shore; the katydids, consistent as a clock, distractions all recognized and put out of mind, made one with her own beingness and the palpitation of night itself.

But then there came a sound she could not banish, a pulsing sound that had yet no noise in it, but seemed to tremble the very boards on which she knelt. She tried for recognition

in order to then be done with it, animal, human. . . . Then
came the flash of recognition, the realization of its rhythm and
her whole body began to throb, her mind to swim with asso-
ciations. She clasped her hands to her head over her ears, but
her own pulsebeat was suggestive and the throbbing took on
color, red for passion, Passion Sunday, red for blood, Christ's
blood, blood-red tears, the menstrual blood, the poppies in
the field, the Sacred Heart of Jesus, the tongues and mouths
of men, the furrowed soil, the slaughtered lamb of pascal, its
wool red at the knife-tear in its throat.

She heard the little choked-off cry—her own, or the
woman's? She felt the pain of sound-held-back within her
throat, and the sobs she could not repress. She muffled them,
her mouth deep in the flesh of her arm, and gradually she
eased herself down prone upon the floor. There, sucking at
her own arm for solace, she said in her mind again and again,
Virgin Mary, Mother most pure, and eased her way past
temptation into silence and finally, peace.

Marc, himself straightened within the poles of sound—he
had been conscious of her every move, and theirs—felt his
sweat grow cold. He knew what she had heard, that exquisite
thumping of human pleasure, and straining for her sounds
when the lovers were at ease, he knew that she was suffering
as he was, the pain of which he could relieve them both.

He forced upon his mind the memory of her as she
looked when the thought had come on all of them to pass
Rachel as the apprentice nun. He cursed and tossed achingly,
and became captive to a repetition of the incidents in that
final day of Rachel's life. His last image, as he passed into a
dream-riven sleep, was of Rachel in coif and cambric. It was
all so ridiculous, so goddamned absurd.

22

IF THE LETTER FROM PARIS HAD NOT BEEN REMOVED FROM THE plate where Moissac had seen it, he might not have contacted the *Sûrêté* to inquire from a Paris source the whereabouts of Jean and Marie Belloir. He assumed the director of the post office in Fauré had given him a correct address for them, but as the morning lengthened and he received no reply to his inquiry of the night before, he wondered. He could not assume anything in this affair now. Little Madame Belloir, if that indeed was her name, had given him a false address for her parents in Marseille. And he might not have checked on that if he had not been making the other inquiry.

He would have liked very much to have an answer from Paris before going into Von Weber's office, but none had come by eleven-five and he had been sent for at eleven-ten. It would take him a good five minutes to navigate the polished corridor.

"So," Von Weber greeted him, "a tankful of gasoline for a security mission. Or were you pulling the wool over my eyes?"

"That would be difficult, Colonel."

"I am glad you think so. But all that gasoline?"

"I was not sure I would get as much as I asked for."

Von Weber gave a dry laugh at such earnestness. "Tell me about this mysterious mission of yours." He gestured Moissac into the chair beside his desk and dismissed his aide.

Moissac began where, being Moissac, he had to begin, getting the dirty part over with first. *Au Bon Coin* was familiar to Von Weber so that Moissac felt there was no outright involvement of Gaucher on his part. He did, however, justify his own presence there by calling the colonel's attention to German Intelligence reports on the bistro.

"I would not for a moment suspect you of clandestine involvement," Von Weber said. "Please tell me about these people—in a relaxed fashion. What are they like?"

Moissac colored at the solemn reassurance. "René Labrière is the man I know best. He is not a very important man—I am speaking now of before the Occupation. . . . "

"The photographer. Why do you make a point of his unimportance?"

"I am trying to give you a full picture, Colonel."

"Give me fact and let me decide its significance, eh?"

"Yes, Colonel. But I do not have what you would call fact: at the moment, I have only suspicions."

"There must be some fact on which you have based suspicion," Von Weber said with an edge that launched Moissac instantly into his story of the arrival of the stranger that night at Gaucher's, the subsequent discovery of him with a bride among the harvesters, the coincidence of René's presence in *Au Bon Coin* and Madame Belloir's visit to his studio for a photograph to send to parents whose correct address she did not seem to have. He omitted no detail: Von Weber could well have intelligence of his own. Finally he described his experience in Fauré.

"What was the message old Belloir gave you for his son?"

"*If* the man is his son. The message was that the cow had calved, a fine bull calf."

"Did you see it?"

"Beg pardon, Colonel?"

"Did you see the calf? Did you *ask* to see it?"

"No, Colonel. There would have been an excuse, I am sure. The message is code."

"Excuses are as good as evidence. I should think as a police officer you would consider that gospel."

"It is so," Moissac said. "But I preferred to show no sign of suspicion to the old one. It is the young man from whom I wish to learn the meaning. Old Belloir is who he says he is, and he will stay where he is until he dies."

"My compliments," Von Weber said with the benevolence of the schoolmaster meting out praise. "You have reasoned well."

The colonel's orderly brought aperitifs on a silver tray. Moissac was flattered, but as he sipped *anis,* he remembered Madame Lebel and Madame Lebel's daughter, and the eerie lapse by which Maman lost track of a generation in time. For just a fleeting instant Moissac wondered if, twenty years from now, tasting *anis,* he would remember sipping it with a man he was trying on his soul to believe a benefactor of France, a German of class, family, and taste who sometimes treated him with a deference he received from no Frenchman.

Von Weber brushed the moisture from his lip. "Shall we speak now of the young Belloirs, if, since you question it, they are the Belloirs? If they are not, what do you see as their purpose?"

"They are very intelligent. Not like the others this year. There are not many students. I will say it, Colonel. Since I no longer suspect him of being a Gestapo man, it occurs to me they might be members of the *Maquis.* The harvesting would make an excellent cover for recruiting."

"It is interesting that you equate intelligence with terrorism."

"They are better educated, that is what I meant."

Von Weber set his glass down carefully. He took off his spectacles, polished them, and put them on again. Moissac braced himself. "Let us reconstruct saying the couple are Belloirs. A medical student and his wife come home from Paris for the harvest. They cannot have been home in many months, and yet within a day or so, they set out among strangers to harvest the fields of strangers. Most curious."

"My very logic."

"Thank you, *Monsieur le Préfet.* And does your logic not suggest that if they are not Belloirs, they may be Jews trying to escape across the Spanish border?"

Moissac tried hard to control the muscles of his face. He did not dare to lie. "No, Colonel."

"And yet it happens quite frequently, wouldn't you say?"

"Yes, Colonel. I am always alert to it."

"To you they must seem very Aryan. You mistook him for a Gestapo man." Von Weber sat and laughed silently. He ended it by rubbing his mouth with the handkerchief on which he had polished his glasses. He threw the handkerchief into the bottom drawer of his desk. Instantly, his orderly brought him a clean one. "Ah, Moissac, Moissac, love looks not with the eyes but with the mind."

Moissac shook his head that he did not understand, and shaking it, he felt the weight of his jowls.

"I am fond of Shakespeare," Von Weber went on. "I used to teach school, you know. Have I told you that?"

"No, Colonel, but I have thought so."

"And do you think I am right now about the Belloirs?"

"I do not think so, but it is possible."

"What you mean, Moissac, is that you do not feel so." Moissac shrugged.

"Some men feel truth," the colonel said, "and some men feel so much that is not true, the truth eludes them like a rabbit a St. Bernard."

Even the choice of dogs in the comparison made him uncomfortable, Moissac having but the moment before felt jowlish.

"It would be pleasant for you perhaps if they were Jews," the colonel suggested.

"I do not understand," Moissac admitted again.

"Think about it: you are responsible to me for the clearance of all these harvesters. Is that not so?"

"In St. Hilaire, yes, Colonel. That is why I have consulted you."

"In the district, Moissac. That is my jurisdiction. You will operate in liaison with Military Security, but that should not be too difficult. . . . After all, your first suspicion was security, wasn't it?" He sat thinking for a moment. "Do you enjoy the hunt?"

"Sundays, I do a bit. Yes, Colonel."

"The wild boar is my favorite. You would have thought so, wouldn't you?"

Moissac was not sure he was not himself being baited. He would not think a schoolteacher the likeliest hunter of the wild boar at all. He took a chance: the colonel did not have much more humor than he had himself. "Yes, Colonel. I would have thought that."

"Why?"

"It is one of the oldest sports of aristocrats. Is that not so, Colonel?"

"It is exactly so." Von Weber looked at his watch. Moissac started to rise. "Don't go for a moment. I should suppose my ancestors would have hunted the boar through this very country. There is nothing like it, Moissac, except possibly what you are engaged in now. He's a clever fellow obviously."

"Yes."

"And he will be protecting the female of the species?"

Moissac flushed to the roots of his hair. The German studied him for a few seconds. He leaned back then and said as though unleashing a dog: "Go get them!"

As Von Weber again hiked his cuff to look at his watch, Moissac got up. "But suppose it turns out that they are not Jews, Colonel?"

Von Weber took his arm. "That would be a pity, but I have every confidence in that great nose of yours, *mon préfet.*" He walked him to the door of the Rotunda. "The court martial has acquitted Lieutenant Heinrich, by the way. The old woman was adjudged mad."

"I have said so myself," Moissac said.

"You would agree, then, a bullet was a mercy?"

"I could not say that, Colonel, and long remain a peace officer of the republic."

"You could under the New Order. You ought to think that way, Moissac. It is a great tonic for men who are not sure of their own worth."

Moissac left Von Weber's office in a state of high excitement, something he had not been able to conceal from the German so that he pretended it was the prospect of the hunt that had infected him. And in a way it was, but only in a way. Moissac could not account even to himself what was happening to him. He went out from the *Hôtel de ville* feeling in all ways the German's equal, for which he supposed he would have to thank Von Weber himself. It did not even seem extraordinary to him that the colonel should treat him with such camaraderie.

To Maman it seemed extraordinary that he should speak to him at all. "There will be something he wants of you, some dirty work."

"A policeman's work. That's all. Some people call it dirty, some duty. It has profited us, maman, and until lately you have praised me for it."

"I will not entertain the German in this house, Théophile. I will not cook for him."

"I have not asked it. I don't intend to now, but if I did, I would expect you to do your duty too."

She looked up at him, the little black eyes trying to pry their way into his. "It is not the German we are really talking about, is it?"

He did not answer. He could not meet her eyes. Instead he looked at the goose where she had hung it from the beam over the sink, naked as sin, stripped of its feathers.

"Come, I want to show you something," she said.

She led the way through the house to the front door which was rarely used, overlooking the river. She opened the door. On the dark wood a huge scythe had been painted in white. They spoke simultaneously.

"What is the meaning, Théophile?"

"When did it happen, maman?"

"Tell me what it means."

"There was a woman shot in the field."

"I know that. By a German. What does it have to do with us?"

"She was a crazy woman, but the Resistance is making a martyr of her. That is their symbol now."

She gave up trying to get a direct answer from him and resorted to an old weapon. "You will have to paint the whole door white. And maybe yourself as well. A pretty sight."

He caught her by the wrist. "Don't you make fun of me, maman. You have my thanks for what I am. I happen to like it just now."

As always when he asserted his will over hers, and he kept forgetting this until pricked by necessity, she gave way. She made her arm go limp in his grasp. "I have always liked what you are. That is why I get angry with you. You are not a collaborationist, and that is what they mean, isn't it?"

He let go her arm and closed the door. "I don't know. I want a change of linen packed, maman. I may be going away for a day or two."

She began to rub her wrist. He had not held her that firmly. "Take me with you, Théophile. You need me to look after you."

"No, maman. It is not possible."

"It is not possible because you do not want me. You can't even look at me. You hide your eyes like your father did. I used to loathe him for it."

"Why did you marry him then?"

"Close the parlor door," she said, and herself returned to the kitchen.

Moissac closed it. Why they had a parlor he did not know, except to entertain the monsignor in. The monsignor, he thought, would wait a while for another invitation.

Maman brought the plates from the warming oven to the table. She looked at her bony hands and twisted the wedding band, much too loose except that the joint was swollen so the ring would not come off. "He was such a pathetic man, always trying to please me. Never a complaint. . . ."

Moissac had thought she had chosen not to answer and he wished now that he had not started her on his father.

"Like St. Joseph," she said suddenly, and with a defiant

toss of her head. "I have always thought St. Joseph pathetic."

"That's enough, maman."

"I thought you'd say that." She was enjoying herself. It happened the instant he reproved her. "Oh yes, a really pathetic man, pushed from one thing into another with no idea of what was going on."

He caught her by the elbows and shook her even as she had shaken him as a child. "Aren't you afraid at your age to talk like that?"

"Of course I'm afraid. That's why I do it."

"I do not understand you."

"Nor I you, my son."

He had just removed his coat and sat down to the table when the telephone rang. He went into the vestibule and answered it. The call was from the prefecture. An answer had come from Paris: Jean Belloir and his wife had returned to their flat in Rue Vanquelin after several days' absence. If further information were required, he was to so instruct.

Moissac wished no further information for the moment. In terms of time it was just barely possible for the couple to have left the harvesters and returned to Paris: that this was not so was the first thing of which he had to be certain. He instructed the desk man to have René picked up that afternoon, and to have him available for interrogation on Moissac's return.

When he hung up the phone he saw Maman standing in the doorway. "So that was all Von Weber wanted from you, Théophile? The arrest of your friend."

"Do you not think there is something for which to arrest him, maman?"

"There is always something for any man. If that wasn't so where would the martyrs come from? Men make martyrs. They are not made in heaven."

"You are in a strange mood, maman. It is a shame I have to go so soon. Put up some soup for me and let it cool." Moissac glanced at himself in the hall mirror, wishing he had

shaved more carefully. He lingered, studying his face. It was
the dark beard as well as the nose.

"What do you see, Théophile? Open your eyes and look
well, my son. Then tell me what you see and you will feel
better."

"I feel just fine. Please, maman, the soup."

A few minutes later she watched him pour wine from his
glass into the soup. "You will not permit me to go in the car
with you?"

"No. I do not know what may happen or when I will get
back. I will send someone to paint the door."

"I will paint it."

"If you like."

"I do not like, but I will do what must be done."

"Leave it. I will probably be home tonight," he said,
exasperated at her melodrama. "You sound as though I were
going away forever."

"That is how I feel. But that is because I want to feel
that way. I admit it. Self-pity is an overcoat you slip into very
easily in old age. It is a shoddy fabric, but no one cares.
Everybody knows they won't have to wear it for long. I will
pack your valise now."

23

MARC AND GABRIELLE HAD WORKED APART THAT DAY. IT WAS Gabrielle's wish and Marc had responded by assigning himself to the machine, working at the grain spout, filling and replacing the bags. In fact, he had placed himself as far apart from her as possible, behavior he recognized as more becoming an adolescent than a man three days widowed.

The morning's move had brought the harvesters twenty kilometers closer to the border. The patrols were more frequent, the examination of papers more careful despite Colonel von Weber's promise of non-interference. Marc, working near the dwarf, where he pranced and danced over steps and platforms like Quasimodo in the tower of Notre-Dame, found his nerves on edge by the end of the day. Artur delighted in announcing the imminent arrival of a Nazi patrol by jumping up and down on the iron seat atop the thresher and shaking his fist in the air. Then at the last minute, Marc cursing at him, he would plop down on his plump little backside and bury his legs from sight. Between them, Marc and Jacques, who was hauling the grain from machine to storeroom, composed a litany of abuses which delighted the dwarf. He begged them remember and write them down for him. . . . A two-stemmed mushroom, sawed-off and hammered-down, Napoleon the half. . . .

When the machine was silent at last and Marc could shake the dust from his head as from a mop, he went out from the yards of this estate called Champs des Corbeaux, and stretched himself on the ground where he could look down to the far fields and see the others starting in. The *marquis*, their host-employer, saw no reason to send a horse to carry men and women who, he said, were better able to carry his horses. They were a sorry lot to look at, his half-dozen horses, but an old man who had long worked on the estate, told Marc that the master had sold his good ones to the Germans at a fine price. Marc prophesied a thin soup and watered wine. So he fed himself on the setting sun. He could not get enough of sky. He rolled over on his back and stared up at it trying to fathom its depth for stars.

She had wanted to stay apart from him so that she would not need to talk, of course. Or was it that she could no longer bear the nearness of him as he was finding hers too painful, being that near and no nearer? He turned onto his side and watched her come, the last and most solitary, not only alone but with the mists of evening threatening to overtake and vanish her. On the next day, according to the map, they would come into a more hilly terrain, and within two days they would near the mountains, and after that day's work the harvesters would swing away in another direction. Two days.

Gabrielle saw him and raised her hand. Marc rose from where he lay and all the weariness flowed out of him as he ran toward her, leaping with but a touch of the hand for balance over the stone hedge. And yet she did not speak when he came abreast of her, nor even look up to meet his eyes, nor let him take the pitchfork from her.

And so they walked, side by side, up the lane. It was not enough, Marc thought, but it was something. At the end of the lane they found the St. Hilaire prefect of police waiting for them. He offered his hand to Gabrielle as she came over the stile. Now she gave the fork to Marc, and at the last moment, her hand into Moissac's. His was as soft as putty and as coldly moist. In the days when hands were meaningful, such a hand would have made her uncomfortable, making her think of dead and slimy things. Once as a little girl she had dreamt of hands, hundreds of them floating in the pond without arms or bodies or meaning. "They intend you no harm," her father said, so that she must have told him of the dream or wakened crying. She remembered saying, "But what will the people do without them?"

Marc took his time getting over the stile. After the day's

encounters with the Nazis, Monsieur Moissac was even more difficult to deal with. The Nazis were strangers, Moissac a native. Nor did the policeman's greeting reassure him.

"Your father asked me to give you a message, young Belloir."

"I hope no one is ill."

"Who would be ill?"

"People when they get old are often ill," Marc said.

Elusive as a fox, Moissac thought. "He said to tell you that the cow had calved, a fine bull calf."

"Thank you," Marc said. "I am glad to know it. It is good news, Marie."

Gabrielle was not sure: was he asking her to respond? She did know why a farmer would rejoice in a good bull. "It will be good for the herd, is that not so?"

"Yes," Marc said, but what the message was meant to convey to him he had no idea at all. American slang sometimes referred to the police as "bulls," but it still made no sense, except to tell him that Moissac had gone to see the elder Belloir. And the fact that Moissac brought the message seemed to mean that Belloir had covered him. "I am most grateful to you, monsieur. I hope it did not bring you out of your way?"

"On the contrary," Moissac said, quite as amiable.

"We ought to go up," Marc said. "They will serve the meal soon and I doubt there will be very much of it tonight."

"I have been asked to dine," Moissac said, starting up alongside Marc.

"But with the *marquis,* so you will not need to hurry."

"I will eat at the harvesters' table," Moissac said. "I am a humble man."

Marc could think of nothing to say to that. He found himself again commenting on the meal and its provider. "I'm told the old boy is a miser."

"Your father made me a gift of a goose."

"Which one?" Marc said, an absolute inanity, he thought immediately, but he had done enough mumbling.

The question, of course, threw Moissac off-balance. Indeed it made him wonder for the moment at the accuracy of his Paris informant. He said, "No. Not Monsieur Hercule."

Marc got off the subject. "Will you wish to wash up, monsieur?"

"Thank you, but I will talk with madame."

"She too must wash," Marc said. "We can all talk afterwards." He nodded to Gabrielle to go.

Moissac curbed his temper, but not his authority. "One minute, madame. You will tell me, please, why you gave me the wrong address of your family in Marseille."

Gabrielle said, trying to make her consternation seem surprise, "They are not there, monsieur? It will be the Germans then."

"Why should the Germans be interested?" He did not want to ask that. He had not even wanted to question the address yet, but the insolent husband had provoked him.

"My father is a strong man," Gabrielle said. Her father had been strong, and that day she had listened to the story of Philomène's husband and the German labor camps.

Marc said, "We plan to go to Marseille afterwards if we can get travel permits. It has been much too long, as we said yesterday, since Marie has seen her parents." To her he added, "I think it is simply a matter of their having moved. We must not worry until we know for certain."

Again Moissac felt he could almost believe them. He needed more certainty, and until he had it, he too must be disarming. "You wonder why I checked the address, madame: the photographer you visited is under suspicion of black-market activities. It is my duty to check on him in every way possible."

Marc, leading Gabrielle to where the other harvesters were washing, considered the plausibility of Moissac's backing down. Or was it the truth? René had said in the loft, stripping their ration books of coupons, that if he were picked up they would think him on his proper business, the black market.

"Is it true, what he said about checking on Monsieur René?" Gabrielle asked when they were by themselves.

"We must believe it," Marc said, "until we know otherwise."

Her face had the glow of two days' sun, and there were flecks of gold in her eyes. Marc said, "I don't suppose I ought to say this to you, but I will: I missed you today."

"You must not say it." Then, her eyes wide so that he saw the beginning of tears, "And you must not miss me. You must not!" She turned and ran from him.

Moissac, watching covertly, was troubled again by his own deductions. Surely two people on the run would not quarrel at such a time. Something was not right in the way he saw them, but what? What? He decided to learn what he could by ingratiating himself with the harvesters. The young people would barely give him the time of day, but Jacques and Philippe were men who liked to talk. They sat on the lowest of the wagons, stretched themselves and watched the night come down on them. Jacques, reminded by the mists of a fog at sea, told of a phantom ship he saw come out of every fog, the same ship no matter where on the seven seas he was sailing. Philippe told of watch duty once in the army when a stump crept up like a wolf in the moonlight. Artur came and sat among them and Moissac tried not to see his legs. When the women came Moissac got down and helped Philomène and Céleste aboard. He then insinuated himself between them which made them giggle.

The first stars had come out when the dinner-bell sounded, and the harvesters, as well as tenants and neighbors of the *marquis* whose grain would be threshed in the early morning, went up the graveled path to the chateau. It was a procession of some thirty people and they were led by a servant of the house with a torch.

"It is medieval," Marc said. "I've not been here before, if you know what I mean."

Gabrielle had rejoined him at the ringing of the bell. "I know."

"Will there be music, do you think?" Jules asked.

Marc glanced back at him. "Where's the guitar?"

"I hid it."

"It will be a long walk if the *marquis* asks you to play."

"I do not intend to entertain him. He contracted to feed us, and we to do his field work only."

Marc remembered his rebellion the night of the feast at Madame Fontaine's: that too now seemed a part of far history. Then as he stooped to enter the arched passageway that lead through the cellars and servants' quarters of the chateau, a passageway lit by torchlight, Marc underwent an experience that shook him badly: he was afraid, but in the context of the Inquisition. It was such self-consciousness, such awareness of his Jewish origins as he had not experienced ever before. He hung back and Gabrielle turned to him, and what he remembered of her at that moment was also flame-lit and terrible: she and her partner leaning over Rachel, the sense of ritual somewhere deep in him as suggesting a life for a life, the primary sacrifice.

"It is too terrible," he said.

"No. It is only strange to you. To me it is like going home."

"You do not understand."

The others were crowding in behind him, wanting to see what lay ahead, and hungry. Some of the boys pushed past him, looking back and grinning as though he were merely awestruck with the place.

Gabrielle held out her hand to him. The palm was down as she might offer it to a child. "Come," she said, and her eyes coaxed him as well. It was at that moment that Moissac came up also behind Marc. "You must not stand and gawk, Jean," she said. "*Monsieur le Préfet* wishes to pass."

It took but a few seconds all, in happening. Moissac would have prolonged it, seeing her. The man was no more than a shadow between them. Moissac closed his eyes. The prayer was habit, but the content new: Please, God, let her be a Jew. The dwarf skittered past him, and then past Marc and

caught Gabrielle's hand where it was outstretched. He put it
to his lips, his cheek.

As nothing else would, this sprung Marc into motion. He
caught the little man by the collar and pushed him behind
him, going on then with Gabrielle although her hand was no
longer there for him to take. Moissac put his hand into the
face of the dwarf, his thumb beneath the chin. He flung the
creature backwards with all his might. Nor did he look back
hearing the thud of flesh and bone as Artur hurtled into the
wall. Artur lay and whimpered, but when no one who passed
stopped and then no more came, he picked himself up and
scurried after the procession.

They moved through the kitchen, where the cook and her
staff looked them over contemptuously. On they were led over
the flagstoned floors into the great dining hall, where as in
centuries past, the family table was on a dais, and the long
table for guests and workers below. A fire roared in the hearth
beside which a man could stand his full height and scarcely
reach the chimney. There were areas of darkness in the room
and the dampness prevailed despite the fire.

"You see," Gabrielle whispered, "except for the hearth—
and once there was one but it no longer works—this is like
the place where I live."

Everyone spoke in hushed tones.

"Do you miss it very much?" Marc said.

They stood beside benches at the table. Gabrielle
frowned, trying to be honest with herself at least. She nodded,
knowing the answer she must give to him. She was not sure
that her vocation was not being taken from her for this abuse
of it. There were times when she had spoken and it was not
necessary. And she had sung, and laughed aloud. Away from
Marc she had missed him too. But all day she had told herself
that that was because she missed the responsibility he was to
her, and it was so. She would not have put her hand out to
him except to help him. Poor little Artur. God's littlest
messenger—could she not call him that? He had come and

snatched her hand, and she had been reminded of the rule
she now seemed to so easily violate.

Leaning forward a little and putting her fingertips on the
table, she closed her eyes and remembered how the refectory
was on the last night she had been present, the sisters from
Normandy had come and Sister St. André had spoken when the
lights went out. What came to her, just letting her mind roam
at random, from Sister Marguerite and her rheumatic shuffle
to Ursula and her stomach's noisiness, to Sister Agathe whom
she loved, to Reverend Mother whom she loved more than
anyone on earth—what came to her was a feeling of kinship,
of family. She did miss them and it was good.

She opened her eyes. The *marquis* had entered the hall,
followed by his family, a very old woman whom he helped to
the table himself, a younger one who doubtless was his wife,
and numerous children. Gabrielle started to count them, but
the *marquis* made the sign of the cross and began the blessing
in a deep voice that echoed in the cavernous room. It was a
long blessing of his own composition.

Moissac came and asked if he could sit with Jacques and
Philomène. They made room for him, and he was opposite the
Belloirs. Even as he had blessed himself, he had noted the
awkwardness or—as he corrected his own impression—the too
careful way in which madame made the sign. That she should
do it at all filled him with pleasure. Her husband had stood,
his arms folded with the expression on his face of someone
about to spit.

For all Marc's cocksureness, he had been wrong about
their dinner. The soup was not thin: it was clear, but it
swarmed with vegetables that had not lost their identity. So
he described it and looked Moissac in the eye.

Indeed, as the meal got under way, Moissac found himself uncomfortably under the eye of the suspect Jew. Marc,
seeing the policeman's choice of seats, anticipated the niggling
questions throughout the meal, the leads and snares with
which any fool could trap him, his knowing so little of the

Belloirs, much less the farm and town they came from. So, he
did the only thing he could do: he launched into what he
hoped might be called a virtuosic performance on the subject
of student life in Paris. He caricatured some of his own pro-
fessors giving them parallel authorities in medicine; he spoke
of the café life before the war, the streets around the Pan-
théon which he knew well, of body snatchers and of disappearing whores who were sometimes recognizable cadavers.
He shocked purposely to rivet attention; he spoke openly of
the Resistance so that Antoine, sitting a few seats down from
Moissac, tried to signal him to caution. Marc shrugged and
went on talking: he was only talking legend, the places, the
names now months obsolete. He found himself playing his
talent as he might an instrument, discovering with every
laugh new wells of wit within himself. Once launched on the
gambit, he enjoyed it. He might even come to enjoy the food.
He did enjoy the wine. It had a dark softness that soothed the
palate and then just before you swallowed, it gave the tongue
a nip, declaring the authority of age.

"An aristocrat," Marc said, turning the glass in his hand.
"One must not take liberties."

Moissac, giving a dry little cough at the catch the wine
had left in his throat, said, "Well put, monsieur."

"Thank you, *Monsieur le Préfet*," Marc said, and looking
down at his plate of white beans and goosemeat, he thought
he might just enjoy that now too.

"You were very bold," Gabrielle said afterwards.

"He will come back and back and back," Marc said, "like
a hound momentarily thrown off the scent."

"There is not that much longer."

"Then he will come the sooner. He knows there is something, but he's not sure."

They sat on the floor in front of the fire. Others were
bringing benches from alongside the table. The floor was
damp, sweating. Marc had put down his coat and they both
sat on it, needing to speak of Moissac. The policeman had left

suddenly after the *marquis'* withdrawal. The harvesters were
welcome to the fire if they wished, the master of the house
had announced. The doors would be open until half-past ten.

"Maybe he isn't gone at all," Gabrielle said. "Maybe he is
waiting for us outside."

"No. He is weighing the burden of proof. Poor little
Monsieur Lapin. That is the terrible thing of being what we
are. . . ." He smiled and corrected himself: "What I am, the
danger in which we place others, asking their help."

"It is hard for you to ask help, isn't it?"

"Yes."

"It is much easier to give than to take. I have found it
so."

"To take," Marc said, "you give away a little pride in exchange, and all your privacy. I don't have much of that left,
do I?"

"Neither do I, I'm afraid," Gabrielle said.

"But you do. You have it all. I do not begin to know why
you are—what you are."

"I am nothing in myself, in God I may become more
worthy."

"More worthy of what?" he said with an edge to his
voice.

"Sh-sh-sh. More worthy of being alive perhaps, of serving
God."

"If you are not worthy now, no one is. You will forgive
my saying this, but you are talking rot. Look at me. . . ." He
lowered his voice, but he articulated the more clearly for the
whisper. "Of what single thing or person or luck are you not
worthy?"

"I am so imperfect . . . it is like having spots," she
blurted out.

Marc, coddling a rising anger, lost it all. He laughed
aloud, and his laughter leaped around the room in echo.

A moment later Antoine came and squatted down beside
him. "The policeman, what does he want?"

"Philomène," Marc said facetiously.

"Are you on the run?"

"Look, my friend. What you do not know will not harm you."

"What I know doesn't harm me either. Nothing does."

"And does nothing heal you?"

Antoine glanced back to where Michèle was waiting. "It heals me to heal her," he said.

"You are a good man," Marc said, "and if I needed help, you would be the first one I would ask."

"That is because you know how I feel about policemen," Antoine said. "They are bourgeois inventions. They turn my stomach." He straightened up and limped back to Michèle.

"I do not understand them," Gabrielle said.

"They are lovers."

"Is that all? I know that."

"It is very important," Marc said. "If all the world were destroyed except them, the world would not be destroyed."

24

MOISSAC DID NOT KNOW EXACTLY WHAT HAD HAPPENED TO HIM
at dinner. He had listened to the magician-sorcerer, whatever
the imposter was, with a pleasure that could only be accounted for by his awareness of the woman in every pore of
his body. He had by sheer will power avoided staring at her.
Yet not a movement of her arm, her lips, the rise of her chin,
the tilt of her breasts when she straightened her back, nothing
was missed, and the husband's self-obsession as a teller of
vulgar tales had woven a music in itself seductive. When, to
end the meal, the heavy sweet plums of Agenais were served,
Moissac had with the first bite sickened. Actually sickened. It
was to save himself from disgrace that he fled the table at the
first opportunity.

The man, Jew or Jesuit, was diabolical, and the one
person Moissac knew who might be able to stand up to him
was Monsignor La Roque. He had no intention of going to
the monsignor on the matter, although, thinking about it as he
drove back to St. Hilaire, he felt certain the monsignor would
say he was doing his duty in pursuing these two. What the
monsignor would say about his feeling toward the woman,
Moissac was not sure. In the instance of some men, men
worth his thinking about because they were looked up to in
the community, the monsignor would say of their sensual
accommodations, man is only human. But Moissac, blunder-
ing through his admissions of lust, was likely to be told to
pray to the Holy Ghost.

As soon as he reached the prefecture, he had René
brought to him in the interrogation room. "I am sorry I was
delayed. I hope you were not uncomfortable?"

René did not answer. His face was ashen, his hand
trembled when he took the cigarette Moissac offered him.

Moissac thought he would himself keep his hands in his pockets. The waiting had badly shaken the little man. Moissac adjusted the lamps: they were an innovation of his predecessor in office, who had taken instructions from the *Sûreté*. By keeping his head held high, René could avoid the direct glare. Most men found it difficult to keep their heads that high.

Moissac watched him for a moment or two. "You would be more comfortable in my office. If you would agree to tell me what you know about the couple who are passing under the name of Belloir, we could go in there and talk."

"You flatter me, Théo," René said, having to clear his throat.

"So that is how it is going to be." Moissac sat down on the edge of the table. "Maman will be very disappointed. In which one of us I am not sure. She has become very patriotic. Is it out of patriotism you work for people like that, that you risk your skinny little neck, René? It is so easily stepped on. Or is it only for money? Jews always have money. I have heard they put a great deal of it into the Resistance. What have you heard?"

"Not enough," René said.

Moissac laughed. Then, "Oh, I see. What you mean is they do not put in enough money. René, these people whose photographs you took—you and I both know it was for new I.D. cards. Shall I tell you? I asked the woman for the address of her parents in Marseille. You remember? She gave me a wrong address. I don't think she knew the address of the Belloir in-laws. It was all done in a hurry, wasn't it? The young Belloirs are back in their Paris flat today after a few days' absence. Long enough supposedly for these people to get away? I should think that's it. It is not likely they will risk coming home at all now if they find out that I was in Fauré."

For the first time René reacted, just the contraction of the eyebrows, a reflex.

"It's too bad if you deceived the old folks into thinking their son could still come home, René. Now God knows when they'll see him. I wonder what would happen if I told them

that. Would they still cover for these people? You know the
answer to that. I don't. I would have to find out. Don't you
agree that it would be better to settle this just between you
and me? Tell me who these two harvesters really are and I
won't press the matter any further. I won't ask why they came
to you, how they found you. Not even a word about Gaucher
and who meets at *Au Bon Coin* between curfew and the
dawn. Just tell me who they are."

René was trying to get out of the light in order to see
where he could put his cigarette.

"Drop it on the floor. I'll step on it."

"If you know they are imposters, Théo, why don't you
arrest them?"

"I want to know who they are."

"Why don't you say it? You want me to throw you a
Jew."

Moissac struck him with the back of his hand. René put
his hand up when the blood began to spurt from his nose.

Moissac had not known that he was going to strike him.
He could hardly believe that he had done it, but he saw the
blood and he felt the stinging in his knuckles. He averted the
lamps and gave René his own handkerchief. "Maman used to
hit me like that when I stuck my tongue out at her."

When René thought he had stanched the blood, he tried
to rest his eyes, his neck. The room was small; a man could
take no more than four paces in it. And everything was
painted white, walls, woodwork, the table, and two chairs. A
white windowshade closed out the dark of night through the
one small window which a man could not reach in any case.
The light was white. Everything. There was but one more
thing needed to drive a man from his senses in time, silence.
White silence.

"You called him a Jew," Moissac said. "May I take that as
your answer to my question?"

"I said you wanted a Jew. I did not say they were Jews. I
don't know what they are."

Moissac focused the lamps again. "René, I will not implicate the Belloirs. I will not question Gaucher. I will not even ask why or who expects you to pass these people." He wet his lips. "I will not say to any authority that they would have had to have been passed by the prefect of agriculture. Monsieur Dorget must be a vital man to the Resistance, and that is something the Germans would like to know."

René, his chin still high, his eyes closed, the blood beginning to ooze again, said, "How do you know the Belloirs themselves didn't go back yesterday to Paris? Maybe they decided they did not need to work in the fields of rich men."

"I thought of the possibility. I ate my dinner with the harvesters tonight and sat across the table from this couple. They are thirty kilometers further away from Paris than they were yesterday, thirty kilometers closer to the border. I gave him a message from Belloir, the elder. Whatever it meant, it would have warned him that Moissac was on his trail. That should clear your conscience, René. They could go tonight. They may be gone already. If they care about the safety of you and the other people who have helped them, they are gone now. Permit me to send you home from here. Protect your friends, not these strangers."

René sniffed and said nothing. The blood burbled in his nostrils.

"For God's sake, wipe your nose."

René cleared his nose, blowing it into his fingers. He slashed the bloody mucus through the air so that it spattered the white wall.

Moissac turned his back. "I wonder if you would have done that if it was the Gestapo asking the questions. They are the proper channel for Jewish affairs. I have found a discrepancy in papers. They could find the other discrepancies much sooner than I could." He started for the door and then turned back, motioning for René to come. "You might as well come with me, René. Captain Mittag's going to want to see you anyway."

René said, "He is a Jew, Théo. Hunt him down. Enjoy yourself."

Moissac went out and let the door lock behind him. The

room was almost soundproof. He could just hear René's voice. He went to his own office, past the desk where two teen-aged boys were being questioned on violation of curfew. He sat and thought about the woman. Were all Jews sensual? The husband looked as sensual as an umbrella. He saw her again in his mind's eye as she beat at him while he carried her from the dance. He was again beset by doubts. René could be lying now to save himself.

Going out he instructed the duty officer to leave René where he was until he cleaned the wall. Moissac would call in further instructions. He was tempted not to go home. He had his valise and he could stay at Madame Fontaine's. But that would cost money, and with any luck Maman, not expecting him home, might be asleep. There was not a light in the house. He shone his way with the electric torch up the back walk and in through the kitchen. The place was spotless as usual, but it also seemed empty. This is what it would be like, he thought, if she were dead. It was peace at least, if it was peace that a man wanted. He hung up his coat and listened for the old lady's snoring. The only sound was the ticking of the clock on the kitchen sill. He stood a moment trying to puzzle out why that should make him so uneasy. He realized: the clock should have been in the bedroom with Maman. Every night she took it with her, winding it on the way.

He crossed the kitchen in very few strides and pushed open the door to her room. The big bed had not even been turned down. He went through the house, room by room, down with his torch to the cellar, where, before she had gone off, she had hung the goose. Moissac went back upstairs and looked for a note. There was none. And her hat was gone from the corner shelf.

If he had not known where René was at the moment he would have turned his anger on him. He could imagine her having gone out of the house for spite. She might have got a ride to Gaucher's. She could have walked it. But it was past curfew, and he did not feel that this was what had happened. What did he feel? Relief. The moment he could be sure she was not lying in a heap somewhere in the house, he was very glad to be alone. But where was she? And at what hour had she left the house? He remembered the scythe that had been smeared on the front door and went to see if she had painted it out. There, tacked on the freshly painted door was an envelope. He did not open it until he returned to the kitchen. Then he read:

> Your mother is safe as long as Labrière is safe. Do not give him to the *Boches*.

That was all. No signature, the handwriting as simple as a child's. Maman had been taken hostage for René. He stood for a moment trying to grasp it. Then he laughed aloud. He put on his coat and returned to the prefecture, this time however using his bicycle to conserve the fuel in the Peugeot.

René had managed to clean the wall, and he had stretched himself face down on the table, protecting his eyes from the glare of light.

Moissac said, "Wake up, my friend. I have news. Maman has been taken hostage for you. How do you like that? Her safety for your safety. René, are you listening to me?"

"Yes, Théo, her safety for my safety." He sat up and swung his legs off the table.

"You are fond of Maman, are you not, René?"

"I like her."

"Is that all?"

René shrugged.

"Let me tell you something, René. I am not jealous. It is quite the opposite."

René just blinked trying to look at him.

"It is you who are going to have to save Maman. The kidnapping of Maman is not going to save you. They say in their note: Do not give him to the *Boches*. Which is an admission that the *Boches* would be interested in having you. Is that not so, my friend?"

"What do you want of me?"

"I want proof. I want the identity of the Jew and his wife."

"His name is Marc Daridan, and he has enough trouble

without you, Théo, so try to have a little pity on him. Or have you sunk so low that you would turn a man over to the *Milice?*"

"Why do *they* want him?"

"He infiltrated them on behalf of a Paris Resistance group."

"A Jew in the *Milice?*" Moissac said after a moment.

"Didn't you think yourself he was Gestapo?"

"So I did. I was right: he is a chameleon. Tell me the rest."

"That is all I know. I did not want to know more."

"But you do, René, and you will tell me. Listen to me and stop shaking your head. From what you have told me, I am not going to raise a hand against him. I am going to help him escape. Yes, René, I am going to help him escape. The *Milice* are filth. They deserve to have a Jew in their midst."

"Let me out of here, Théo. I am going to be sick."

"Soon, my friend, soon. It would not have been under his own name that he enlisted in the *Milice*. Under what name?"

"Renard. Claude Renard."

"Renard," Moissac repeated. "And they got this far under the identity of the Belloirs?"

René did not answer.

"I will keep my word."

"Yes, the Belloirs. Now may I go home?"

"As soon as I have checked on this fox and his vixen."

"You will find no record of the wife. He was not married until a week ago."

"Thank you, René. Now I believe you."

"I am a brave man," René said, and buried his face in his hands.

"You did it for Maman's sake," Moissac said as though to console him. "It is understandable."

"For my sake," René said.

"That also is understandable—as Maman would be the first to say."

25

THERE HAD BEEN AN INCIDENT THAT MORNING ON THE HIGHWAY
just two kilometers from the *marquis'* gate: a bullet had
dented the helmet of a German patrol officer. Since the gun
had been fired from the *marquis'* property, the patrol as well
as contingency troops from the nearest post all converged on
the chateau. The harvesters proceeded in their threshing of
the tenants' grain, but they were surrounded by the soldiery
who lingered in the yards awaiting the outcome of the meeting between their officers and the *marquis*. The women were
not working that morning, the smallholders having reaped
their own fields and stored the sheaves for threshing, so that
the idle soldiers sought out their company. The *marquis* sent
them wine.

Marc, aware of the general tension, did what he could to
hold the morale of the harvesters steady. He sent Jacques top-
side, to keep Artur in place and out of mischief. He put
Antoine on the grain spout and left himself free to ward off
emergencies. The feeling that one was imminent was very
strong.

One after another of the *marquis'* employees, then his
tenants, was summoned before the council. Those who left off
work to go and later returned said among themselves that
they did not think the *marquis* would give sanctuary to anyone who could not clear himself of suspicion. Marc would
have guessed that most of them were in agreement with the
marquis' policy.

The return of Moissac was but one more aggravation.
Marc intended to ignore him as long as possible. Then he
looked up and saw Artur with his thumbs in his ears, his
hands wagging, and his tongue stuck out at the prefect of
police. Jacques was making his rounds with the oil can. Marc

himself climbed up, dug his fingers into the shoulder of the
dwarf and leaned close to his ear. "You little bastard," he said.
"If you don't sit up here and behave yourself, he'll get you
on some charge or other. We can't save you. Don't you know
that?"

"Why not?" the dwarf shouted over the roar of the
machine.

"Because he has the whole Nazi regime behind him and
they don't like dwarfs."

Artur began to grin and nod at someone below. Marc
looked around. It was Moissac who was also smiling and
nodding. Marc found himself doing the same thing.

He turned around to see one of the German soldiers
beckoning to Jules to come to him. When Jules ignored him,
continuing to spread the unshucked grain as it passed along
the conveyor, the soldier shouted at him, *"Kommen Sie hier!"*

Marc went down as quickly as he could. Jules had started
toward the soldier with a pathetic swagger and the brushing
of his nose with the back of his hand, a gesture straight out of
American films. What in God's name made them all feel in-
vincible, this little band of cripples? Marc leaped down the
last few feet, landing between them.

"Go back to work," he ordered Jules.

To the German in his own language he said, "I am sorry,
sergeant, but we are working on a schedule. It is important
that he stay at the belt."

"Who are you?"

"Jean Belloir, a student. He also is a student." He indicated Jules.

The sergeant, a young man with a round, chubby face
whom Marc would have supposed a baker's or butcher's
apprentice, said, "I also am a student—of music. Before the
war, at the folk festival at Bâle. . . ." He nodded toward
Jules.

The conversation was never resumed, for Jules, glancing
around, was suddenly jerked backwards. He began to scream.
One of the rotary prongs had come down on his hand, not

merely piercing it, but forcing it down on the metal cleats, dragging it and him toward the maw of the machine.

Marc shouted up to turn off the machine. Artur was prompt: he threw the gear stick.

Jules lost consciousness, slumping over the conveyor, his hand still prisoned. Marc lifted him and held him while the German soldier with his bare hands lifted up the prong and bent it. Marc eased the hand free. The back of it was as torn as the crucified Christ's, and the palm mangled. Gabrielle had come. She took over the support of the hand wrapping it in the handkerchiefs both Moissac and the German soldiers gave her as Marc carried the boy a few feet and laid him on the ground.

"Get a doctor," Marc said. "I am not competent to deal with this."

The German soldier kept saying over and over, "He is a musician. I know he is a musician."

"Give him first aid," Moissac said. "I will see that he gets to a hospital."

Someone had already gone to the steward's office for the first aid materials.

And Marc knew this much also: he said to the German sergeant, "Do you carry sulfa powder?"

"Yes, yes."

In the end there could have been no better first aid possible than the ample dusting Marc did with the sulfa. Cheese cloth was brought from the dairy, and a great loose bandage was made, and then a sling. Jules gained consciousness when Marc spooned brandy down his throat, Gabrielle cradling his head.

Perhaps he was also a medical student, this Daridan, Moissac thought, but he was more likely the chameleon who could manage the disguise the occasion demanded. He was beginning to understand the survival of the race.

Everyone was standing by now, even the Germans, in a bemused admiration, as though the boy's opening his eyes was the signal that all was healed. Gabrielle stroked his head.

The boy put up his good hand, trying perhaps to reach his own forehead, but instead his hand seemed to cup her breast before falling back on his own. Moissac fairly leaped, seeing the way so marvelously, so simply open to him.

"Monsieur—madame, I will bring my car to the platform. Madame will ride in the back seat with him and we shall get him at once to the hospital." He did not wait for their reaction, turning to the German soldier who stood, still wringing his own hands: "If you please, sergeant: get a message to the hospital in St. Hilaire to have a surgeon standing by, Dr. Lauzin if it can be managed. And you may say the prefect of police so ordered."

The way was opened for Moissac as the parting of the waters, and the feeling of his own power was exquisite.

It would not have been easy in any case to question so reasonable a proposal, but when Jules murmured, "Please, madame," the matter was sealed for Gabrielle.

Marc dreaded to see her go, fearing she would not return, yet wanting to tell her the choice must be hers. "Perhaps it would be better," he started, then amended, "it would be safer. . . . "

Gabrielle reached across and touched her forefinger to his lips. She did not dare make the sign of silence by raising it to her own. Marc moved his head quickly and managed to brush her hand with his lips.

"You are making it difficult," Gabrielle whispered, and the color flamed in her cheeks.

"That is my intention."

He stood up. Above him on the platform of the machine, Jacques waited, one hand on his hip and the other on the shoulder of Artur where he sat on his perch. Marc nodded and Jacques passed the signal to resume work.

Marc and Antoine between them carried Jules to the car where Gabrielle was already waiting. Moissac held the door. The German sergeant had run alongside them. He shouted in to Jules, just before Moissac closed the door, "I will pray for you."

Moissac said to Marc, "Where do you go from here, monsieur?"

"Lacroix," Marc said. "It is a village on the Adour river."

"We shall find it, never fear. Your wife will make a reliable navigator."

26

JULES BEGAN THE JOURNEY SITTING UP, BUT WITH THE JOGGING OF the car, for Moissac drove as though the fire were behind and not inside him, he again became faint. Gabrielle made him stretch out on the seat, his knees in the air. She sat on her heels on the floor, and made sure his arm was secure. Her discomfort was its own solace, and she was grateful to travel with her back to Moissac. The prefect, outside of an occasional inquiry as to the boy's condition, did not try to talk to her. Nor was she questioned at the several checkpoints where they stopped on command.

Jules began to cry, and his mind wandering, he called for his mother. Over and over. Then, lucid again, he would beg Gabrielle, "Don't tell my mother, don't let them tell Maman, please. . . . "

"For the love of God, talk to him," Moissac shouted back to her. "Say you're his mother. You say you are a Christian, say you're his mother. He'll believe you."

Gabrielle glanced over her shoulder at the prefect. His face was a dark red, the color starting in his neck where it bulged at his collar. *You say you are a Christian. . . .*

She brushed the boy's forehead with her hand, and she said, close to him, "It will be all right. There will be a doctor waiting to fix your hand. Everything will be all right. Jules, would you like me to pray out loud? We could pray together."

"No, do not pray. . . . I do not want to die. . . . "

"Yes," Moissac called back. "Pray. I want to hear you pray."

The man sounded mad, and again she thought: *You say you are a Christian.* She was confused: to pray now seemed a betrayal of Marc. A Catholic prayer and the policeman would know. . . . What would he know? What did he know?

"He does not wish it. I will pray quietly," Gabrielle said. To Jules she said, "I was not going to say the prayers for the dead. You are not going to die. You must be brave. Your mother would want that. My brave little Jules," she crooned.

And then the boy himself was praying, "Hail Mary, full of grace, the Lord is with thee. Blessed art thou among women. . . . "

She said the words to herself.

Gabrielle felt rather than saw their approach to the Convent of Ste. Geneviève. She tried to keep her eyes averted, concentrating on Jules' face, a sweet face really, the pain strangely softening it . . . but at the last moment, catching sight of the wall out of the corner of her eye, she looked, and then strained to see through the gate when they passed it. There was no one in sight, not a solitary figure. "Thank you, God," she murmured.

Moissac caught her just before she turned away. "That's a convent," he said, "nuns . . . sisters. The Sisters of Ste. Geneviève. Did you ever hear of Ste. Geneviève?"

"Yes, monsieur."

She was saying it to please him, to placate him. "One of the sisters died at the hospital the other night. I was there. I helped get her to the hospital, I got the doctor out of bed, I brought the Reverend Mother, and then afterwards I drove her out here again. . . ."

Gabrielle listened as though to a voice in a dream. He had spoken of Reverend Mother but she could not even bring that revered face to mind. Then for an instant she had it: as she had looked round at her in the barouche on the way to the station.

" . . . The nun . . . She was a novice actually—that's a young nun, a nun before she takes the vows—she was going to be all right. Then something happened at the hospital and she died." He maneuvered the mirror to get her in view. "Maybe it was the will of God, but I have the feeling somebody at the hospital didn't care if she lived or died, her being a nun."

Please, God, make him stop talking like this.

" . . . A communist maybe. Maybe a secret Jew. You come on them once in a while, you know." He saw her bow her head and bite her lip. He was satisfied then to concentrate on his driving. As he turned into Rue Louis Pasteur he began to sound the car horn regularly, clearing the road before him.

As soon as they stopped at the hospital entrance, Jules sat up and swung his legs to the floor. He looked out to see where he was. Moissac opened the car door. Gabrielle did not move for a moment, watching the boy.

"Don't be afraid," she said. "We'll all come and see you when we come back to St. Hilaire, and you'll be healed by then."

"I'll be fine," he said. "It's my left hand." Then, "I shouldn't have left it lying around." He gave a short, hurt laugh. "Will you tell them I said that? Remember."

"I'll tell them." She got out and beckoned him, coaxingly, to follow.

"Tell Jean. He'll think it's funny. And Antoine. He will really understand it. Antoine can bring my guitar. And if he wants to play it, tell him I said he could."

At the desk when they asked for his identity card before allowing him to proceed up to the surgery, Gabrielle got it out from his wallet for him. The admissions clerk repeated the name as he copied it: "Jules Laffite."

Sister Marie Gabrielle: Sister Agathe would have said it when the clerk asked the name of Marc's wife, and somewhere the records showed Sister Marie Gabrielle to have died. As clearly as though he had human voice, the devil implanted the words on her consciousness: And so you are free, Madame Daridan.

But in fact it was Moissac who had spoken to her, using that name for the first time: "Let us go, Madame Daridan."

She stood and watched Jules disappear with the attendant who brought the elevator down for him, Moissac waiting behind her. Marc had said, If you are ever in trouble. . . . Marc was in trouble now, his identity known. But if that was so, why had he not already been arrested, or charged, or taken prisoner? The prefect then could not be certain. He would be hoping now to get his information from her, counting on a woman's weakness.

"Madame Belloir!" he said in that voice that made the softest of words sound like a growl.

But he had called her Madame Belloir again, and so she turned and went with him out the hospital door and into the car.

Moissac maneuvered the Peugeot carefully past the cars crowding the driveway, all official vehicles of the Occupation, some medical, some military. He remembered that the second floor of the hospital was occupied entirely by the Germans. He stopped suddenly as an officer backed out of his car. He slammed the car door, saluted Moissac, and then stooped to look into the car at the woman as the prefect drove on.

"The Germans are everywhere," Moissac said. "That was Captain Mittag of the Gestapo."

Gabrielle said nothing at first, feeling that there was a threat implicit in the identification. Then, as she felt Marc would likely have done in the situation, she asked clearly: "Do you know him, monsieur?"

The boldness of it, the nerve, the calculated insult. And yet it only excited him more. He would not have wanted a wilted, beaten creature. It was one thing to go to a tired whore. This was to be something quite else. "Shall I say, madame, they have forced their acquaintanceship upon me?" There was an answer, Moissac thought, the woman remaining silent. If he could give such parries to his peers, they would no longer be his peers.

He drove alongside the river, avoiding the Old Town. It crossed his mind that Maman might be somewhere on Rue Michelet: he would not have wanted her, prisoner or no, looking out at him just now. He could not help feeling, now that turning home he thought about her, that she was enjoying her captivity. She would be counting on her domination of her son to insure the safety of René. Perhaps, if she had seemed to be enjoying herself too much, they would have dumped her home this morning.

The fear of that possibility became so vivid that when he reached the house he had the woman wait in the car a moment while he went up to see. There was no one and no new message. Going down through the garden, he glanced surreptitiously at the windows of the nearest neighbor. The drapes were drawn. They always were on the Moissac side.

"Now, madame, if you will come with me please, I will ask you to wait for me in the house. My mother is not home, but you will be more comfortable there than sitting in a public place in a hot automobile. I will not be more than an hour. I know how anxious you are to return to your husband. And I know how anxious he is for your return."

"They will have gone on by now," Gabrielle said.

"We shall follow them."

It seemed most plausible, the way he said it, and seeing the man in his own garden, stooping to pull up a weed as he came along the walk, made of him a human being, that and the mention of his mother. She was further reassured, going up the walk, when she saw a little grotto to Our Lady among the marigolds and lupin.

Moissac said, not going into the house at all himself, "Perhaps you will be good enough to look in the larder and put together a lunch we can take along with us. There's bound to be something there."

But in the house alone, hearing only the buzzing of flies and the droning of bees about the honeysuckle bushes at the window, and no sound at all from the clock which had stopped at a quarter past two, she thought again about his having called her Madame Daridan. Or had she imagined that he said it, so thinking of herself at that very moment? Which was a sin. Or the very gravest of temptations. The trouble was she had no real measure of what was evil, except in herself. It was a peculiar thought, but she sat down at the scrubbed, bone-white kitchen table to think about it when it occurred to her: Christ and all His saints were human. Why wasn't the devil human also?

27

PERHAPS HE SHOULD NOT HAVE LEFT HER ALONE. BUT HE HAD TO leave her alone: it was part of the ceremony, that she be allowed a kind of retreat, a time alone in a Christian house. It was also necessary that she be there when he returned because she wanted to be there. Alone now she was free to run. There were people enough in St. Hilaire to hide her. A call to Gaucher would probably arrange the matter. And if she did not love her husband, she would run. It was essential to the ceremony that she be given that choice first, and then the other choice.

He went to the prefecture and cleared his desk of an accumulation of paper-work, forms and counterforms, reports in triplicate and quadruplicate, all requiring signatures and stamps and seals, and not an item among them that would stir the republic a jot if it had not been prepared. That was not true. It was part of the fabric . . . a shoddy fabric. What was it Maman had said? She was talking of self-pity. She was right. The shoddiest. He was done with it. All done with it. He glanced at the clock over the door. The allotted hour was almost up. The very hair on his head seemed to bristle. He had never felt more alert, more in control.

He went out and chatted at the desk for a few minutes just to prove his command of himself. Finally he stopped at the prison annex to the prefecture. René was its only occupant at the moment. Moissac gave the jailer the money out of his own pocket and instructed him to see that the prisoner was served the best luncheon available in St. Hilaire.

28

GABRIELLE, HAVING GLIMPSED IN THE ROOM OFF THE KITCHEN THE ivory crucifix above the bed, was drawn toward it as a moth to flame. She did not pray. She merely sat on the edge of the blanket chest and gazed at the crucifix until at last she said, You must speak to me, Lord. I don't have anything to say. But she heard nothing.

Not that she expected to hear the word of God, only to be moved toward self-expression for being herself so utterly empty. So many things had cancelled one another out, like a game of Trafalgar, checks and zeroes. You did not put things off in the religious life: tomorrow never brought again today's opportunity. Which was not to say that failing today, you could not try again tomorrow. Slowly, slowly, her self-contemplation deepened: to know yourself could not be sinful: what else could it mean, to examine your conscience? Therefore to blame yourself, having no real guilt: was this less a sin than to excuse yourself having guilt? Guilt—it was a word itself to think about. Every time Marc heard it he would almost gnash his teeth. And that brought her thoughts to Marc: would she ever be able to get him entirely out of her mind? Not so very long ago, in school, she could remember—not in school, it was her sister on the way home from school—saying she thought she was in love. How do you know? I'd die for him . . . Lord, I must think these things unless you turn my mind to other thoughts. So her mind proposed one thing and then another, but never once focusing on where she actually was—or on what lay immediately before her for which she was subconsciously trying to gather strength.

Moissac returned. She heard the car, then the slamming of its door and his step on the walk. She waited in the kitchen, watching him come up the walk. She wondered why she was not afraid. Or were there kinds of fear as there were kinds of love? Unrecognized, or but dimly so. She did not like to think about Monsieur Moissac. She knew that. He was ugly-looking, for which no man could be blamed. And having refused to blame him for being something that might have frightened her, she had conquered fear. So simple. It was the same with Moissac as it had been with Artur, the dwarf, when she had permitted him her hands and danced with him.

"No lunch?" he said, coming in and removing his hat and coat, and hanging them behind the door.

Gabrielle had thought that they would go at once, but he sat down at the table in his shirtsleeves. "I am sorry, but I did not look, monsieur. I did not like to look."

"You do not like to look at anything. I have observed that. Or is it only me you do not like to look at?"

"No, monsieur."

"Whatever that means. I am wearing a clean shirt."

She glanced his way to see him pluck at the sleeves, hiking up the cuffs. There were dark marks of sweat under his armpits.

"Come, madame, and sit down where you can hear what I have to say to you."

Gabrielle sat on the opposite bench at the far end of the table.

"You are very modest, madame. It is becoming in a bride. And you are a bride after all, in spite of what the Belloir papers say. Do you love your husband?"

Gabrielle flushed, then shivered, for a feeling of ice had come over her, and her mouth was dry. It was hard to speak but she said, "Excuse me, *Monsieur le Préfet*, but I do not think it is your business."

"Maybe you don't think so, but I do. I am now making everything that is your business and your husband's business mine. You see, I know enough right now about Marc Daridan to send him to a concentration camp, perhaps to his death. Quite probably that, or you would not be trying to reach the Spanish border disguised as Belloirs. Is that not so?"

Gabrielle sat silent, her hands clasped in her lap. Because he had commented on the downcast of her eyes, she fixed them now on the middle button of his shirt. It was a thin shirt and the hair of his chest shone darkly through it.

"On the other hand, there is no reason if I say so, for him not to make the border. I cannot take him there, but I can refrain from sending the dogs after him."

This time in spite of herself she nodded her head a little.

"That's better. There's no reason for us to pretend that you are Madame Belloir any longer, is there?" When she did not respond, he said: "Answer me!"

Gabrielle moistened her lips and said: "I am Madame Marie Belloir. I do not know the other name."

"I see," Moissac said quietly, "you are ashamed of being a Jew. I do not blame you for denying it."

This time her eyes flew to his. "Christ was a Jew, monsieur."

Moissac grinned, his yellowed teeth then parting as he darted his tongue between them. "Ah, but you weren't long in denying Him. You must admit that thirty-three is no great life-span for a man, eh? How old is your husband? Ten years left at most, I'd say. Suppose down through history every Jew was permitted to live only to the age of thirty-three? Now there's an idea—you see, your husband's not the only one who can make up a tale. Would you believe me, I've only just now thought about this. Every Jew must die at the age of thirty-three. Every male Jew, that is. Otherwise we might breed a race of giants, everyone like your husband. That simply would not do. No, we must saddle them with their aging crones, their matriarchs, their witches at the hearth. If I was not a religious man I could draw you a picture of hell, madame, for I can see it now in my own mind's cauldron."

Gabrielle again moistened her lips. "I will go and find

something to make for lunch, monsieur." She put her hands on the table, about to get up.

Moissac sprang to his feet, jogging the heavy table so that it must have hurt him. But he pounced his hand on hers. "Later, madame." He held her hand down with a cruel tightness for a moment, then let it go. "I did not mean to touch you," he said. "Not yet. What I mean to say is, please do not move until we have finished talking. What I want to say, I will say directly, for I am a plain, outspoken man. . . . No, I am not that either." He sat down again. He put his hands behind his head, tightening and freeing the muscles in his arms, his shoulders. "I wish you would catch fire for me again—the way you did when I said you were ashamed to be a Jew."

He half-turned and pointed to the room where she had found the crucifix above the bed. "I want you to go in that room and take off your clothes and wait for me. It is a fine large bed."

The words seemed very strange, but the idea must have already crossed her mind; that she did not know precisely what it meant or how he expected to achieve this thing was true. But this she did know: if he did not believe she was a Jew, he would not have dared to so approach her. She did not move. She kept her eyes on her hands where she had folded them on the table. "I do not understand, monsieur."

"I want to fuck you," he said.

And the word she did not understand, but she could not help but feel that having said it was a new agitation to him.

"But with your consent, madame. You must understand, I am offering you the life of Marc Daridan for the pleasure of your body. I am a man of honor. I am a man of religion, let us say that, and I will swear to you upon the Bible at the bedside there that your husband will go free insofar as my life can manage it."

"If I do not consent?"

"It would be very bad for him, madame. Not merely the concentration camp as it would be for you, but the *Milice*, you see, are something else. I have heard that they put out the eyes of men who could identify their spies. You must admit, it is a fair exchange I'm asking of you."

"Monsieur, if I was not a Jew, would you ask it?"

"How dare you put that question to me?" But even as he spoke, he knew the beginning of his supremacy: she had said the word, *If I was not a Jew*. He said almost tenderly, "You have a choice. You are not my prisoner. You may either go in and wait for me in the bed, or you may go out and wait for me in the car."

Gabrielle sat quietly for a long-seeming time, the silence of which time broke only with the rasps of his heavy breathing. Then she got up. She did not speak until she reached the bedroom door. "Must I take off my clothes, monsieur?"

"No, of course not. I will take them off for you."

29

SHE MADE NO SOUND, NO SOUND AT ALL EVEN WHEN IT MUST HAVE been most painful, and when to have heard her cry out in pain would have helped him. And so he had to help himself with every lewd name that he could conjure and prefix all of them with Jew. Thus was it consummated.

When at last he rolled the stone weight of himself from off her, she lay in a kind of sick fear, not of him, but of the emptiness, the wetness, and the smell, as of earth at first, and then, she knew, of blood. She was afraid to go from the bed for fear of what might happen to her, standing. And so she lay, her hand between her legs, holding herself as though it were still possible to put back something that was no longer in its place.

He sat up on the side of the bed, a fat, hairy, heaving hump of a thing, and looked around through swollen eyes to where the cream-colored limbs were crimsoned and Maman's sheets blotched and soaking. He sat and stared at the hands and the hair and the blood and tried to think what it could mean that she should be a virgin. Was the Jew impotent? What else could it mean? He remembered her fists in her husband's face, them beating against his breast for having taken her from the dancer where they had fallen upon the floor together.

He began to laugh, laughter such that he needed to contain in his hands, covering his mouth, for there were sobs in it, great joyous sobs. He, Moissac, had succeeded where the Jew had failed! He had consummated the marriage act of the tall, muscled, virile, blue-eyed Jew. That he had done: his triumph was marked in blood.

He did not touch her. He did not stand up until he had

gathered his shabby bathrobe from the floor and wrapped it round him. He went to the wall at the head of the bed and straightened the crucifix where it had gone awry. Her eyes followed him. He stepped back and pulled the quilt over her to hide the filth of it all. "I will bring you warm water," he said, and motioned to the washstand. "You will feel better afterwards. Dress quickly and we will leave as soon as you are ready."

They had driven twenty kilometers and still she had not spoken: it was as though she had been stricken dumb. He stopped at a farmhouse where, before the war had changed so many things, he and his colleagues on the force had come for a Sunday's hunting. He was able to buy dark bread spread with pâté and a bottle of wine which he brought back to the car. She would not eat.

"You'd better keep it and take it with you," he said, and folded two slices of the bread into a sandwich. "When did you plan to go?"

She did not answer.

"Look, madame. Théophile Moissac keeps his word. I will not interfere. I will punish no one, not even René. Do you understand?"

"Yes, monsieur." Finally, words.

"You ought to thank me," he said with self-conscious irony. He was sitting at the wheel of the car. He maneuvered round so that he could watch her face.

"Thank you, monsieur," she said in the same monotone, and continued to stare ahead.

"I mean for everything."

She turned and looked at him, her eyes wide and frank and saying something, but in a language he could not understand. He did not have to: that little triumph would last him a while yet. He made himself comfortable for driving and turned on the ignition. "What will you tell your husband?"

"Nothing, monsieur."

"But when he finds out. . . . Some day, you know?"

After a moment she said, "I will tell him what he will believe."

Which, Moissac thought, was the way and wisdom of all women, to tell a man only what she knew he would believe.

30

BEFORE NOON THE HARVESTERS HAD ARRIVED IN LACROIX, FORTY kilometers on, a village from which the oak forests could be seen patching the hillsides like the shadow of clouds; beyond, dimly, rose the high mountains. The children came out to see the combine and the tractor and the van of workers as though it were the circus that had come to town. The threshing machine did resemble some huge, lumbering beast, and when it was set up quay-side by the river, for the grain was to go directly to the mill upstream, and its grain spout lowered to the barge, a child called out that the tin beast wanted water.

This village too had its medieval aspect, dominated entirely by the *châtelain* who also owned large holdings in the cork-oak forests. As soon as the harvest was in, the men of the village would go into the woods for the beginning of the bark-stripping season.

Marc, arranging the loading of the grain, which would go that night to St. Pierre-sur-l'Adour, arranged to also travel there on the same barge. It would wait for him until ten p.m. He had confided in Antoine after they left Champs des Corbeaux, Antoine already suspecting Marc's purpose. He foresook Michèle that afternoon to work alongside Philomène and Céleste, one or the other of whom, he told Marc, ought to be able to ride the night through with the prefect of police.

As the afternoon lengthened and Marc calculated the time it should have taken Moissac to drive to St. Hilaire and thence to Lacroix, and that time passed by an hour and then another hour, he wondered if he would ever see Gabrielle again. Then the car came, Moissac parking in front of the water fountain. And Gabrielle had come back.

Marc stayed at his place with the grain shute, but he watched her step from the car and pass among the wagons

and along the dock toward him. She walked, he thought, as a
woman might who carried something on her head, a carefulness that without the burden had the appearance of great
grace. Moissac had stopped at the fountain for a cup of water.
Jacques came down and took the grain shute. He called out to
ask how Jules was.

Gabrielle answered, speaking to Marc: "We left him at
the hospital. That's all I know. He would like Antoine to keep
his guitar and bring it to him."

Marc signalled Jacques to say that Jules was all right,
which was not necessarily so, but he jumped down beside
Gabrielle to speak to her before Moissac came up. "You've
been gone for a long time."

"Yes."

"Did he question you?"

"I did not tell him anything. There were not many questions I could answer."

She would not look at him at all. She had not wanted to
return, Marc thought. His fantasies—and he had had them,
hardly knowing it—were idle. He said, "Thank you for coming back."

"When shall we go, monsieur?"

Monsieur again. "I have made arrangements to go up the
river tonight on the grain barge. Why do you ask it? Because
of him?"

"Because I can see the mountains."

"Why does he keep following us? Do you know?"

All afternoon she had been thinking about the lie that she
must tell him, the lie he would believe and therefore save
himself, and ask of her no more questions. "It is not us he
follows." She watched his face until she saw the sad little
smile that came after the first brief look of surprise.

Artur was waving wildly at her. He cupped his hands
and called the name, "Marie, Marie, Marie!" When she looked
up at last, he blew her a kiss. It was not easy, it never had
been easy to pretend so much. Now only an act of will en-

abled her to make the little gesture that would satisfy him.
She mimed the catching of the kiss mid-air.

She walked to the van and got her pitchfork. Then she
rode into the valley with the next wagon that left the dock.

Marc went back to work, jumping down into the barge
and spreading the grain with a shovel, and while he worked
he thought about the blindness to the plight of his fellow
voyagers that must be the greatest affliction of the refugee.
And he remembered, thinking of this, his impatience with
Rachel when she complained of the pain. Once more he felt
the pangs of grief, having, just for an instant, an intimate
sense of her and the way they were together that afternoon
before she died.

Moissac sat outside the dockside bistro for a little while
and watched the threshing while he drank beer. A great thirst
had come on him. He saw Marc remove his shirt and work
stripped to the waist, but only after his wife had gone to the
fields. Hairless and pink, the virile Jew. What had she told
him that he would believe? When Philippe rode in atop a
load of sheaves, Moissac beckoned to him and ordered a
pitcher of beer and glasses. Jacques came also on the motioned invitation, and Antoine, after Philippe had gone, all inquiring after Jules. Moissac promised to get word to them
that night. Finally when there was a lull in the arrival of the
wagons he poured the Jew a beer also. But the dwarf he
could not bring himself to invite, not in daylight. Marc, instead of drinking his, carried it back and handed it to Artur.
He came back expecting another beer. But then, why not?
Moissac met his eyes: steel blue, Moissac could not get over
it. Moissac let his eyelids fall to where they were comfortable.
He gestured to Marc to pour himself the beer.

"Thank you, monsieur."

"It is nothing."

Moissac, his eyes level with the Jew's waist, lowered
them, and he thought about the mark of the Jew and wondered if that might affect their potency, the circumcision

badly done. He shuddered at the thought of the operation and looked about to throw his mind entirely off that track. There atop the machine, Artur was pouring the beer over his head.

Moissac watched him for a second, then glanced up to see the Jew shaking his fist at the dwarf. Moissac burst out laughing. He put down his own glass and clapped his hands, applauding. To Marc he said, "What does he do ordinarily, a carnival? Sideshow?"

"He's a mechanic," Marc said. "Otherwise he is a fool."

"So. Who is not?"

"Your health, monsieur," Marc said and drank the beer.

Moissac just sat nodding, his eyes half-closed.

31

MOISSAC TOOK THE JAILER'S KEY AND WENT IN HIMSELF TO WHERE
René was lying on the bench. The moths circled thickly
around the naked light bulb. The whirr of their wings and the
burble of the urinal drain were the only sounds in the place
his men called The Tomb.

"Wake up, my friend. . . . "

"I'm not asleep."

" . . . And let me tell you about the Jew."

"I don't want to know about the Jew."

"They will go tonight, I think. I watched him on the
barge—as though he owned it. That is how they'll go. I'm not
a policeman for nothing. And tomorrow on a coal truck into
the mountains and there they'll find a passer. . . . "

René slowly sat up and looked at him.

"Or is that arranged already? Do not tell me. You do not
need to tell me anything." He put his hand on René's thigh.
"But let me tell you something: the woman, the bride. . . .
She was a virgin and she gave herself to me. I, Moissac, did
the honors for the Jew."

René, slowly understanding, doubled in on himself and
buried his hands in his face. His shoulders shook, his whole
body rocked to and fro.

"Yes! Go ahead, my friend, and laugh. Why not? This
time I'll laugh with you."

René took his hands away and there was something wild
in his moist eyes. Then he said: "So it was a triumph! You
finally found a woman you could take, Moissac, a woman you
could. . . . "

"She gave herself to me, René! The Jewess gave herself."

"The Jewess is dead. She's buried in the nuns' graveyard
at Ste. Geneviève. You had yourself a nun, you pig. . . . "

Moissac felt it like a blow at the back of his head that numbed his neck and spine. The cell was tilting and he could not stop himself from falling until his knees hit the stone and then his hands, and he had to stay in that position or pass out altogether.

"She gave her name and clothes to the Jewess to get her into a hospital where the Nazis have the second floor. Remember, Théo? You picked me up that night with the Reverend Mother in the car. . . . "

It came back to him, all, kaleidoscopically, the *camionnette* on Louis Pasteur, the sudden funeral and the nun, the shyness of the woman with the man. "Let me be, René. No more! For Christ Jesus' sake, no more. . . . The doors are open. Go. Leave me."

René got up. "I gave her to you, Théo. In the end I gave her to you. I made her go with the Jew to keep him safe."

Moissac beat his fists on the floor of the cell. He began to retch and René went out quickly and closed the prison door behind him.

32

A GERMAN PATROL, TWELVE MEN IN ALL, SAT AT THE QUAYSIDE bistro, their rifles leaning against the stand for bicycles. They ordered beer and used the *pissoir* while Marc and Gabrielle watched from among the bales of straw. The engine of the barge was stoked, the charcoal smoke fouling the air. One of the Germans went down to the dock and ordered the bargeman to proceed. He spread his hands, then shone his torch on where presumably a valve refused to work. The bistro owner came out and pleaded with him to pole the barge away, but very soon the Germans took their guns and left.

The bargeman collected his fee and the refugees buried themselves to the neck in grain.

"At least we can see the sky," Marc said.

She did not answer.

"Do you know who it is the policeman wants?"

She did not answer.

"He will want us when we are gone. Otherwise, I would have left you with our friends. They were a kind of family. I think they'll miss us. While I live I will remember them—and you, friend-sister."

"Do not talk," she said at last. "It is too painful."

Before they docked at dawn in St. Pierre, the bargeman asked Marc where they wanted to go from there. Marc gave him the name of the mountain village where he was to find the guide René had promised.

"Come home with me," the bargeman said, "there will be a coal truck going up if you don't mind getting dirty. It has worked before."

"And I've been dirty before," Marc said, and to Gabrielle, lightly, "and you, madame, it will be like having spots. Remember when you said that to me?"

At last she smiled.

They were seated with the bargeman's family for breakfast, brown bread and milk in bowls. Six children watched them eat while the oldest boy watched at the door. This was no new experience for any of them, Marc realized, even before the bargeman's wife took him up a ladder to a loft where they were to hide if the signal was given. "It has never happened, monsieur, but that's more reason to be careful."

When the children had gone from the house and the woman to milk the cow, Marc and Gabrielle watched at the window alone. He remembered that other vigil from the mill. "Are you praying?"

"No."

"Why not?" he said with tender teasing.

"I shall pray again," she said, not looking at him.

"Who knows but I will too—some day."

"Do you mean that, Monsieur Marc?" So briefly her eyes sought his.

"It is not a promise, and probably I won't, but I will understand."

"It is enough."

"You've not said that for days, but then we have not talked for days. Or so it seems. Gabrielle . . . will you come with me?"

"Until you are safe."

"I won't ever be that safe."

"I shall go back when there is time for you to have got across the mountain."

And so she was resolved. He said, "Remember once you said that perhaps the Reverend Mother would not have you now?"

"She will! She will!" The tears welled up in her eyes.

"I said it then," he went on quietly, "and I repeat it now: she would be the greatest fool not to, and I do not think that of her."

"Thank you."

"For what? Sending you back? I want to ask you a question, Gabrielle."

"Please do not, Monsieur Marc."

"I will ask it, but you do not need to tell me the answer. Do you want to come with me?"

"No."

"You have not wanted to at all?"

"I did not permit myself to think about it."

"Then you have not wanted it," he said.

"That is probably so," she said almost in a whisper.

"Then there is something I do not understand: why have you done so much for me? Why are you here with me now?"

"Because I believed you needed me."

"And would you have done the same for any man, any creature on the run?"

She did not answer.

"Suppose the dwarf, Artur—no, better, suppose the policeman, Moissac—they call him the Jew—suppose he had been in my place?"

She felt the numbness coming over her again, the cold dead numbness. But that she could feel it again meant that it had gone away a little. "He would not have been in your place."

"You are right," Marc said after a moment. "He would not have been in my place. Forgive me, little sister, but I was searching for the truth for both of us. You see, one of the things you have given me: you have made me a person who wants to know, to understand. That is a great gift in times like these."

"I am glad," she said, and saying it, she knew it to be true. She could feel the gladness awakening in herself.

"One more question," Marc said, "to which I have no right, but I shall ask it anyway. Do you feel that you have sinned in helping me?"

"No, Monsieur Marc, I do not believe that I have sinned."

"You are not saying that to make it easier for me to go on?"

She shook her head. "And I am not saying it to make it easier for me to go back. I believe it to be so."

He put his hand to where he might have touched hers.
She did not draw away. Nor did he touch her, just letting his
hand hover over hers. "I wish you great joy, Gabrielle."

The novice bent her head until she touched his hand with
her lips. Then, removing Rachel's ring from her finger, she put
it in his hand and folded his fingers over it. She turned away
from him and Marc resumed his watching.

When the bargeman's wife came in with the milk, Marc
said: "Madame, would it be possible for my wife to stay here
for two days? She is not Jewish, and I will not have her go
with me just now."

The woman looked sternly from one to the other of them
and shook her head. It was, he suspected, her disapproval of
mixed marriages. "You must speak to my husband," she said.

When the bargeman came to say the coal truck would go
within the hour, Marc spoke to him and arranged the price
not only of Gabrielle's staying there, but of her return by a
series of barges to St. Hilaire. Gabrielle went up to the loft
and stayed there until he was gone.

It was near nightfall of the third day afterwards that
Gabrielle returned to St. Hilaire, but before anyone was
allowed to leave the barge, the police came aboard to inspect
the cargo. The pilot objected, and there was an argument
which Gabrielle and two other passengers had to wait
through. She stood, as the others, with identification in hand.

"It has never happened before," the pilot said. "I will
take it up with the prefect of police."

"Do, monsieur, do. He will meet you in hell. He hung
himself in his own jail three nights ago."

She had to walk almost the length of Louis Pasteur, past
the mill, and she had to wait while a German convoy passed.
No, she thought, he will rest in peace if it is God's will. I shall
not say it, and when she reached the fork in the road leading
up to Convent Hill, she began to run, and she did not stop
running until her breath was gone, and when she had breath
enough she ran the rest of the way.